APACHE WELLS

APACHE WELLS

ROBERT STEELMAN

ISBN-13: 978-1-957868-51-6

Published by
Cutting Edge Books
PO Box 8212
Calabasas, CA 91372
www.cuttingedgebooks.com

CHAPTER ONE

Old man Coogan was the dirtiest man I ever saw. He wore buckskins, the way they did back in the forties, and they were black and stiff and grease-shiny. A crusty ring was on his hide everyplace it stuck out from the buckskin, on his neck and wrists and ankles. But he was the best guide in the Arizona Territory, they said, and for a hundred dollars in gold he was getting us through the Apache country and on to California. I guess it was worth it if you didn't have to stand downwind of him.

"There it is," he said, pointing with the barrel of his old Hawken rifle. "Chiricahua Wells. Looks purty, don't it, Joey?"

I looked, but I didn't see anything. Nothing but dry grassy plain, baking in the afternoon sun. The wind was like a furnace, and a dust-devil picked up handfuls of gritty sand and threw it in my eyes. Away in the distance a feather of smoke curled up from the purple mountains like a question mark.

"I see an Apache smoke," I said. "I see that, all right."

Coogan coughed and spit, and wiped his scrubby chin.

"They ain't gonna jump any seven wagons, and guns to match." He sat on his pony, real contented, and grinned when I sneezed and coughed in the dust. "Tastes real good, don't it? That's Arizona Territory, boy. Dod-dum it, there's a country fer you."

I was only seventeen but I didn't like anyone calling me *boy*. I'd swung my weight all the way from Columbus. I'd killed me a Comanche in Texas, and I had his coup-stick back in Saul's wagon to prove it. I felt pretty big, all right, but if I'd known what was going to happen at Coogan's damned Chiricahua Wells that night I'd never have stopped there with the rest. I'd have kept right on to California, and maybe ridden right into the ocean.

"They can keep it," I said. "How far's Tucson?"

"You'll feel better, hoss, time we come to the Wells," Coogan said. "Cottonwoods, and a big fat spring. Plenty grass for the animals, too. Tucson's fifty mile or so, anyone wants to go there. But I mind me of Oregon, now, when I was up there with Parkman. He was just a kid of a boy, too, like you. But the whole country was green, like the Wells. Sure you want to go to Californy? Oregon's a whole lot more comfortable."

He was a liar, too. To hear him tell it, he'd met Columbus at the boat and shook hands with him. But we had to depend on him.

"Let's get back to the wagons," I said, sawing my bay Buster around. "Saul will start fretting." He would, too. Coogan might show us where Chiricahua Wells was, and palaver with the Indians for us, but my brother Saul was the boss of the wagon train.

"All right," Coogan said.

He ambled after me, the Hawken propped across the saddle in front of him, and he was still talking about Parkman, back in forty-six. That was thirty years ago, and he hadn't forgot a thing, or he was making it up as he went along, which was more likely. I hope I never get old and windy like that.

When we got back to the wagons, he was still talking.

"We stopped that night at Fort Laramie. I tell you, I never seen so many Sioux in all my days. We—"

"Coogan says there's water up ahead," I told Saul.

He straightened up from the hub he was greasing, and wiped his hands on the seat of his jeans.

"How far?"

"Eight mile," Coogan said. He shifted his cud to the other side of his mouth. "We kin make it easy before sundown."

Edie Gorman stuck her head out of our old Moline wagon, holding the flapping canvas around her like maybe she didn't have many clothes on. She probably didn't. She was Edie Boston, now, and Saul's wife, but I never could get used to it. I don't think she could, either, because she spent most of her time with my brother Dave on some excuse or other. She was pretty, with a head of hair like red silk—raw China silk—and her skin was rich and smooth as cream.

"Is there water?" she asked. "Because if there is, I want to take a bath. Saul, is there water?"

He took his time, wiping his big hands on a bandana and working it around his knuckles real careful. That was his way.

"Mr. Coogan says we'll make it by sundown, Edie."

She closed the flap, but first she winked at me, because I'd blush, and she liked that. Then I heard her picking at the dulcimer, and I knew she was lying half-naked in the hot wagon, her hair falling over her shoulders, teasing at the strings the way she teased at Saul. She was only a couple of years older than me and a lot younger than Saul, but she knew how to be a woman like she'd been at it for a thousand years. "By God, now I like music," old man Coogan said. "She plays that instrument real sweet, Mr. Boston. You take your brother Dave and her pounding at that harp or whatever 'tis—him singin' and her plunkin'—why, it's a real nice sound."

It seemed like Saul would never get done wiping his hands. Finally, though, he stuffed the bandana in his pocket and clucked to the mules.

"Get along," he said. "You, Sodom, and you, Gomorrah."

Even the mules never fooled with my brother. They leaned into their collars and pulled. Behind us, the rest of the wagons creaked along, dust hanging low around the iron wheels. The wind had died, and you could hear a long way. There was Leo Nation and his outfit, and behind them the Galloway family with seven noisy skinny kids, and the Thorpes, and Finn Crozier and his wife, that owned the madstone, and the Ogg wagon with milk goats yammering and Carl Ogg's buggy tied behind. Gus Moon's wagon brought up the rear. Gus was never on time for anything. It was sure a patchwork outfit, but Saul had talked them all into going to California, all the way from Columbus, Ohio, where us boys lived. I guess if anyone could get them there, Saul could.

"Where's Dave?" Saul asked me. "Doing the devil's work someplace?"

He walked along at my stirrup, and his broad back was as wet as the mules' hides.

"How do I know?"

It was a touchy subject between us. When Dave said he'd go along, it didn't please Saul too much. Dave took the whole thing for a big joke, like he took everything. Saul never approved of Dave gambling, and drinking, and laying in bed on a Sunday morning instead of going to church. So it was up to me to smooth things over between them, and carry messages back and forth, and I thought the whole thing was pretty silly.

"He went out for game this morning," Saul said. The beat of his boots in the sand never stopped, but he turned his head over his shoulder and looked back along the train. "I warned him not to stray."

"He can take care of himself," I said. Dave could, too. A man that's handy with women and cards and liquor is apt to be handy with a gun. Once I saw Dave plug the pip on an ace at fifty paces. Did it with a borrowed gun, too.

Saul wasn't much for conversation, so I rode ahead to look for Chiricahua Wells. Now that we were in Arizona Territory, we were near the end of the trip, and I wasn't exactly looking forward to it. Anyone else going to California would have come for a gold mine, or Spanish treasure, or something lively, anyways. But not Saul. He was a farmer, born and bred, and that was all he could think about. He'd heard of a valley below Sacramento where there was plenty of water and black soil six feet deep and mild winters, and that was enough for him. That was how he talked the Nations and the Thorpes and the Croziers and the rest into striking out for the Coast. Now me—I'd had enough milking at four in the morning, and tromping behind a plow, cutting hay with a cradle. So I figured I'd better enjoy my last fling before Saul put me to work again.

Whatever else old man Coogan was, he had a sharp eye. I could see the Wells now—a low green smudge in the heat waves, a snake wriggling on the horizon. A creek came foaming out of a cleft in a granite shelf, and pooled in high-piled rocks before running off to sink into the barren grass and disappear. It wasn't very far from the eight miles Ike Coogan had guessed.

"This here is what they call the Sulphur Springs Valley," Coogan said. He waved a skinny fringed arm around. "Shame it's so pestered with Apache. A man could make a good living here."

I watched the dusty wagons pull in, the canvas flapping and harness creaking. There wasn't much talk—everyone was too tired after that day's long pull. The last time we'd stopped for a decent camp was Fort Bowie, fifty miles back. There'd been a lot of grumbling because Saul was in such a hurry, but tonight they were all too spent to argue. Men moved around the ring of wagons with a kind of shuffling walk, unhitching stock and helping the women and children down to stand stiff-legged till the feel of the ground got through to them. Mina Ogg was already milking her goat, and young ones stood in a quiet circle, each waiting for his turn at the bucket. Saul told off two men to gather wood, and two more to bring water from the pools that lay among the big rocks. But I didn't see Dave.

"What's for supper?" I asked Eda.

She was still lying in the wagon, only her red head poked out, but when I said that she gave me a queer look, and her lip trembled. It was a joke between us, about supper, because she couldn't boil water, and Saul had to do all the cooking for the Bostons. But I guess she was overly tired, or maybe upset like a woman gets sometimes over nothing, because she started to cry, and then she jerked the flap shut and left me standing.

I went over to where Saul was slicing bacon into a pan.

"What's the matter with her?" I asked.

He pulled the knife through the pink meat.

"Eda?"

"She's crying."

He laid the slabs in the pan like he was laying a wall, the joints all matching.

"She'll be all right soon's she's had a bite to eat."

"There's Dave," I said. "Looks like he got us a deer."

Saul didn't look up.

"About time."

Dave had a fat buck slung over his saddle, and there was blood on his jeans and hands and down the withers of his horse. Everyone was glad to see him, and old man Coogan dragged the deer down and went to work on him with his old Green River knife.

"Here, kid," Dave said. "Take Queenie and rub her down for me, will you?"

I guess Dave was the handsome one of the Boston boys, if any of us were. Anyway, he always said he was, and I was the smart one and Saul was the strong one. Dave was small and compact—not skinny, but tough and brown like a strip of saddle leather. His face was small and brown and wrinkled—perfect, in a way, like a walnut is whole and complete. He was always grinning about something—it didn't have to be much. I heard a man say once that Dave was smiling the night he shot Jake Earnshaw in a poker game back in Columbus. But Jake had it coming. He always was a loudmouth. And you couldn't get mad at Dave, because he took Jake to the doctor himself, which he didn't have to do. Saul was the oldest, all right, and the boss, and Dave came next, but I always wanted to grow up and be like Dave. Dave and I were real blood brothers, and I had our bloody fingerprints in solemn compact on a piece of cloth in my pocket.

When I came back from watering Queenie, it was getting dark. The sun got redder and redder as it sank, and the whole rocky glen where we camped was spilling over with red light. Some of those boulders were as big as houses, and the light slanted between them and around them and splashed red into the pools of water and then out again, so it hurt your eyes. The campfires didn't count for much in that red light. You could hardly see them.

"Here," Dave said. He tore off a piece of liver from the chunk he was roasting over the coals and handed it to me. "Eat some of that and you'll fill out a little, kid."

He was only five years older than me, but he called me kid all the time.

"Sure," Coogan said. His jaws worked in the red light, gumming at the liver. "A man could live on deer's liver, if he had to. And drink the blood. Ain't nothin' healthier."

I looked over toward Saul. He was hunkered down with a tin pan, staring into the fire, his big black hat pushed back on his forehead.

"Maybe I better take a piece of this over to Saul," I said.

Dave looked up at me and grinned. His face split and creased into a thousand dark wrinkles.

"You'll get along, kid," he said.

When I handed the roasted liver to Saul, he shook his head.

"I'm not hungry."

He hadn't eaten the bacon, either. It was still on his plate.

"Maybe Edie would like it," I said.

He looked across the grass to where Dave was sprawled on his elbows, swapping lies with old man Coogan.

"She took her wrapper and went down below to take a bath." He got up. "It just come to me, I haven't set a guard for the night."

While he went off to round up the guard, I climbed on a wagon wheel and sat there, my boot heels on the hub. Well, if no one else wanted the liver I'd eat it. I chewed, watching the red light get darker and darker, like blood turns black when it stands.

Mina Ogg put her young ones to bed in the wagon and Leo Nation got out his mouth-harp and started to play, soft and quiet. I think it was Sourwood Mountain. There was something about the Wells right then that didn't call for any loud noises, and everyone just laid around with their bellies full and stared into the fire or hummed along under their breath, or maybe thought about Columbus and little farms and places they'd left to go to California with Saul Boston. Pretty soon the stars came out, and the wind stirred a little. I remembered that signal smoke Ike Coogan and I saw before dusk, and I craned my neck around to look, but it was too dark. The last light was gone, except for the winking of our cook-fires. Some of the women and children went out to take baths in the deep cold pools, and came back shivering and giggling, the women with their wet hair piled high on top of their heads. I didn't see Edie, though. She never liked to go with the other women. Come to think of it, I didn't see Dave, either. I went over to where Coogan was dressing out the skin of the buck Dave had killed.

"Where's Dave?"

Ike used that old knife for everything—skinning, gutting, sewing, eating, picking what teeth he had left.

"I dunno. Lit out of here on some kind of a errant."

I sat down beside him and laid his old Hawken rifle across my knees. It must have weighed fifteen pounds. A wind riffled the cottonwoods. I lay there, rubbing my hand along the stock. It was smooth and worn so that it was like glass, almost. Saul went off with Henry Gannon and Gus Moon, them trailing their rifles.

"Ike," I said, "what's California like?"

His knife didn't stop scraping.

"Well, down around San Diego there's a lot of Spanish people, and sheep, and cattle." He wiped finger and thumb along the blade to clear it of the sticky fat. "Now you take them Spanish women, Joey—there ain't nothin' to beat 'em. Kind of soft and plump, like a pa'tridge. They don't put up much more fight either." He gave me a shove, and grinned. "Young feller like you, curly hair and all your teeth—why, you'll lay 'em like mason lays brick!"

The woodsmoke sank low in the glen, like a fog. Someone yelled, "Hey, where's Dave? Where's Dave Boston? Let's have a song to cheer us up!"

"I don't want any Spanish girls," I said.

The yelling kept up, and someone started to pound a tin pan.

"Dave! Davey Boston! Where's Edie? Play us a tune!"

Ike Coogan scrambled up and started to pat his hands and stamp his feet. I handed him his Hawken rifle, and the air was so dry a little spark jumped off the barrel and cracked to his knuckles. He cussed me something awful, but it sounded better than his singing.

"Where's Eda?" he asked me.

I shook my head.

"I don't know."

I went to Saul's wagon to see if she was back from her bath but as I rapped on the tailgate she lifted the flap and climbed out, the dulcimer under her arm.

"Here, Joey," she said. "Take it for me, will you?"

When she put her leg over the high board, there was a flash of white knee—white as milk—and I turned my head away.

She whispered in my ear as she brushed by, smelling sweet and clean.

"Thank you, Joey."

They were gathered around the fire, men and women and young ones, all waiting and anxious. Music was about all there was, in the evening. The train that had a man with a banjo or even a juice-harp was lucky. With Dave Boston and Eda we were high-class.

"Play 'The Buff'ler Skinner'." Ike Coogan begged. He took off his dirty old hat and slapped it against his thigh. "Listen, Dave—Eda! Play 'The Buff'ler Skinners' Oh, I love that piece!"

Dave had the damndest habit of not staying in one place. He'd be standing beside you, talking, and he'd vanish while his last words were in the air. Now he showed up in the circle of fire with Eda, his hat down his back on a string, clearing his throat, while the flames leaped and roared.

"I don't think I know Buffalo Skinners," Eda said.

"You just follow me." Dave grinned, his face screwing up like a juniper stump. "Just strum along, sweet girl."

It looked in a way like Eda was scared about something. Her fingers were clumsy and awkward on the keys, and that wasn't like her. But Dave leaned over her, one hand on her shoulder, and sang a chorus of Buffalo Skinners.

It happened in Jacksboro, the spring of sixty three
A man by the name of Crego come stepping up to me
"How do you do, young fellow, and would you like to go
And spend a summer pleasantly on the range of the buffalo?"

Her touch with the hammers was a little surer, then, but she seemed to be looking, searching the firelit faces.

"Yes, I will give good wages, give transportation, too
Provided you will go with me and stay the summer through.
But if you should grow homesick, come back to Jacksboro
I won't pay transportation from the range of the buffalo."

Everybody joined in on the last line, "... the range of the buffalo ...," the high treble of the children, Gus Moon's wheezing bass, Coogan's quavering tenor searching up and down for a note he liked. I was just thinking it didn't look like he would find one when the chorus died out, real slow, like the church organ when you hold down a note and stop pumping. My brother Saul pushed through the crowd, shouldering people aside. He stopped in front of Dave and Eda, and his face was the color of dead ashes.

It's funny how you remember little small things at times like that—things that don't matter, but you remember. For me, it was a fat gray mouse that skittered out on a slab of rock and picked up a crumb of hoecake, sitting there nibbling, with tiny bright eyes.

"Put up your hands," Saul said.

His voice was thick and blurred as he walked up to Dave. He grabbed a handful of Dave's shirt and ripped it across the chest. Then he slapped Dave, a loud slap that left a welt, even on Dave's hard brown cheek.

"Put up your hands!" Saul's knotted at his sides. "You little sneak!"

Dave stood like he was carved out of wood. The smile was still on his face, and the ripped flap of cloth hung across his bare chest. Someone screamed—I think it was Eda—and the dulcimer tinkled a jangle of notes as it fell. Gus Moon was the first to move. He sidled behind Saul and grabbed his arm, but it was like trying to grab the walking beam of a steamboat.

"What's the matter, Saul?" Dave asked.

I don't think Dave feared anything, or anybody, but that night he was afraid of my brother Saul. There was murder in Saul's eyes, and in his hands that kept twisting and moving.

"If there's anything the matter," Dave said, "maybe you ought to tell us about it. Tell us all about it." He looked around at our people, and old Finn Crozier nodded, his white beard wagging.

Everybody respected Saul, but they liked Dave, and Finn said, "Seems to me that's right, Saul," in his mild old voice.

Saul's head swung back and forth. He looked at Eda with a kind of desperation.

"That makes you even more of a scoundrel," he yelled.

Even behind the brown, Dave's face got white when Saul said that.

"All right." Saul stood thick-legged in the firelight, making clumsy movements with his hands. "All right, then. I'll say it." He was looking at Dave, but talking to us all. "My brother has been hanging around my wife. My Eda. She—she went out for her bath, and he followed her. I come on them by accident, and I wish to God I'd taken another path. But I didn't. I come on them, together. The two of them—her naked and him holding her tight to him!"

A kind of awe fell on us all. Gus Moon dropped his hand from Saul's sleeve, and I could hear breathing—heavy breathing—all around. If the Apaches wanted to spook our camp that night, they could have walked in and carried off every last rifle and cartridge and looking glass and no one would have noticed.

"Dave—" I said.

"Be quiet, kid." He took the dangling flap of his shirt and tore it the rest of the way off. He threw it in the fire and it smoked for a minute and burst into flame. It was charred and black, with only a little red glow along the edges. "Listen, Saul—"

"I won't listen to anything," Saul said. "I saw what I saw."

Eda slipped past me and ran to Saul, her red hair tumbled and flying. Her feet were bare and white and small and her hands were small like a birds's claws where they lay on Saul's chest.

"Listen to me, Saul! You've got to listen! It isn't—I mean I didn't—"

He threw her from him.

"You!"

The word carried a blow like a minie ball, and she shrank away.

"All right," Saul said. His voice was a little clearer, and his words almost rational. "I had a mind to kill you, Dave, but it come to me you were my own brother, and it isn't right, no matter what you done." He looked down at his hands and they were strange to him. "You best get out. Get out of my sight. Tonight. When the sun comes up, you be a long way from here, because if I see you again, I'll strangle you. With my bare hands. Cain or no Cain. I'll do it."

Dave looked at me. He looked at Finn Crozier, and at Leo Nation, and all the rest of the men.

"Saul," he said," "I—"

What he was going to say died in his throat. He put his hat on and walked away. When he passed the circle of light from the fire, he was swallowed up in the night. I heard him whistle for Queenie, and she nickered back, and that was all.

"You." Saul looked at Eda. "Get back in the wagon."

She went away, head down, not caring where her feet walked in the loose shale and rubble that lay in the grass like dead bones. I picked up the dulcimer and followed her.

"Eda?" I said.

Standing before the wagon, she looked up at me. Now, with something like this, she wasn't crying. Women are hard to understand.

"Here." I handed it to her. "Let me give you a hand up."

I made a step for her foot with my hands, and she stepped up and her foot was cold, like marble. I didn't know what to say—what could you say? I heard the canvas flap come rustling down, and I was grateful.

When I got back only Saul was there, hunkered down, poking at the fire with a stick. I went over to where Ike Coogan was rolled in his blanket, and I stretched out beside him, putting my hands behind my head and looking up at the stars. My mouth had an awful metallic taste in it, and my eyes blurred.

Someone was singing. It was a faint tinny voice. I listened. It was old man Coogan. Very softly, he was whining "... on the range of the buffalo."

"Shut up, you old fool," I said.

At midnight it came up Saul's turn to stand guard. He got up, slowly and painfully, and went away into the brush, not looking back.

I don't remember sleeping much that night. I don't think anyone did. But at sunup I got up and kicked at the fire to make some coffee. That was when I found out that Eda was gone, too. She'd gone with my brother Dave, during the night.

CHAPTER TWO

I grabbed Ike Coogan by the shoulder and shook him. "Wake up!"

He sat bolt upright, holding his lousy gray blanket around him with one hand and hanging on to the Hawken rifle with the other. "Injuns?"

I shook my head. "Dave run off during the night. He took Eda with him."

Coogan yawned, and scrubbed at his skull with his knuckles. "Ain't nothin' I can do about, dod-dum it!"

I don't know why I bothered to tell him. With Dave gone, it seemed like he was the only one left, scraggly and dirty as he was. But whatever I might have done, it was too late. Saul knew they were gone. He went from wagon to wagon, talking in a low voice, and then dropping the flap like it burned him and going on to the next. Behind him heads popped out, and a buzz of excitement went round. No one thought about breakfast, except maybe Carl Ogg. He was squatted down over a fire, frying sidemeat in a skillet, and he didn't pay any attention to Saul, even when Saul came up beside him and stood looking down. That was when I noticed Carl's Concord buggy was missing. For fifteen hundred miles and more he'd pulled it behind his wagon, and now it was gone.

"So that's how they went," Saul said.

Carl didn't look up. He wiped the back of his hand across his nose and sat there, hunkered up like a frog. "Sure, that's how they went. Dave slipped back last night while you was out on guard and scratched at my canvas. Give me three hundred dollars for my buggy, and hitched Queenie up and took out like a bolt of lightning. What's it to me if Eda was with him? I ain't so flush I can pass up three hundred dollars, can I?"

Carl was a little man, with a fringe of gray chin whiskers and not much else but children. He was the begattingest man in Columbus. He wouldn't have given Saul any trouble, but Mina Ogg was different. She was big and rawboned, and she climbed out of the wagon in her shift, looking like a gunboat.

"Now, you wait a minute, Saul Boston! Just because your nose is out of joint, there ain't no call to make more trouble. Dave wanted the buggy, and the mister and I talked it over with him, and he had the money and there was a deal made and that's all there is to it! We ain't concerned otherwise."

I never saw Saul look so big and so powerful, and yet he was alone, an animal caught in a trap. He took his knuckles in one hand and cracked them, staring at Mina Ogg. But I don't think he saw her, even.

"He came back, then. After I told him to leave, he came back."

I didn't blame Carl Ogg. The buggy was about all he had, that and the kids and a team of spavined mules. But I wouldn't have crossed Saul for a thousand dollars. I'd lived with Saul for seventeen years, and I'd never seen him like this. He'd been mad at me before, and at Dave, but it was a kind of rough furious anger that passed, and then he was sheepish and tried to make it up in little ways to us. But what he was feeling now came off him like a deadly damp in the coal mines at home. It came off him like a vapor and settled around the camp, and people drew back before it like they would the black damp, and shoved the kids back out of sight in the wagons, and watched with eyes that were little and hard, like glass.

"What did you say?" he asked Carl.

Carl shook the skillet and the meat slid around in the popping grease.

"All I meant was, you got no call to judge him, or her, either. You didn't give neither of them a chance to speak up, did you?"

Saul's chest came up and out and up again, like he couldn't get enough air into it. But he didn't do anything. I'd have given odds he'd kick Carl Ogg into the fire and stamp him down till you couldn't have told him from the ashes. But he didn't. He went away, blundering over a fallen log, holding his hand out before him like he couldn't see.

Old man Coogan had more sense than most of us. He went around bawling at everyone and picking at them like a gray old crow, hurrying them, trying to get the outfit back into the shafts again.

"All right, now! We ain't got all day. Boil your coffee and fry your bacon! Hang me fer bear meat, if I don't push off without the lot of you! Let's make a straight shirt-tail out of here!"

They went at it fast, all of them, looking over their shoulders at Saul. It was his say when they left, not old man Coogan's, but Saul didn't move. He stood beside his wagon, hands deep in his jeans, looking at the toes of his boots. Bit by bit, Saul or no Saul, the train came together. Fresh-filled water barrels slopped, teams plodded into harness, ears flat and eyes rolling. Ike Coogan stamped out the fires and scraped dirt over them, watching Saul from the corner of his eye. I went over to Saul. I guessed it was up to me.

"Hadn't you better get ready?"

He didn't look at me.

"I'm not going."

I thought I hadn't heard him right.

"Not going?"

I said it louder than I'd thought, and the jingle of harness and the noise of kids stopped for a minute. Old man Coogan shambled over, scratching his skinny stomach where it stuck out through a hole in the buckskins.

"Saul, you better get a hustle on. We got a long pull before next water."

"You go on without me," Saul said.

What he was saying was crazy, but the way he said it was quiet and almost cheerful. I'd heard crazy people talk that way, though, in the Mount Olivet Home back in Columbus.

"I haven't got any reason to go anyplace," Saul said. He hooked his thumbs in his belt, and jerked his head at the deep green of the cottonwoods and the big-piled boulders of the Wells. "What's a better place to go than this? Plenty water, wood—" He took off his hat and rolled up the brim in his fingers. I could see his forehead was wet and whitelooking above the brown line where the hat had been. "I'm staying right here, that's all. The rest of you go on. Coogan's been paid. You all don't need me anymore. I'm staying right here."

Whatever the rest of them thought about the fracas last night over Dave and Eda, they still had respect and trust for my brother. There was a chorus of protest. Even Gus Moon, shiftless as he was and drunk half the time, spoke up.

"Now, Saul, you got us into this. It's up to you to stick it out. Come on, now—harness up! What's over is over and done with. Come on, now, hoss."

My brother stared up at the sun. He didn't say anything—he didn't have to. The morning was well along, and they had a long road to travel. Mina Ogg looked at me, and she wasn't the only one. I was supposed to jolly Saul along, the way I'd been doing with him and Dave.

Somehow I was supposed to get him out of this crazy idea and on to Sacramento with the rest. But I knew it wouldn't do any good. I knew how stubborn he was. If he once got an idea, he wouldn't any more give it up than a snapping turtle will let go a man's finger once he's snatched it. There was this one thing—a turtle's got more sense, because a turtle will leave go at sundown. That was where Saul was different.

"Saul," I said. "These people are depending on you."

I knew how he felt. He'd always been boss; that was the way we'd been brought up. But now he'd been humbled and humiliated in front of the people that had trusted and liked him, and that was something he couldn't stand—to be taken lightly.

"Mr. Boston," Coogan said.

The breeze had risen, and it picked at the dirty fringe of buckskin at his elbow. The smell of the desert came to us even there, in the shade at the Wells, and it was dusty and hot, the drawing kind of heat that sucks the moisture right out of you.

"Mr. Boston, you kin stay here or not, as you like. The only thing I'm bound to mention, after we get out of here the Apaches ain't goin' to be long comin' in again. Seven wagons they won't bother, but one wagon ain't got no more chance than a piece of raw meat in a pack of yellow dogs. You stick your finger in a pond, then pull it out and look for the hole. That's where a lone white man goes in this Injun country."

Saul rummaged through the stuff in the wagon. He came out with the tin box he kept our family Bible and papa and mama's picture in. There was money in it, too, and when he put the box down I noticed the lock was twisted and broken.

"Here." He handed me a sheaf of wrinkled bills. "Joey, this is your share of the money for the farm. I was keeping it for you." He seemed to know what I was thinking, and he went on. "Dave got his last night. He broke into the box before he left. Now I guess that makes us all square."

I felt all gone inside, looking at the money. Dave gone—now this seemed to make it final and complete, everything ruined. "I don't want this money," I said.

Ike Coogan cleared his throat and spat a long sticky streamer into the dirt. "Don't never turn down money, boy. If it's yours, take it."

"You'll need it, wherever you're going," Saul said. He slammed the lid of the box shut, and tossed it back into the wagon. "Now get going, all of you. There's been enough time wasted."

"Saul," I said, "don't you want me to stay with you?" I couldn't believe what he was saying. I heard the words, but I couldn't fit them into my mind. "You can't stay here all alone."

He wouldn't even look at me, and I felt a lump in my throat. Two thousand miles I'd come with him, and we were brothers. Up till then, I hadn't known what I was going to do. It was crazy to stay at the Wells with a crazy man, and yet Saul was all I had left. I might have stayed. But the quick way he shoved the money in my hands and told me to leave—I swallowed the lump, and for once I told off my brother.

"All right," I said. I shoved the money in my pocket. I didn't know how much there was, or care. "I wouldn't stay here with you if you were dying. You're like a mad dog, crazy-mad. You hate everyone and everybody, just because of what happened last night. You'll kill yourself, just because you're so crazy-mad, and maybe it's the best thing could ever happen to you."

I climbed into our wagon and put my stuff in a gunny sack. There wasn't much—an extra shirt and a pair of patched jeans, my comb, the little Bible I'd won for knowing the most verse at Sunday School. I put my two best fire-eye aggie marbles in my jeans pocket and threw the rest away. When I climbed out, toting my gunny sack, Saul was still leaning against our old wagon, arms folded.

"Goodbye," I said.

He just stood there, like he didn't hear me. I got on Buster and kicked the bay around toward the west.

"Let's get going," I said to Coogan.

He whooped at the wagons and they rolled out, swinging and swaying and creaking. No one looked at Saul as they went by. Even the kids sensed something solemn and tragic, and one of Carl Ogg's little ones gnawed at his knuckles and then started to cry—a thin sound in the grind of wheels and the scraping of iron tires on rock. But as the Ogg wagon passed, Mina Ogg reached out a fat arm and tossed something toward Saul. It fell at his feet, but he didn't pick it up. I knew what it was. It was the little nankeen sack she kept her madstone in. I guess the madstone was about all the valuables the Oggs owned, and when words wouldn't do any more, she was trying to help Saul, whether he'd be helped or no.

When the last wagon passed, I slapped the reins and rode away, Ike Coogan ambling alongside me. I didn't look back, but in my mind I saw the Wells growing smaller and smaller in the east, a little forest of green in the sunbaked plain and a smaller figure standing beside a wagon. I was riding away from home, it seemed, and it was like a miniature in someone's locket, and the picture would stay with me for a long time.

It was almost dark again when we crossed the old Camino Real. The Santa Cruz was a series of brackish pools there, ringed with green scum and dead insects, but the water tasted good. I squatted beside Ike Coogan while he held a twist of dough on a green stick over the fire. He hadn't said anything to me about what happened last night. In a way I liked Ike; he had sensibilities you wouldn't have thought possible for a fleabitten old rat like him.

He broke off a chunk of the roasted dough and handed it to me. It didn't taste bad with a swallow of coffee to go along with it. I chewed on it, and swallowed coffee, and looked around me in the slanting rays of the sun. Six wagons, now. The sun slid down a notch in the mountains and there was a dusty purple haze all around. The wagon canvas glimmered in the haze, and I heard Gus Moon's team slurping water from one of the green-edged holes. Down the Camino Real came more of Tully, Ochoa and Company's freight wagons. They'd been passing us ever since we made camp, hauling from Sonora up to Tully's store in Tucson—cotton cloth, rum, lard, bacon, hams—Ike knew all about it, and knew most of the teamsters.

"How far's Tucson?" I asked.

Coogan peered into the dusk. "Looks like old man Gulick driving that wagon," he said. "Tucson? Oh, twenty mile up the road. That is, if you go by road. I don't hold much with roads. Too many people on 'em." He cupped his hands and hollered. "Hey, Jake Gulick!" The wagon braked to a halt and the outriders gathered around to watch Coogan and Jake Gulick howl and punch each other in the ribs.

Twenty miles. That wasn't far. I had eight hundred dollars in my jeans—I'd counted it—and Tucson was where Dave and Eda had gone. I was sure of it. Sacramento didn't hold any bait for me. I'd leave the train here and go north to Tucson. Tucson! The name excited me. It was bells jingling and strange sights and romance and adventure. It sounded a lot better than Columbus and Marietta and Mount Pleasant and piddling common names like those.

Old Coogan came back grinning like a baked possum. "Jake Gulick and I went into a whorehouse in Santa Fe together once," he said. "When the madam saw us—" He broke off, seeing me saddling up. "Now where in thunderation you goin', Joey?"

"Tucson."

I think he had consumption, because he started to cough real hard, and pounded on his chest with his fist.

"Night air," he said. "Ain't hardly any other kind at night, but it gethers in my lungs." He watched me yank the cinch up on Buster's belly, and check the quick-loading cartridge box for my Spencer carbine—the one Saul bought for me back in St. Louis. "You think that's where Dave is?"

"I don't know," I said. "Probably."

Coogan rolled another twist of dough and coiled it around the stick. "Don't go, Joey. Tucson ain't no place for a kid of a boy. Besides, you're better off shut of Dave. Dave and me—we got along fine, but then I'm an old rip anyway. You got a lot of promise, Joey. Don't throw it away on Dave. Didn't Carl Ogg offer you a job, onct you get to Sacramento?"

"A lot you know," I said. "Dave's the only one ever did anything nice for me. People just don't understand him, that's all."

Coogan squatted down and stuck the dough into the coals. "Saul understood him."

I saw a bobbing lantern down the road. It was another of Tully's freight wagons. I'd just fall in behind and they'd lead me to Tucson. I climbed on Buster and old man Coogan got up real quick. Up till then I think he'd figured me to be joking about Tucson.

"By God," he said, "you won't last any longer in Tucson 'n it takes a alligator to chew a puppy!" He fumbled in his bed roll and pulled out an old Walker Colt in a worn holster. "Here, you'll need a handgun. Take this."

"I got my carbine."

"Never mind." He shoved it in my hand. "I took it off'n a dead Mescalero. Didn't cost me nothin'." He waved away the bills I held out. "Now git."

I wanted to shake hands with him, or something, but he squatted down at his fire, turning his back to me like he didn't want to see me any more. I waited till the Tully wagon passed and then I reined in far enough behind to let the dust settle, and slumped down in the saddle with a yawn. It would be a long night.

I rode in past the old cathedral at Bac. An Indian family was living there, and they had horses stabled in the chapel. The sun was blinding on the hot white dust, and I never heard so much commotion. Dogs barked and ran under Buster's hoofs, snarling and snapping. Mules brayed fit to split your eardrums. Windmills creaked, and behind every adobe hut was a squeaky burro mill grinding flour. I could smell mesquite wood burning in a thousand ovens, and manure, and garlic and onions and seared hoofs from a blacksmith's shop. Freight wagons, water-vendors with clay jugs on their shoulders, wood-sellers shouting their wares, painted dark ladies looking out through deep doorways and smiling. I kept going, reining up now and then to let a stage by, or watch a fat woman snatch a barebottomed child from under Buster's hoofs. Sooner or later, I figured, I'd come to the center of the town. But it didn't seem to have any center. It was just a big sprawling noisy place, with a lot of soldiers in the middle of the noise, sweating under brushwood *ramadas* in what they called Military Plaza.

Right across from Military Plaza was Warner's store, and I went in and bought a loaf of bread and some cheese whacked off a big moldy wheel. It cost me two dollars and a half. I'd have to watch my money in Tucson.

I lounged around that afternoon, keeping an eye out for Dave and Eda, but I didn't see them. In that hurly-burly, a man would be hard put to find anyone. There were no streets or pavements, and most of the privies seemed to empty right in front of you so you had to watch where you walked. Cockfights were going on all around, and there was a kind of Punch and Judy show every few steps, with a noisy off-key band banging away with a banjo and a drum. It wasn't anything like Columbus.

I ate supper at the Shoofly restaurant across from the Plaza. It cost me three dollars for a plate of beans and chili, with a cup of black Mexican coffee. Well, tomorrow I'd look around for a job of work. And maybe I'd find Dave. I'd forgotten all about my brother Saul, holed up at Chiricahua Wells, fifty miles away.

Whisky was reasonable, I'll say that. It wasn't very good whisky, I guess, but I didn't know the difference. I bought a bottle at Zeckendorf's, like everyone else seemed to be doing, and went out to sit in the evening cool at the Plaza and listen to the soldiers' band play. That was when this dark girl came up to me. She didn't look anything like the powdered and painted women that peeked out of the doorways of Tucson. She had a fine old man with her—a Mexican in a short velvet jacket with silver all over it, and a little beard that waggled when he talked.

I could see at a glance that they were the high type of Mexicans, so I wasn't worried when they sat on the bench next to me. The old man said *"Con permiso, senor,"* and his little beard wiggled. The girl sat on the other side of him eyes downcast in modesty, hands folded in her lap. Every once in a while she would look at me from the corner of her eye. Once, while she applauded the military band with tiny gloved hands, her eye caught mine square, and she blushed so her skin turned a dark warm color.

Ike Coogan! I thought. *What did he know about Spanish women?* I took another drink and offered the bottle to the old man, desiring to become better acquainted.

"Gracias," he said, and tipped the bottle up. He drank an awful lot, but I didn't object. Not with a daughter, or niece, or whatever she was, like this blossom of old Spain!

"Senor," I said. That's Spanish for "mister".

He turned sad eyes on me, blinking respectfully.

"I'd like to make the acquaintance of the lady."

He didn't speak English, but he knew what I wanted. He got up and bowed, turning toward the lady and then me and then the lady again, gabbling Spanish talk. I think her name was Dolores something. Anyway she seemed to answer to that. I pulled the old man's coattails and he sat down, very dignified in spite of the people shouting at him to get out of the way so they could watch the band.

"Senorita," I said, "let us take a little walk in the moonlight."

There wasn't any moon, but the sentiment was graceful. I couldn't let a Mexican outdo me. I looked around for my bottle but her father had it again, and it didn't seem hospitable to take it away from him. Anyway, it was almost empty.

Strolling down a dark lane with Dolores on my arm, the band music dying away behind us and her soft and warm and smelling good when she leaned against me, I felt pretty sly. Saul never liked me to go with any girls but dull ones, like the minister's daughter at home, and *she* was no fun. Dave always laughed and winked when I mentioned girls. Once he gave me a dollar to go to a whorehouse on West Mound Street in Columbus that he recommended. I didn't go. I was scared to when I heard all the things you might catch. But I told him I did and he was pleased. Now, all on my own, I was squiring a real high-born Spanish girl and she liked me, kept squeezing my hand and brushing against me like a perfumed kitten.

"Dolores," I said, "I'm going to kiss you."

The band music was very faint now, but my pulse was loud in my ears. I was unsteady on my feet, too, and when I tried to grab her she darted away and stood in a sliver of light that came from a barred window that opened on the lane. She called to me, softly, and beckoned.

This must be the ancestral home, I thought. Well, this *was* something! High-born Latin people are very reluctant to invite strangers into their homes, but I must have made a good impression because she took a key from her bosom and opened the heavy door, smiling at me to follow.

I think she and her father were aristocracy fallen on evil days, because there wasn't much furniture in the room but a bed. It was a quiet, dusty place, with recessed window sills of dark wood, and a muslin-covered ceiling. Dolores turned the lamp down. While I was admiring some large beetles on the wall, she slipped out of her laces and furbelows.

"Now here!" I said. "Wait a minute!"

She was naked, with a short strong body like ivory in the lampglow. Her breasts nudged against me as she wound her arms around my neck and whispered in my ear. Up till now, the Arizona Territory had only been something to pass through on the way to California. Now it seemed to take on more significance.

I don't remember much else very clearly. It's tangled up in my mind with roses and warm smells and the feel of flesh like velvet, with a texture that excited my fingers. That, and a crazy happy feeling that was a half bottle of not-too-good whisky mixed with love and youth. Then I guess I went to sleep, no longer a virgin, but happy.

I woke up with someone shaking me by the shoulder. Light streamed through an open door, and my mouth tasted like I'd been chewing on brass cartridge cases—old ones, with verdigrease on them. A fat woman with stringy hair hung over me, one hand wrenching at my bare shoulder.

"Get up! Get out of here! *Senor, vamos!*"

I pulled away from her. The effort made my head buzz like a million bees.

"Who—what—" I sat up, and she handed me something. It was my jeans. I think I blushed, but I'm not sure.

"Where's—" I tried to think. "Where's Doña Dolores? The one who—who"

The woman laughed, and blew out her lips in a scornful way. Still fuddled, I got one leg into the jeans and then had a vague feeling something was wrong. There wasn't the bulk in the hip pocket where it should be. My wallet!

I jumped to my feet, not caring about modesty, searching through the pockets. My wallet was gone, and my eight hundred dollars with it! The woman was laughing, fat bosom bobbing, hands on hips. But it wasn't funny to me. The truth was soaking into my throbbing head. I'd been rolled.

"Where's Dolores?" I yelled.

She stopped laughing, and was wary. "I clean this rooms, *senor.* That is all."

"She's—she's—" I was helpless in my effort to tell her how Dolores was—how tall, how favored, the shape of her nose—the nose I remembered kissing last night. Angry, bewildered, acting no different from men immemorial in circumstances like these, I grabbed her fat elbow and pinched. "Where is she?"

That was when the commotion attracted a visitor. A thick smooth man came through the sunlit door, a muscular man with a barrel of a body and legs that seemed too short for the scale of the rest of him. He was smoking a pencillike cigar, and when he took off his hat to me in a kind of mock deference, his head was covered with tiny ringlets, so tight and springy it was almost as if he had no hair at all—only a ginger-colored skull.

"Him!" the woman snarled, rubbing her arm. "He make trouble, Red! You throw him out." She wrapped her fat forearms around her and glared at me, and spat in my direction.

That was how I met Red Chaffee for the first time.

"Trouble?" He chuckled, a good-natured sleek bull, and put his hat on again. "Why, this young man don't look like trouble, Mrs. Gallegos. Are you causing trouble, sir?"

I didn't like him, but till I knew who he was and how he fitted in, I minded my tongue. In spite of his heartiness, there was something about him that made the morning sun thin out.

"Someone stole my wallet last night. There was eight hundred dollars in it."

Chaffee shook his head. "Why do you kids come to places like this? You give us businessmen a bad name."

Mrs. Gallegos said a lot to him in Spanish, and quick. He watched me, smoke from the cigar curling around his half-closed eyes.

"Red own this place," Mrs. Gallegos concluded, speaking in English. "He own the whorehouse across the street, too. By damn, he own mercantile store and flour mill, too!" She was very proud of him!

I was licked and I knew it.

"I'll go to the law," I said.

Red nodded gravely. "I guess you could say I own it, too."

"And Dolores?" I muttered.

"Her, too," he said, "and that drunken Luis Estrada that pimps for her."

As though he had devoted enough time to an entertaining diversion, he moved toward me. Now if he had come at me mean, I'd have known what to do. I was only seventeen, going on eighteen, but I had a pretty heft to me, and I'd been in a rouser of a fight or two myself. But he moved quick, like he was on wheels, and that smile never left his face. While I was figuring what to do, he slapped me across the face, a numbing slam that crushed my teeth against my lips and I tasted blood. I fell back against the wall, and with one continuous movement he grabbed me by the neck and the seat of the breeches and heaved me into the road outside.

There was a lot of whip to the way he did it, and skill. I fetched up in a broken crate of chickens, still trying to hold my jeans up, and the old woman with the chickens screamed at me and beat at me with a stick. I started to rush the door, but Red tossed my boots out and slammed it, and the little barred wicket opened just long enough for the gracious Mrs. Gallegos to spit through the bars. Then it slammed, too.

Around the corner, in the shade of a pepper tree, I put on my boots, sick and discouraged. All I ever got for my share of the farm money was a cut mouth and a lump on my head. Dolores! And her father who was a pimp! I wasn't far from bawling. What hurt most was that I wasn't as grown-up as I'd thought, riding into Tucson. What was it Ike Coogan had said? *Quicker'n a alligator can chew a puppy.*

I got Buster from the livery, glad I'd paid his feed bill while I still had money. I swapped the Walker Colt Ike had given me for a hat and a pound of coffee and a chunk of bacon. Where was I going now?

I didn't know, but I tried to figure it out like a grown man, little as I had any right to the title. I couldn't find Dave. I wouldn't stay here in Tucson, because I'd be laughed at. I had too much pride to try to catch up with Ike Coogan and the wagon train. That left one place. Chiricahua Wells. Somehow I found myself hurrying, pressing Buster on in a way he didn't like. But it was a good thing I did.

CHAPTER THREE

A lot of the Apaches were gathered on the reservations then—General Crook had hazed in most of the organized bands—but a pile of the *bronchos* were around; the wild Apaches that roamed the mountains in the south of the Territory. They didn't recognize any white man's right to put them on a reservation, and as for Chiricahua Wells—well, it had been their prime watering place for hundreds of years, and they didn't want any White Eyes squatting there.

Even from a long way off, I could hear the crack of breechloading Springfields, and I raked Buster with my heels and lathered him good the last mile or so. We dashed through catsclaw and greasewood, Buster sliding and churning in the loose footing, and all the time I could hear that spiteful *crack! crack!* If they were still shooting, though, that meant Saul was alive and giving them a tussle. I flogged Buster and he gathered his legs under him and flattened his ears, going like a catamount.

I couldn't see the Wells yet. The going dropped into a shallow *playa,* it was called; a bare lakelike basin without a spring of green, and hotter than Gehenna. I wasn't far from the Wells, though, because I remembered that *playa* from when Ike Coogan and I went through there with the wagons. Once I heard a low heavy *boom* that must have been my brother Saul's old Sharps fifty, and I sobbed with relief and wondered at the same time why I was bawling. Then Buster broke out of the *playa,* plunging spraddle-legged up a bank, and there was the Wells ahead of me.

There were five or maybe six of the *bronchos* scattered around, skulking behind the boulders that rimmed the Wells. Another was crouched in a thicket of willow, holding their ponies, and it came to me all of a sudden that the way to break this up was to go for the ponies. That was it.

I dropped the reins and snatched up my carbine, and Buster didn't want to go toward those strange horses, but I kicked him in the ribs till he turned. It was all I could do to hang on, but I clamped my knees down like a carpenter's vise and levered in a shell and eared back the hammer, yelling like crazy.

Maybe the yelling did more than the lead, because I couldn't hit a barn shooting from the saddle like that. Anyway, the horse-holder stood there too long, his mouth hanging open. I think what saved me, I came so fast on them he couldn't believe it for a minute, and that was an important minute. I rode right over the top of him, and as he went down he flung himself to one side and let off that Springfield in my face. I scared the hell out of him, but he was only stunned because when he saw me slapping the flanks of their ponies and hallooing at them, he ran quick and low over to a rock and propped his Springfield on it, letting fly again. I remember him now—a squat thick-legged little man in a dirty cotton shirt and nothing much else.

He didn't hit me that time, either. I was moving too fast. But the threat to the horses did what I hoped. The bronks piled out of the rocks at a run, more stocky little men with faded red and green rags tied around short-cropped black hair. Behind them, the big fifty boomed, and one of the attackers suddenly bowed out like someone had kicked him, head back and stomach thrown forward. He ran a dozen yards that way, and then his brown legs buckled and he fell.

I got out of there quick, whipping Buster into long jackrabbit leaps. The bronks were too busy catching their mounts to bother with me, but right then Buster snagged his off front hoof on a root and drove to his knees. I flung my hands off and ran right off him, right over his ears, but I was going like a bullet and I tripped and fell, knocking the breath out of me.

I lay there for a good minute, trying to suck the air back into my lungs, arms and legs spreadeagled. I tried to get up but I couldn't. It seemed like my limbs belonged to someone else. I was dimly aware I still had the carbine in my hand, but I couldn't drag it to me. How far away were the bronks? Did Saul scare them off? Or was one of them bending over me, hatchet high for the kill? I couldn't even hear for the ringing in my ears, but I could see a shadow pass between me and the sun, so that the sand at my face turned sudden dark and cold.

I tried to roll over. With one wrenching effort I got the carbine up, but I knew I couldn't work the lever. Then I saw it was my brother Saul. He laid the Sharps down on a flat rock and dragged me to my feet, gasping like a beached bluegill.

"Joey!" he said. "I knew you'd come back. I knew it. Thank thee, Lord!"

I sat down on the rock. My face felt cold, and when I put my hand up it was wet. But it was only sweat. Cold sweat.

"It's a good thing I did," I said. "Are they gone?"

Saul nodded.

"I—I saw one fall."

"You all right?" Saul asked.

I nodded. I didn't have breath for more.

"Wait here."

He picked his way through the clumps of greasewood, the Sharps ready. Suddenly he stopped, looking down. He stood that way for a long time, fixing every detail of the bronk in his mind. Then he lifted the butt of the Sharps with a slow deliberate movement and slammed it down. Again and again he did it, and when he was finished, he found a clump of some kind of wiry grass and wiped the butt on that. Then he poured a handful of dust over the butt, and wiped that off with his hand, and came back to me.

"Was he—dead?" I felt sick.

"He is now." Saul threw me a rawhide string with some shells and feathers and a couple bird's feet strung on it. "That was a good idea, to go for the horses."

It was the closest he'd ever come to talking to me like I was a man, and it surprised me. But I remembered the eight hundred dollars I'd lost in Tucson, and I knew I wasn't a man yet, nor likely to be, till I learned to take care of myself better. Saul would jump down my throat and gallop my insides out when I told him about it, but I figured this was the time, right now, while he still felt good toward me.

"Saul," I said, "I had some bad luck in Tucson."

He still had the Sharps under his arm, and he took a step away, toward the Wells, in a hurry to get back. But when I said that, he stopped.

"It's about the money." I felt my face turn red clear up under my hair. "I—well, someone stole it from me in Tucson. The whole eight hundred dollars."

I wouldn't tell him the rest of it. Dave, I wouldn't mind telling it to—he'd laugh and guffaw and slap his knee and have a sly joke about it I didn't ever mind Dave joshing me. He had a way of doing it. But I took Saul wrong, I guess, or he'd changed already, somehow, in this hot rainless land, because he just scratched the stubble on his chin and said, "My fault, I guess, Joey. I should have kept it for you. Leastways, part of it. Tucson isn't any place for a—a—" He hesitated for a minute. "Someone that isn't used to a place like that."

He helped me corral Buster, and we went back where his wagon was sitting in the shade of a black rock that was as big as the capitol dome back home in Columbus. The creek purled through the shallows, and the shade was cool and dark, even at noontime. But it didn't look good to me. I remembered that dead Apache, with his head smashed in. How clear I remembered his face now, when I came down on him flogging Buster and yelling at the top of my lungs! He had a flat big-holed nose, and his face was pockmarked, and his hair was cut low in coarse bangs over his eyes.

"Saul," I said, "let's get out of here. Now, while we've got a chance. There'll be more of them around soon's they find out what happened."

He poured me coffee from the pot on the fire. "I was just cooking me up some meat when they jumped me."

For a minute I thought he hadn't heard me. But he heard me, all right, because he pointed to the bed of the creek, kind of proud. "Does that look like I intend to leave here?"

He'd been making dobe bricks out of the wet clay, and dry grass was spread in the sun for straw to make the bricks. Already there was a couple dozen of the big fat bricks drying in the sun, and a rough frame to mold them in, and batterboards set up with string stretched between them to lay out a house.

"I'll build it good," Saul said. He handed me a tin plate of bacon and biscuits. "A foot thick, with rock slabs on top, and narrow windows with shutters, to shoot through. There's cottonwoods up that draw there—good straight-grain stuff for rafters. I'm here to stay, and the sooner those devils realize it, the better we'll get along."

I chewed on a biscuit, feeling it dry and floury in my throat Somehow or other, I'd had the idea in the back of my mind all the way from Tucson that this was just a whim on Saul's part. He was steady and reasonable, even though he was a sobersides. Once he got over the shame and the hurt of Eda running off with Dave the way she did, he'd see it was all for the best, and we'd push on together to San Diego. But things weren't working out right.

"I've thought it over," Saul said. He waved his hand, and I noticed the back of it was brown and hard. The hand had changed, in this country, and the man that was back of it, too. I didn't know him any more. "I've figured it real good, and if it's good land I'm looking for, what's the sense of going any farther? Even Ike Coogan said this was good land. All it needs is water, and we've got water to spare here. Look." He got up, slapping dust from his jeans. "I'll build a dam where the creek narrows. Then it's a nice gentle drop to that level spot there. With good sweet water, I can grow com and beans and melons, and good sweet hay. I'll get me a sow and some pigs, and beef cattle, and a cow for table milk and cheese and clabber. I don't need to go to Sacramento. The Lord's given me everything I want here—right here."

Losing Eda had turned his mind. And yet, there was a ring in his voice that almost convinced me he was speaking sense. It would have, if it hadn't been for that dead bronk lying out in the scrub, not fifty feet away.

"Saul," I said, "Tucson's a boom town. They need help there, all kinds of help. You always were good with a hammer and nails and a saw. You can go to Tucson and sell your team and wagon for a stake, and make ten dollars a day abuilding. You won't have to fight Indians to do it, either."

There was something in his eyes I didn't quite understand, but the words hurt. "Scared, Joey?"

That stung me. "If I'm scared," I yelled, "why did I ride into that beehive and fetch you out of the comb the way I did?"

"That's right," he admitted. "I oughtn't of said that."

I decided to play my right bower then, even at the risk of getting him riled. "Tucson is probably where Dave went," I said. "Him and Eda. I didn't see neither of them there, but where else is there for them to go? That's probably where they are."

You never really know anyone, even your brother that you lived with for seventeen—almost eighteen years. It was almost like I'd said names to him like the Great Khan and Ptolemy. They didn't turn a hair on him. They didn't mean anything.

"I don't care where Dave and Eda went."

He sloshed the grounds out of the coffee pot and went over to the creek. A minute later he was puddling clay into a board form made from mama's old bureau, stripped to the waist in the sun, the muscles of his arms cording and knotted as he worked the mix with a hoe.

"All right," I shrugged. "I don't care either, I guess . . . "

When the sun set that night, a dusty yellow moon came up over the mountains and hung there. When it came bedtime, the desert was lit up with a white torchlight, and the air was full of dry spicy smells. You wouldn't think an Apache could get within ten miles of the Wells without us seeing them first, but Saul kicked the fire out, and made up our bedrolls on top of one of the big rocks, a hundred yards or more from the wagon.

"I'll take first watch," he said. "First though, I better go out and bury what's left of that Apache or we'll have varmints around."

I laid there a long time, watching the moon sail higher and higher. The rock was warm from the sun, and in spite of myself, I drifted off to sleep. The last thing I remembered was that slutty little Spanish girl in Tucson, how short and straight and solid her body was, like a good horse. Short-coupled. Then I went to sleep, thinking how nice it would be to hear rain again.

Sometime in my life I may work harder than I worked those next few weeks, but I doubt it. I laid 'dobe brick till the whole world seemed made out of 'dobe. My hands split and cracked till I could hardly hold my carbine, but every night I perched on that high rock, fighting to keep my eyes open, taking watch and watch with Saul. We dug ditches and planted com and beans and potatoes, and Saul traded papa's old key-wind Waltham watch to a passing wagoner for a sick cow and a pair of new lambs. The house took shape, only it seemed strange to call it a house. A house meant a veranda and doors and windows and curtains. This was a Texas house, Saul called it; two squat earth-colored boxes with a common roof that made a dog-walk in the middle. The doors were heavy and studded with nails, and deep slits were all around to poke a rifle through.

I watched Saul dig a shallow trench from the creek and roof it over with stones and brush. "What are you doing that for?"

"Water." The flies always hung in that dog-walk, and he slapped one, and leaned on his shovel. "This way we got water when we're holed up. Water's important."

How come him, a farmer from Ohio, to think of something like that I didn't know. He was studying this country, straining against it and planning to make it bend his way. Everything he did—everything he said—it was part of a plan to hang on and make do here. It was like he took all the part of him that had been concerned with Eda and with Dave and turned it loose on a wild plan to carve out a place here, at Chiricahua Wells. He was fighting the desert and thirst and Apaches and flies and the heat, and I think he was beginning to enjoy it. But I wasn't.

"Saul," I said, "how would it be if—" I was going to say, how would it be if we just took a little *pasear,* they called it, into Tucson and looked around. Maybe buy a bottle of beer and listen to the band and walk around Military Plaza.

"How would it be if what?" He didn't even stop digging, and I just walked away. Even the cow, sick as she was, was better company.

When the real summer heat came, the trickle of bull-wagons and freighters and emigrants dried up. No one wanted to come through the Wells with the temperature at a hundred and seventeen in the shade. The creek dwindled to a trickle, and the big boulders never cooled off. All night long they baked you, and then the sun was up again and it was another long brassy day, with the light so white and hot it made you close your eyes and even then feel it ringing around in your head like a gong. Up till then, we'd seen an occasional Apache on a rise in the distance, looking us over in early morning or in the dusk, kind of thoughtful and calculating. Maybe they were remembering what we did to them that first day. But now we were strictly on our own, and they had plenty of time to haze us without worrying lest a stray freighter haul in to give us a hand.

"The thing to do," Saul said, "is to encourage other folks to settle down here with us. There's plenty of land for all, seems to me. There's protection in numbers. I'd sure like to talk someone into throwing in with us here."

I took Saul's brassbound spyglass and rested it on the fence he'd built around the garden to keep varmints out. There were deer back in the high-piled rocks of the Wells, and they liked Saul's new carrots.

"There's another rider," I said. "See him down there, in front of that patch of greasewood?"

In a way we'd been living in a fool's paradise or whatever they call it, because when the com greened and the cow got better and began to give a little milk and the lambs got frisky and fat, we forgot about the Apaches and that this was their land, and old man Coogan's warning about them. The two or three we'd seen at a distance didn't seem real; they were like views in a stereopticon we had at home. I thought about the stereopticon again as I focused the lens and the Apache and his paint pony fuzzed in and out, and then stood sharp and clear. He raised a rifle in one hand, and his lips moved in probably a shout, but we couldn't hear it from there. He was half a mile off, although in that shimmery heat distance was hard to judge.

"I'm not scared of 'em," Saul said.

It seemed awful quiet to me all of a sudden. The midday breeze dropped, and all there was was the dying gurgle of the creek and the heat of the sun and a leather-squeaking noise as Saul shifted from one boot to the other.

"I'll give 'em what for," he went on. "This is good land—too good to waste on a pack of naked savages."

I wondered what that bronk was doing out there, just sitting. He couldn't do anything that way. It seemed like a foolish thing to do. Why didn't he get in out of the sun and sleep, or go away, or do something—anything? I felt a prickle in the short hairs at the back of my neck.

"I'm going to make my mark in this country," Saul said. "I'll show 'em. All of 'em. Nobody better get in my way. Indians, bronk Indians, soldiers, gun-slingers—nobody!"

What happened then proved how foolish we were, both of us. After a venison stew with some of Saul's new onions in it, we'd swilled coffee till we were full and fat and content, and the two of us went out to the shade of a big rock next to the garden—we called it The Old Man, after a big rock at home, down around Lancaster. Sitting there in the hot shade, we took a nooner, and our guns were in the Texas house, fifty yards away. But even from there I could hear the little sucking sound when one of the Apaches made a mis-step and went to his ankles in a mud-bank along Boston Creek. That was what Saul called it now.

I dropped the spyglass and reached for my carbine, but it wasn't there. Saul dug in and sprinted for the house, yelling over his shoulder for me to follow, and it was that split-second that saved us. The bronks poured from the rocks, not bothering to waste lead because they were sure they had us cold. But Saul was a big man, and he had long legs, and I was almost eighteen and I won a footrace once at the Circleville Grange picnic. I almost ran Saul down once, but he lost a boot and it seemed to lighten him some, because he was ahead of me when we reached the door. He grabbed me as I came in and flung the door shut and barred it. Just outside, one long jump from my shirt-tail, came a yell of pain. It was that narrow a squeak, we caught that bronk's fingers in the door when it closed. And there we were, boxed up in one half of our Texas house. It was lucky it was the half where we did most of our living, the half that had the spring water flowing through it.

"Close the shutters!" Saul yelled.

It was a good thing the bronks were spreading around the house in the same direction we were going to close the shutters, because every shutter we slammed went home in the face of an Apache. If they'd gone the other way, they'd have climbed in the far windows while we bolted the shutters on the near ones.

Saul poked the Sharps through a slit, chest heaving with the run. "That 'pache out there, he was just a decoy! Keeping us interested while the rest sneaked in behind!"

For a moment it was still, and dark, too, with motes of dust swimming up in the shafts of sunlight from the rifle-slits. I poked my carbine out and squinted into the sunlit world beyond, now suddenly a grim and terrible world. Just then they rushed the house again, screaming and hollering. They'd hacked the tongue off our Moline wagon and were using it for a battering ram. It thudded and thumped against the door, but Saul had done a good job. The door heaved and bent and shook, but it stayed in place. The angle they were at, we couldn't get a shot at them, and after a while they drew off and held a conference. We could see an occasional head bob up from behind a rock, and then down again, like in a shooting gallery, but they weren't about to give us a good shot.

"Reckon what they're doing?" Saul said, rubbing his chin and staring out the crack.

"I don't know." My mouth felt filled with milkweed down, and I dipped up a cup of water, and handed some to Saul, too. "Ike Coogan says—"

Just then we found out what they were doing. Four or five of them ran up to the house carrying armfuls of dry grass and brush and set a fire against the wall. At the same time the rest of them laid down a scattering volley against the slits on that side, and the fire brigade got away while Saul and I were wiping 'dobe-dust out of our eyes and cussing. At least, I was cussing, because I remember Saul saying, "You stop that cussing now, Joey. You hear me? How many times I got to tell you not to take the name of the Lord thy God in vain?"

The fire didn't do any good, not with that sun-burned 'dobe. The Territory sun had been working on that 'dobe for a long time, and even it hadn't been able to faze it. The Apaches got real feisty when they saw the fire burn down, and us still fine as silk inside.

One of them jerked up his skirt and showed his butt to us, which is the supreme Apache insult, and Saul whipped up the Sharps to plug him but the man ducked behind a boulder and that was that.

"Saul," I said, "Ike Coogan says Apaches are unpredictable. He didn't use that word, but that's what he meant. Maybe if we just sit tight and don't rile them—"

There was a thump on our roof, and then another thump. We looked at each other. Had those red bastards got on the roof somehow? But all it was, it was some burning sticks they tossed up there, trying to start another fire. It was a good thing Saul made our roof out of those flat slabs of rocks. They didn't burn worth a damn. So they gave that up, and it was quiet for a while. Just sunny and quiet. To look out the crack, you'd never have thought the rocks were full of death—squat, bowlegged death, with knives and lances, and what was worse, breech-loading Springfields.

"I built this place good," Saul said. He rubbed the stock of the Sharps. "I guess they ain't never seen a place built like this. I come to stay, I tell you."

Just then a squall split the silence—an unearthly squall, shrill and screaming, and as we listened it died into a bubbly crying sound.

"What was it, Joey?" Saul ran from one slit to the other, trying to see what was doing that awful crying. "What was it? You see anything?"

I did, all of a sudden. The bronks had got at our mule, Sodom. The mule that had pulled our wagon all the way from Columbus, along with Gomorrah. Through the slit at the end of the room I saw them at Sodom. They hadn't cut his throat like they'd ought to, or hit him in the head the way the butcher did with a steer at home. No, they'd brought him down with an arrow through his hindquarters. They were squatted around slicing off thick red slabs of meat, and Sodom still bawling. I guess Sodom had busted out of the corral and they'd run him down where they figured they were out of rifle shot.

"Move over!" Saul's voice was thick and excited. "Do that to a mule! To any animal!"

I remembered how he'd been with the stock at home—patient and careful, and the animals liked him. Seemed he always got along better with animals than people, maybe because animals took to bossing a little better.

"Move over!" He tried to get the muzzle of the Sharps in the slit where I stood. "Get out of my way!"

I didn't budge. "No. Don't. Just wait."

He looked at me wild-eyed. "Wait? For what?"

"You'll get one of them. Maybe two. But there's a dozen or more of them. If we lay low and don't bother 'em, they'll go away, like old man Coogan said. They know they can't get at us holed up in here. They got their mule meat, they'll go away. Ike Coogan said if you can't lick 'em all by yourself, let 'em have their fun and keep an eye on 'em. That's what he said."

Angry, Saul pushed me aside, shouldering me, fighting to get the muzzle of the Sharps out the slit. He was crazy to get a shot at them. But I grabbed his arm and the Sharps went off, blasting a hole the size of a hat in our roof. A little shower of splintered rock and dust sifted down.

"Goddam it," I yelled, "now see what you've done!"

It didn't seem to bother the bronks, though. One of them stood up and held his hand over his eyes, looking our way, that was all. The bubbling cry got weaker and weaker, and the bronks sliced off more and more mule meat till Sodom's hindquarters were sticks of white bone. They loaded the stuff, hot and dripping, on their ponies. One of them fired a round at us and yelled, shaking his rifle. Then they rode away, not even looking back, like they were scornful.

"They're gone." I put a hand to my forehead and it came away cold and sweaty. I felt cold all over, and dizzy. "Saul," I said, "I'm scared."

He grunted, scratching his chin again. "Maybe it's a trap."

"I don't think so. They're superstitious, Ike says. All of a sudden they probably figured it was a bad day for shooting up white men, and they've probably gone off to barbecue meat and do a medicine dance or something."

He looked up to the hole in the roof, thoughtful. "Maybe you're right. I guess the Lord put out his hand and saved us."

I wanted to tell him the Lord had a little help from me and Ike Coogan, but it didn't look like the time for it. Especially not with him looking at that hole. So I didn't bring it up. "You know something funny?" I said. I think I was a little light-headed. "This is my eighteenth birthday. I clean forgot."

Saul went to the slit that faced south, looking, and the sun came in and licked his face like fire, almost. It still wasn't but early afternoon. "I guess the mule's dead. Stopped bawling, anyhow. An animal couldn't live all cut up that way. Not for long."

We waited till the sun was teetering on the far mountains. Once we thought we heard them coming back but it was only a skunk, sniffing around some sour milk Saul had dumped on the ground near the door. I wondered about our cow, and I hoped maybe she'd got away. And the lambs.

"We got to go out some time," Saul said. "Anyway, I left a boot out by the garden."

When he went to open the barred door, he stopped for a minute, looking down. Then he stooped and picked up two brown things. They looked like short stogies, the kind Dave used to smoke. Only these stogies had fingernails on them.

"That was a good tight-fitting door I made." Saul looked down at the severed fingers in his palm. "Clipped that 'pache's fingers off like a cleaver."

I felt my stomach turning over. "Throw them away."

He rolled them around in his palm, almost proud. "Next time he comes, I'll get the rest of him. They can't drive me out of here. This place is mine. I'm going to keep it."

"Throw them away," I said. "Bury them. Get rid of them." I began to feel sick to my stomach, and dizzy cold. A pressure began to build up back of my eyeballs.

"They're mine," Saul said. He dropped them in his pocket like they were coins paid for a debt. "You, Joey," he said, "you better change your jeans. You wet 'em when they rushed the house that first time."

My face turned red, and then white. I didn't look down. I didn't think he'd noticed. I stood there stiff, not saying anything, waiting for him to go out. Then I stumbled over to the old packing case where we kept our duds and got my other pair. I was eighteen years old that day.

CHAPTER FOUR

If you work hard, the way we did, time goes in a hurry. When old man Coogan stopped at the Wells one day, it came to me with a shock that it was almost a year since I'd seen him. He looked older—a lot older, and thinner. At home, an old man like him would have been sitting around the stove in Hewicker's General Store toasting his shins and chewing Wedding Cake plug. But Ike Coogan had been trapping that winter up on Horseshoe Creek in the Black Hills, in Dakota, and he'd made him some money, too.

"Joey!" he said. He climbed down and tied his horse, kind of stiff. "Dod-dum it, boy, you been growin'!" He turned to Saul. "Hain't he, Saul? Might near as big as you be, and that's a lot of man!" He looked around at the plowed furrows, the thick tangle of bean vines, the melons half-hid under the leaves. "Got yourself a real spread here, boys."

He took a hitch in his side all of a sudden, maybe from being in the saddle so long. Saul and I had to carry him into the house, and I rubbed his back for a while till he quit squalling.

"You oughtn't to gallivant around like this," Saul said. "Haven't you got people anyplace?"

Ike looked scornful. "My people's all been dead for twenty years, hoss."

"How old are you?" I asked.

He cackled, and dug me in the ribs. "Nine years older'n God." Rummaging around in his possibles sack, he brought out a pipe for Saul, a hand-carved twisty thing. "Bought that in San Francisco, off'n a sailor just come in from China."

Over fried meat and red gravy that night, Ike Coogan got talkative. He found a bottle of bourbon liquor in his stuff and we drank it out of tin cups. It went down good with a mouthful of gravy, but by itself it burned my mouth.

"I got as far as Chimbley Rock," Ike said, "but my—that country's changed since I was up there with Parkman! Too many people. And the Sioux ain't friendly any more. Too many soldiers in the country. They're busy as a bumblebee in a bucket of tar, tryin' to get the Sioux onto the reservation. But it's agin nature, and can't be did."

"Did you come back through Tucson?" I asked. The reason I brought it up, Saul and I had talked some about selling our crops there. But what it brought to Ike's mind was better left alone.

"Yes, sir, I sure did." He wiped gravy from his chin with the sleeve of his buckskins. "And I want to tell you who I saw." He turned to Saul, grinning. "Dave. Dave Boston. Good old Dave."

Saul's face turned white. I passed Ike some more biscuits, quick, but he waved them away and went on, happy as a coon in a fishpond.

"Doin' real good. Got himself a checkered vest and a set of single-action Colts. Workin' for Red Chaffee, they tell me." Ike slapped his thigh and guffawed. "I tell you, Red Chaffee's a big man in this country, but he better watch out for Davc. Old Dave'll cut himself into Red's business like a Philadelphia lawyer, that's what he'll do. Dave's clever."

Chaffee, I thought. Red Chaffee. Dave's working for Red Chaffee. I forgot all about Saul, and how the news of Dave hit him. But of a sudden he got up and stalked out, and Ike Coogan and I sat there looking at each other.

"What's the matter?" Ike asked "Did I say something wrong?"

I started to clean up the dishes. "No."

Ike plucked at my sleeve. Standing near to me that way, he didn't smell any better than he ever did. I don't think water had touched him since I left him that day with the wagon train. "I didn't mean to cause no trouble."

"Ike," I said, "don't you remember why Dave left that night? Why he and Eda went away?"

He rubbed his forehead, frowning. "Eda? Seems to me—" Then he remembered. "She was Saul's wife!" He made his skinny hands into fists and beat himself on the temples. "Christ, I'm an old fool and my brains is dusty!" Shaking his head, he picked up his stuff and started out the door.

"Where you going?"

He pushed my hand away. "I dunno. Santa Fe, mebbe. I—I know a man there owes me some money."

"Not tonight," I said. I took the possibles bag and threw it on my pallet in the corner. "You sleep there, Ike."

He sighed. "That's your bed, ain't it, Joey?"

"I'll roll up in a blanket alongside you."

"All right. If you're sure Saul ain't mad at me."

"I'll take care of Saul," I said.

When I got Ike bedded down, I went out to look for Saul. That was when I heard this faint whispering sound, like music. A harp, maybe. The night was still, and the stars stood out like gas mantles, with no moon. It was still dark, though, and I stumbled onto Saul before I knew he was there. He had Eda's dulcimer with him, the one she played that night there was all the trouble. When he saw me, he shoved it away in a hurry, but his hand raked across the strings, and there was a jangling noise came out of it like a complaint.

"Saul," I said, "I'm sorry. I guess you know Ike didn't mean anything. He's an old man, and he's awful forgetful."

"About Dave, you mean? That name doesn't mean anything to me. It's like I never had a brother named Dave. Forget it."

He couldn't fool me. There was a tightness in his voice that wasn't natural.

"He'll hear of you someday," I said. I looked around at the black shadows of the Wells, listened to the com rustling in the night air. I wanted to say something to make him feel good. "Some day you'll be an important man in this Territory. As big as Dave ever hoped to be."

"Bigger," Saul said. He got to his feet so quick it startled me. "I'll be the biggest man from here to Tucson. I'll own more land, I'll have more stock, I'll pile up money, I'll make people do what I want, I'll—I'll—" He broke off, grinding one fist into the other. "I'll show 'em. Make a fool of me, will they!"

He grabbed me by the arms. "I'm doing something here Dave Boston could never do! He's a free-loader, that's all he ever was—he never had the guts to work for anything in his life. When he left that night, it was good riddance. And I knew then there wasn't anything left for me but to work, to work hard. Work's good for you. Some day I'll be a rich man. A man will ride for three days and not pass out of my land. And someday Dave Boston'll reach for something that isn't his and he'll get shot in the back and die in the gutter, and I'll laugh. I'll laugh because I outsmarted him at last."

From the house I could hear Ike Coogan snoring, a wheezing mournful sound. Now that the wagons were passing again, we'd left off our night guard.

"I'm going to bed," I said.

I walked away and left him standing there. It was all his, the Wells. Saul was doing it all himself. I didn't count for dirt. I wrapped myself in my blanket and stretched out beside Ike, still mad. But after a while I forgot my mad. Ike smelled too dammed bad for me to keep my mind on my hurt. I finally got up and went out to the *ramada* we'd built on one end of the corral, for our stock. I climbed up on that and went to sleep. I think Saul was still up. And I remembered, just as I went to sleep, that he hadn't said anything about Eda. Nothing at all.

Ike pulled out the next morning to follow a train of freight wagons.

"I git tired of ridin'," he said, "I'll tie Lightning to the tail gate and chin with the boys. I know the wagon boss. Old Mike Hersey, trapped beaver with me one winter on River La Bonte."

"Ike," I said, watching him cinch up his red pony, "did you see Eda in Tucson?"

He scratched his chin. "Eda? Oh, you mean Dave's woman? I mean—" He floundered for a minute. "Saul's wife, she was, if I remember. Anyway—" He looked around cautiously. "Yes, I did, Joey."

"Is she all right?" I asked.

He looked surprised at my concern. "Well," he said, seeing to the priming of his old rifle, "I guess she's all right. Depends on what you mean." He stuck it into the saddle boot. "I guess you know she left Dave."

"No. I didn't."

Coogan took a deep breath. "Now understand, hoss—I ain't got anything against Dave. He's more fun 'n a pack of monkeys, and mostly he's goodnatured and free with a dollar. But he didn't treat Eda right, accordin' to what I heard. So she left him, her bein' a high-spirited gal. Served him right."

"Where is she?" I asked.

Coogan shrugged. "Ain't much of a place for a woman like that in Tucson, less'n it's in the cathouses around the Plaza."

"That's a lie!" I blurted.

Coogan blinked at me. Then he climbed on his pony. He looked down at me with pity. "Joey," he said, "you ain't growed up as much as I thought."

The bullwhackers' cries were faint in the distance, and the dust of their wheels was settling. Ike kicked Lightning in the ribs and trotted away. Once he looked back and waved his hat to me. Then he was gone into the dust cloud, and I was alone. Only I wasn't quite alone. I had a picture of Eda in my mind. Lying in the back of Saul's big wagon, red hair spilling out over the tailgate, laughing at me, and teasing. Once she'd touched me with her hand, a pat, and the remembrance of the feel made a shiver go through me. Eda and the soldiers at Military Plaza—no, that wasn't possible! Ike Coogan was an old liar. I'd known that for a long time. He just liked to tell a good story, that was all.

Winter in the Territory was dry, dry as a bleached bone. The wind would come whooping and fill the air with sand driven like a bullet, so that a rusty old pan would scour clean and shiny again. The days were still sunny, but come sundown the night sucked all the warmth out of your body so you just stood and shivered, feeding the stock. We had stock—Saul bought beef cattle from a Mexican drover that was taking them into Tucson for the army, and a couple more mules. That was my job, the stock. While Saul harrowed the vegetables and planted corn, I hazed the stock on Buster.

We had other animals, too. It wasn't fair to call them animals, because they just didn't know any better. A family of tame Apaches built a wickiup near us. Saul wanted to run them out, but I figured maybe we could learn something from them, so I talked him into letting them stay. I never did know how many there were—they went in and out of that brush hut like rats in a trashpile. There was at least old Nacho, the grandpa, and a woman or two and a passel of naked children. That is, he said his name was Nacho, but an Apache won't ever give you his right name. Most of them were scared of us at first, but the old man was a tough nut, a bowlegged feisty little man in a dirty white shirt and not much else. He could speak some Spanish. He finally made me understand they came to live with us because we were great chiefs, and would protect them. Life was hard, and someone named Cut Finger didn't cotton to Nacho and his family, and so the white *nantans* could look out for them.

Whenever Saul wasn't around to yell at me, I'd sneak over and sit in the wickiup with Nacho. That hut smelled worse than

Ike Coogan after a rain, but I learned a smattering of Apache. Once, when I had a bad cold, the old man sprinkled some sacred hoddentin powder on me and threw a handful of owl feathers into the fire, and my cold got better. I'm not saying that was the cure of it, but it did get better.

One thing I'll say for them—they were blue-white honest. We never had to worry about letting things lie around. They wouldn't touch anything that belonged to the *nantan*. But after the first awe wore off, they were nosy about how we lived—what we ate, the way we dressed, Saul shaving in the morning. The big Argand lamp we bought from a passing freighter fascinated them. At night they'd sit in a circle around the door, blinking in the yellow light from the mantle, and draw in their breaths with a sucking sound. I didn't mind—it was kind of like being God—but it got on Saul's nerves. He found out a way to get rid of them, though. They hated and feared fish, any kind of fish. The pools in the Wells were foaming with fat trout, but they wouldn't touch one. Instead they snared field mice and picked berries and baked *mescal* three days in a pit to make a sweet chewy stuff, but they wouldn't eat fish. So whenever Saul got annoyed, which was often, he'd take an old tin of salmon he'd opened and come storming out the door waving it. That was enough. The whole tribe would take off and hide in the wickiup.

Something else they were scared of, too, was the U. S. Cavalry. One morning a half dozen soldiers rode up out of the *playa*, led by a bucktoothed sergeant in a fur cap. I guess he'd been up in the Dakotas once, and that was his way of showing it, though it looked silly in the Arizona Territory. They were Third Cavalry, all the way from Fort Bowie, and they were after a bronk named Cut Finger. I remembered what old Nacho had said about a man by that name, but when I looked around, he and his whole tribe had lit a shuck. The wickiup was empty. They'd been sitting in the sun all morning, playing cards with some little squares of rawhide they'd painted up, but I think they could smell cavalry all the way to Tucson. They were gone.

"No," Saul said in answer to the sergeant's question, "we haven't been bothered for several months. Last time a band of them butchered my milk cow, but we gave them a drubbing and they left."

The sergeant took off his fur hat and fanned his red face with it.

"By God, you couldn't pay me to settle out here like you two fools! No sir, I'd want me a company of cavalry and three field-pieces." He swallowed another gourdful of our milk and licked his lips. "You and the boy better get out while you got a headful of hair. That Cut Finger, he's the meanest 'pache in the Territory."

"Why do they call him that?" I asked.

The sergeant whistled, and the cavalry got back into the saddle again.

"Lost a couple fingers in a melee somewhere. But if you ever get clost enough to notice, you'll get a lance stuck through you like a pig, my boy."

Saul reached in his pocket and drew out the two brown fingers he'd been carrying around for months. They were mummified now, from the heat, and they were shriveled and dry, but you could see the fingernails.

"Goddamighty!" The sergeant reached out and touched them where they lay in Saul's palm, and they rolled around and then were still. "Well, all I can do is warn you people. I can't make you move out'n here. It's on your own head."

We gave them some Mexican figs, and they filled their canteens, and they rode away again. The Wells seemed empty and scary when they were gone. Even Nacho and his family were gone. Nobody but us—Saul and me—against the Indians and the heat and the dust and the country that didn't give a damn for us.

"Saul," I said, "do you suppose he'll come back?"

"Who?"

"Cut Finger."

Saul laughed, a sharp hard laugh. He didn't answer my question, just went back to chopping weeds in the deep green shade of the corn.

That winter we sold a lot of produce to passing wagoners and bullwhackers and the occasional emigrants that passed, wagons loaded down with rosewood bureaus and rocking chairs and chamber-pots. I couldn't help but feel superior to them, the gaunt pale-faced men and the worried-looking women and the kids that sucked their thumbs and stared. Maybe I did look different from the boy that came to the Wells a long time ago. I was burned almost black, and my hair hadn't been cut for a spell, my jeans had worn clear out and I was wearing a pair of buckskin breeches Nacho made for me. The men Apaches did most of the sewing, and they were good at it, almost like a city tailor, considering what they had to work with. Still, I probably looked like a homed toad to those tenderfeet.

"Saul," I said one day, "we better get rid of some of this garden truck we got here. Melons and beans and corn. Look—it's rotting on the vine, some of it. And that wheel of cheese you made, it's going to spoil. Why don't I load up the wagon and take it to Tucson, like we talked about? The soldiers there at the Plaza will buy all of it, and more. All they get is salt beef and biscuit, usually. I can make us some money."

I don't know what was in his mind. Maybe he was thinking about Dave. Maybe he figured I'd sell the stuff and then go looking for Dave and never come back. It wasn't fair, to think a thing like that, but maybe that was it.

"No," he said. "There's too much to do here. Besides, some of these wagons are bound to stop here and take up land when they see how we're doing. There'll be plenty of market for our stuff then. What cause is there for a man to go all the way to the coast when he can settle here? I'll sell 'em a plot of land and stake 'em to seeds and the loan of my mules and plow. That's the way a lot of big cities got started—just like that."

I couldn't see the Wells ever looking like Columbus, Ohio, but maybe Saul was right. Anyway, it would be comforting to have a few more guns around if the bronks jumped us again. But when we had the chance to talk someone into throwing in with us at the Wells, I was the one that ruined the deal.

It happened like this. I was chasing a steer down a gully that opened into the *playa*. He was playing hard to get, dodging in and out of the catsclaw, and I was sweating and cussing, trying to get a rope on him. Then, over the edge of the gully, I saw a wagontop, and a scrawny man in a paper collar yelled down at me.

"Which way to water, sonny?"

I let the steer go and jumped Buster back up the wall of the gully. It was the mangiest outfit I ever saw—a shabby Studebaker wagon with a broken off front wheel held together by baling wire. A thin gray-faced woman sat on the seat beside the man, and the sides of the wagon were rolled up. I think I counted an even dozen kids. It was hard to tell how many boys and how many girls, even if I'd wanted to know, because they were all covered with clinging gray dust. One of them licked his lips and there was a pink circle around his mouth that made him look like a circus clown.

"Name's Warner," the thin man said. "This's my wife Africa. We was following a wagon trail but I guess we got off it."

There was an older girl sitting on the front seat, too, but she was gray and dusty like the rest, and she didn't catch my eye much, at first.

"You just follow me," I said. "There's plenty of water at our place. Bear to the left and turn down that *barranca* there. It's a good hard sand bed, and it'll lead you right to the Wells."

The girl gave me a scared smile and then turned her face away. Even in the sack-like gingham, I could see she was ripe-looking and neat, and I clucked to Buster and rode ahead like Kit Carson himself. Saul would be pleased, I knew; these people didn't look like much, but maybe they'd like the Wells and want to stay. I didn't hold the paper collar too much against Mr. Warner. Maybe he was just a dude.

Like I thought, Saul was pleased when I brought them in, especially when Mr. Warner got down from his wagon and looked around and said, "You got a real nice place, Boston. Yes, sir, a real nice place. My, them are big melons you raise here! Must be good soil."

Mrs. Warner liked the Wells, too, and she was real taken with the way Saul helped her down, and bowed and scraped, and said "Yes, ma'am" and "No, ma'am." Ordinarily Saul wasn't much for the social graces, but I knew as well as he did what was in his mind. One family at the Wells (if you could call Saul and me a family) didn't mean more than some stubborn blockhead trying to draw the case ace, like Dave used to say. But two families meant there might be a chance, and others would follow along and throw in. So far, the few wagons had stopped for water and to swap for fresh vegetables, and that was all. But the Warners looked interested. And while Mr. Warner looked kind of poorly to farm this country, you never could tell.

"Yes, ma'am," Saul was saying to Mrs. Warner. "Plenty of water—good sweet water. This soil'll grow sweet com ten feet high if you give it water. That's all it needs."

Old Warner frowned and rubbed his chin.

"Mister, if you got a little piece of baling wire—just a couple feet long, say—I better look to that busted wheel of mine. It ain't goin' to hold out much longer. Been that way since a couple miles out of Fort Bowie."

Saul took him by the arm. "No sense in bothering with that wheel now, Mr. Warner. Let me show you around."

While he showed the Warners around the Wells, I helped Effie—that was the grown girl's name—I helped Effie catch the kids, and I held them while she washed their faces for supper. The sun was low in the west and the Wells was hushed and peaceful.

"How old are you, Joseph?" she wanted to know.

"Eighteen," I said. "Nigh on to nineteen."

"My, it's nice here," she said, wringing out the rag she'd been scrubbing faces with. I liked her already. She was kind of hearty and—buxom, I guess you'd call it, with a cheerful way about her. She made those kids walk the chalk line, too. No nonsense. She had them all lined up on the wagon tongue, and she said, "Now you sit there, you Lemuel and Foxcroft and Asa and Rachel and Henry and Bibbons and Louisa. I'll start supper directly."

I helped her. I carried water and started a fire and pulled new carrots out of the garden and brought a pailful of milk for the young ones. They sat wide-eyed on the wagon tongue and never moved, watching me like I'd just arrived from the moon. But I didn't mind. It was pleasing just to be near Effie Warner, and watch the way her slim waist pinched in and the firm pink look of her arms when she beat up a pan of biscuits. The best part of it, she wasn't silly and mysterious by turns, the way most girls were. She was just simple and clean and nice, like a healthy heifer. I could see right through her. I mean she wasn't any puzzle to me.

"Where you from?" I asked her.

"Burlington. That's in Iowa. Papa was a miller there. There wasn't much money in it, though, and he sold out to go to California. Have you ever been to California?"

"No," I said, "but I've been to Tucson."

"My!" she smiled. "Tucson!"

"Effie," I said, "after supper you come with me. I've got a private place up in the rocks where you can see almost to Tucson. Even Saul doesn't know about it. There's like steps, almost, and when you're up on top there's a flat place to sit, and you can lean back and feel the rocks all warm and see the moon come up, too."

She got a little flustered. "Papa—"

"I don't mean anything by it. Honest, I don't. It's just a secret place of mine. I wouldn't ask just anybody up there."

"Well," she said, "I—I'll see."

Saul came back then with Mr. and Mrs. Warner, and we had supper together, like a picnic, sitting on the grass. It was good, too—Saul cut steaks off a venison haunch and Mrs. Africa Warner made gravy to go with Effie's biscuits. Afterwards Mr. Warner passed around a sack of lemon lozenges. I hadn't had a lemon lozenge since I was a boy. It seemed a long time ago.

"Well, now, I don't know," Warner said to Saul, sucking at a corncob pipe. "I been a miller most of my life. I guess there ain't much to farming, but I admit I ain't rightly no farmer." He turned suddenly shrewd. "What about when a drouth comes on you, Boston? Do them springs dry up?"

Saul started in on him. He was like a bulldog after a bone, and he didn't notice when I took Effie by the hand and pulled her away after me.

When we got out of the circle of firelight, she stopped and made a whimpering noise. "I don't know if I ought."

"They don't need you any more," I whispered. "Henry and Rachel and Foxcroft and all the rest are bedded down in the wagon and the dishes are washed up. The old folks'll sit there and talk for hours. No one will miss us. "I'll show you the Apache necklace I got."

I took her hand, surprised how bold I was, and how warm and soft it was. I pulled her along after me in the shadow of the boulders.

"Isn't the air warm and soft!" Effie said. "And—oh, there's the moon! It's like a big fat gold piece, low down in the sky."

We picked our way higher and higher, and the rising moon lit the rocks till they looked like gray elephants, standing patient while we climbed on top of them. I could smell some plant on the night air—spicy and dry and musty. Down below the Warners' fire winked a red eye.

"There!" I stood on top of the pile and waved my arm. "Over there, that's where Tucson is. If everyone in Tucson was to light a candle tonight, I'll bet you could see the light from here."

Her face was pale in the growing moon, and one hand rubbed at her throat. "I'll bet there's Indians out there, too. A lot of Indians. Mama's frightened to death of Indians. I am too." Effie moved close to me. "You and your brother must be brave, to stay out here all by yourselves."

"I'm not scared of any Apache," I said. "Saul isn't either. They jumped us a lot of times, but we always give them what for. I reckon I've killed over a dozen myself. I got me a Comanche in Texas, once, but a Comanche ain't nothing to an Apache. Why, they're the fiercest Indians there is, I guess! Like old Cut Finger. The last time, he killed our cow, and the whole passel of devils just sat out there and sliced her up while she was still bawling."

She shivered, and I put my arm around her. Me being tall the way I was, with long arms, my hand kind of crept around her and laid on her breast. It gave, just a little. It was a nice feeling.

"Once they had Saul all boxed up here. I'd been to Tucson, see, and when I come back I heard shooting and I knew there was Apaches. I come busting in on them and ran their horses off. That spooked them, I can tell you!" I made a little bolder with my hand, but she didn't move. It seemed like she was paralyzed, and I felt pleased. An Apache was good for something, it seemed. As long as I had a string of stories about the Apaches, she was content to snuggle against me.

"Yes. sir." I squeezed her waist. "Why, this place is a regular hotbed of Indians, I guess you might say! But you don't need to worry none. Not as long as I'm here, Effie."

She made a little scared noise and turned up her face to me. I kissed her right on the lips, which startled her some. I guess she was more used to milksop Eastern men.

"Oh, Joey," she said. "Hold me tighter."

The Warners moved out early the next morning. Matter of fact, they were packed up, kids and all, before dawn. Saul wouldn't talk to me till after they left—just stood there, red-faced, watching them go. Then he turned to me, and his voice was like a handsaw cutting through a nail. "You and your loose tongue!"

I looked at him, his face set hard and big dark sweat circles under his arms. "What did I do? Is it my fault if they don't like the Wells?"

He made a howling kind of sound, and beat a fist into his palm like he was trying to break his hand. "You scared that girl of theirs half out of her wits, you and all your loose talk about Apaches and Cut Finger and all the rest! While my back is turned you take her up in them rocks and undo all the hard work I did!"

That Effie Warner! She believed everything I said. She'd gone right back and told her pa. That was why they left without a how-de-do or how've-you-been. I'd made too good a case for the Apaches. I thought for a minute Saul was going to hit me, but I stood my ground and he just glared at me, one big fist doubled into a club. I didn't say anything. What was there to say, except I'd been a damned fool? But I did try a weak defense.

"I didn't mean to cause trouble. Honest, Saul. But if you don't tell people the truth about the Apaches, they'll find out sooner or later, and then they'll be mad at you. They—"

"I had it all planned!" Saul yelled. "They would have stayed! More would have come! We could farm this place in peace, and I wouldn't have to sleep all the time with one eye open watching for Apaches. Old Warner was going to give me a hundred dollars for that piece of grassland south of the house." He ranted and raved on, long after the Warner's wagon had dwindled into a dot and then disappeared over the edge of the *playa*. He talked awful mean to me. Finally I had enough.

"Saul," I said, "you better get out that old madstone Mina Ogg gave you."

"Why?"

"Maybe you can use it to suck some of the meanness out of you," I said.

He stared at me a long time, the muscle in his jaw twitching. Then he sucked in his lips, and spat. "It ain't any of your business what I do. But I tell you what you're going to do." He pointed to our vegetable patch, the lush melon vines and the beans on their twig supports. "You get out there and pick vegetables till I tell you to stop. Then you load up the wagon and make a straight shirt-tail to Tucson and see can you sell it. Maybe with you out of here I can get some peace."

"You'll be alone," I said.

"That's the way I want it. I don't want you around messing up my plans."

"All right," I said.

Out in the melon patch, piling up the big fat globes, I sweated and cussed, watching the house out of the corner of my eye. The big dumb ox! Leave him out here all alone, Cut Finger'd get him, and that was what he deserved. I didn't care. I knew where Dave was, and that was where I was going. It seemed like Christmas.

CHAPTER FIVE

On the way to Tucson I had a lot of time to think over things. I hated Saul—there wasn't anything else for me to do. He wouldn't let me do anything else. Even if there couldn't be the free and easy way between us there always was with Dave and me, at least we were kin! But that wasn't enough. Once, a long time ago, I heard some one say there wasn't any hate could compare with that between brothers. Now I was beginning to see the truth of it. A stranger you don't like—you just up and fight him, or leave him alone. But I couldn't fight Saul, and yet he was all I had in the world unless I found Dave. Yet, in the back of my mind, I knew losing Eda had unhinged Saul's mind, and every day he was drawing more into himself, snapping at the world, angry when it didn't go his way, and filled with a bitter pride. Well, what was it Ike Coogan used to say? *Life's short and full of blisters.* It was too nice a day to stay grim very long, and in a minute I was singing "The Buffalo Hunters" to the mules, cracking the whip over their bobbing haunches, hurrying them on to Tucson.

That night I holed up in a shallow *barranca*, tying the mules under the raw edge of a bluff. I didn't dare make a fire, even in the cover of the gully, so I chewed on some jerky and had a drink of water from my canteen and let it go at that. Hunkered down out of the wind, I squatted in the lee of the wagon with a blanket around me and waited for the dawn. Old man Coogan said the Apaches never poked around at night, but I wasn't so sure. They were supposed to be scared of owls, because they were a kind of evil spirit, and they thought there was an old man called Ostin somebody prowled at night, putting spells on people. Anyway, I wasn't taking any chances. I kept my carbine in the crook of my arm. But along before dawn I guess I went to sleep, because when I just opened my eyes after forty winks, it was light again, a chill gray light, and cold enough to freeze water.

The desert was misty and unreal in that half-light, and when I went to get the mules a high stalk of *mescal* loomed up and I felt my heart leap up in my throat. But then I saw what it was, and I felt foolish. You never knew about this country, though. Just when you thought you had it figured out, something happened. Like Saul and me watching that Apache all by himself out on the *playa.*

I was well on my way when the sun came up, wet and hazy-looking in the east. There wasn't any warmth in it and I shivered, huddled in my blanket on the high seat. The moisture ought to be good for the vegetables under the canvas, though. They'd be crisp and fresh, and bring good money.

Not more than five or six miles from the Camino Real, I heard a faint far-off whoop, and a rifle shot slammed through the tailgate of the wagon. It must have hit one of the iron braces, because it sailed away with a whickering sound. It was funny the effect it had on me. Maybe I was learning, because this country was a hard schoolmaster. I lashed the mules a couple good licks and then tied the reins to the brake handle, giving them their head. Hanging on with one hand, holding the carbine with the other, I scrabbled over the canvas to the top of the load, where I could lie down and rest the muzzle of the carbine on a hillock of potatoes and cabbages. Not till then did I see the Apaches, fanning out behind me in a kind of V, the outriders whipping their ponies to get around and turn me. They were still only small black dots in the thin sunlight, and I could see the plume of dust under their hoofs better than I could see the Apaches, but they were coming fast. The mules were no match for them, pulling that heavy wagon.

I was too busy to be scared, this time. The load shifted and rolled under me, and the mules ran away with the wagon, their ears laid back flat and their big hoofs pounding. It was all I could do to hang on, but I managed to check the cartridges in the magazine, and put a handful in my shirt pocket where they'd be handy. One of the Apaches must have had a Sharps to reach me with that first shot, but the range was closing fast. Another shot ripped a long feathery gash in Saul's canvas cover, and it made me mad enough to squeeze off a round that kicked up dust in front of the lead pony.

"Go, you mules!" I yelled. "Go!"

I didn't think the Apaches would dare come too close to the Camino Real. There were too many freighters and wagon trains passing. Once I got there, I'd be safe. But it was like a school problem in geometry, the Camino Real one line, the Apaches flogging their ponies on another, and me and the mules flat shirt-tailing on the third. They were closing in fast on the wagon, but the wagon was rocking and swaying like an express train, and the haven of the Camino Real couldn't be far. Already, over my shoulder, I imagined I saw it—a thin dusty trail winding in and out of the *nopal* and greasewood. I squinted down the barrel and caught a naked Apache dead in my sights, but just as I pulled the trigger the wagon hit a chuckhole and it rolled like a ship at sea, throwing me across the canvas so that I had to clutch and grab to hang on.

That last shot seemed to change their minds, or so I thought. The outriders, seeing they couldn't turn the wagon, fell back with the rest of the band. They all came to a stop, bunched in a little group like they were palavering. And then, big as life and lovely as a fresh apple pie, I saw a long wagon train snaking down a pass off to my left, and I knew it belonged to Tully, Ochoa, and Company. That was why the Apaches broke it off. I scrambled back down to the seat and unwrapped the reins, but it took me a good ten minutes to stop the team. They were all wound up, shivering and lathered with foam, chests heaving and eyes rolling. But we'd brought the vegetables through. Saul couldn't blame me for anything, not this time.

When I pulled in behind the wagon train, one of the bull-whackers came back, coiling up his whip, and offered me a chew of tobacco. He was a big man with long black mustachios, and his head was shaved balder than an egg.

"What's your hurry?"

I told him about the Apaches, and gave him a couple heads of lettuce and a piece of Saul's cheese. He was real nice to me—took me up to the *cocinero* and got me a tin plate full of sow-belly and beans. I tied the mules to his wagon and gave him a hand watering and feeding his oxen at the noon stop, and that was the way we came into Tucson the next morning.

Military Plaza looked about the same as I remembered it. I tied the mules and went up to a captain that was lounging under a brushwood *ramada,* sucking a cigar. "Captain," I said, "I've got a load of prime vegetables in my wagon. I'd like to sell 'em to the Army."

He put one hand under his shirt and scratched his ribs. "Ain't got any blueberries, have you?"

I thought at first he was ragging me. "No, sir," I said. "Cabbages, potatoes, carrots—stuff like that. I'll make you a good price for the load."

He called for a sergeant, and when the man came, he pointed to the wagon and told him to take a look.

"Yes, sir," the captain said, "up in Michigan we used to have blueberries. Whole thickets of them. My wife used to bake pies. There ain't nothin' like a fresh blueberry pie settin' on a window-sill to cool." He broke off, staring out at the blue mountains in the distance. Then the sergeant came back, and the captain got up, chewing on the cigar.

"Give you ten dollars for the load."

"Ten dollars?" I shook my head. "There's a whole wagonload."

"Make it fifteen, then."

"Where you going?"

I started to walk away.

"I can sell it around for a nickel a basket and make more than fifteen dollars," I said. "The Shoofly restaurant'll take half of it, anyway."

He crooked his finger at me, and I came back. "You from Chiricahua Wells? Where that crazy feller's trying to farm?"

"He isn't crazy," I said. "That's my brother."

The captain reached in his pocket and took out a handful of bills. "There. Twenty-five dollars. That's my last offer."

"Done." I shook his hand. "You got a good buy, captain."

His stogie went out, and he scratched a sulphur match on the seat of his corduroy britches. While we waited, the sergeant and a detail unloaded the wagon and carried the vegetables to the cooktent.

"You ever get back this way again," the captain said, "stop by. We can use vegetables whenever we can get 'em. A handful of carrots and a few potatoes helps a piece of salt beef something wonderful."

I folded the bills and put them in my shirt pocket, buttoning the flap. "We've got a good crop of hay coming on," I said. "And we make cheese, too! ... I gave the last piece to a bullwhacker on the road, but I'll bring you some next time. A dollar a pound, if you want it."

"I'm your man," the captain said. "We'll do business together, boy, if you and your brother hold out down there."

"We'll hold out all right." I climbed on the empty wagon. "Don't you worry about us."

As I drove away, he called after me. "Plant some blueberries, why don't you?" I don't know why he was so crazy about blueberries. They never seemed so special to me.

I thought it would be nice to take a present to Dave, so after I tied my mules at the Plaza I bought a bottle of Clubhouse Gin at Zeckendorf's, and had them wrap it in a piece of white paper with a gold string around it. It cost three dollars but it was worth it. I couldn't wait to find him and hand the package to him.

"Dave Boston?" the clerk said. "No, I don't know no Dave Boston."

"He works for a Mr. Chaffee."

The clerk's face got a sly look. "Oh!" He bit off the string, and handed me the package. "Fifty cents extra for the wrapping. Well, if he works for Red Chaffee, I daresay you'll find him over at the Paradise Bar. That's where Red's people hangs out."

I went out on the street again, pushing my way through the din. The Mexicans had a kind of Punch and Judy show they called *romeriomarias* and there was one on most every corner, with a crowd of people around. The streets, if you could call them that, were ankle-deep in dust. Till I die, I'll remember Tucson by the dust. It got up your nose and tickled, it whitened your face like flour, it got into your teeth and made them grit, and it smelled of horsedroppings and burning wood and garlic. It was a rich smell, kind of, after you got used to it.

The Paradise was on Camp Street, a weathered two-story building with glass in the windows. Inside, it was dark and smelled of stale beer. I asked the man at the bar where I could find Dave Boston.

"Who are you?"

I looked pretty frowsty, powdered with dust, my hair long and ragged, and my carbine under one arm and the package under the other.

"I'm his brother."

The bartender wrung out his rag and stuffed it in his hip pocket "Upstairs. First door to the left."

I don't remember anyone else being in the Paradise, except for a grim blue-jawed little man with heavy eyes who looked at me once and then went back to the bottle on the table before him. For a big place like that, the Paradise was pretty empty. It seemed almost exclusive. Maybe Mr. Chaffee didn't like just anyone coming into the Paradise.

I knocked on the door. No one answered, so I turned the knob and went in. I found Dave all right. He was in bed with a woman, a woman with bleached hair and a thin red mouth. She cursed me, pulling the covers up tight, but Dave told her to shut up and get out. She dressed while I turned away my eyes, and went away, slinking out like an animal, lips drawn back over her teeth.

"Joey!" Dave shut the door after her, pulling on his jeans and his shirt. He grabbed me by the shoulders, grinning at me from his brown wrinkled face. "Old Joey Boston!"

I felt kind of sick. Dave always had women—all kinds of women—but this seemed different. It was like I bit into a red apple and found a worm in it, and I guess my face showed it. But he made out like he didn't notice.

"What you got there?" He grabbed for the package. "For me?"

He unwrapped it, and then when I didn't say anything, he laid it down on the table.

"Thanks. Thanks for thinking of me. I like gin—I guess you remembered."

I took a deep breath. "You been all right, Dave?"

He wiped his hands on the thighs of his jeans, looking at the bottle.

"You been all right, Dave?"

"Oh, hell," he said. "Sure, I been all right, Joey. Don't I look all right?" He put on the checkered vest and buttoned it, and hung the gunbelt with the Colts around his narrow hips. "Look, what you're thinking—"

"You don't know what I'm thinking," I said.

He grinned, a wry twist of his mouth. "You're thinking about Eda."

"What if I am?"

He pulled the cork out of the gin bottle with his teeth. "Hell, she wasn't for me! I made a mistake, that's all." He handed me a tincup. "You don't expect me to join a holy order or something, do you? A man's got to have women. I've always told you that. They're all alike, anyway. One ain't got anything the next one ain't."

I pushed the cup away, and Dave's face got stubborn, the flush of it staining through the tan. "Drink it!" he said.

I did. It seemed to take away some of the hollow feeling in my stomach, but it still tasted like medicine.

"Lay that damn popgun down," Dave said. "It ain't friendly to come in here carrying that thing like you was looking for a bear." He dug me in the ribs. "Good old Joey! Say, how's Saul? What you two doing in Tucson?" Then, suddenly, his eyes narrowed and he set the cup down so hard, it splashed. "Is Saul here?"

I shook my head. "He stayed on at Chiricahua Wells. I stayed with him. He sent me in with a load of vegetables to sell." I showed him the money. "I got a real good price."

Dave sprawled on the bed, chin propped on his fist. "I'll bet he sweats the tar out of you, that holy old rube."

"We both work."

His eyes sparkled. He was almost like the old Dave. For a minute I forgot the bleached woman and her snarl. "Farming ain't no life for you, Joey. You listen to me, now. You keep that money. Don't go back to Chiricahua Wells. This is your old friend Dave telling you." He sprang up to tap me on the chest with a long finger. "This is the place, Joey. Hell, Tucson is wide open! I got a good thing here. Red Chaffee is a good man to work for. I tell you, he makes things go! All I got to do is give him the word and you got yourself a job."

I folded the money into a tight roll. "Doing what?"

Dave shrugged. "A lot of things. Mr. Chaffee's got a lot of connections. I'll take you in right now to see him."

I didn't want to go. I remembered the time Red Chaffee threw me out of the whorehouse he owned, and I was afraid he'd remember. I don't mean I was afraid of him. It wasn't that. It was just that there was something embarrassing about meeting a man that had booted you in the rump, right out of the door and across the street into a crate of chickens.

"Wait a minute," I said. "Let me get my carbine first."

Dave was always in a hurry. He never stopped to get the right of anything. "Hell," he said, dragging me down the hall, "for all the money he's got, he's just as common as an old shoe! All I got to do is say the word to him, and you're in, Joey. You're in on something big."

Down the hall was another door that looked just like the first one. Dave knocked, head bent over, listening. While we waited I looked over the rail and saw the silent man with the heavy eyes still hunched over his bottle, and the bartender picking his teeth and staring out the window.

"I know he's in there," Dave said. He knocked again.

"Come in," a deep voice said.

Dave grabbed me by the elbow and hurried me in, almost like someone was chasing us.

"Who you got there, Dave?" Red Chaffee asked.

He was sitting at a roll-top desk beside an open window, looking down at Camp street. He looked like a barrel sitting there—a red-headed barrel in black broadcloth.

"This is my brother, Joey," Dave said. "He needs a job, Red."

Chaffee still didn't look up. He kept his gaze fixed out the window, and one big pale hand, a fringe of reddish hair on the back, rubbed at his skull.

"I don't neither," I said. "I don't need no job." But Dave banged me in the ribs so hard it made me grunt, and the sound seemed to attract Red Chaffee's attention. He turned to look at me, and I remember now the way the reflected sun glinted in his close copper curls.

"What can he do?"

Dave slapped me on the back. "He ain't but eighteen, but—"

"Almost nineteen," I said.

"All right then. Almost nineteen. But he's hard as nails and he c'n ride anything you can throw a saddle on."

Chaffee stared at me with the same single-mindedness he had a moment ago spent on the street below. Finally he smiled, a planned kind of smile. I thought for a minute he remembered throwing me out of that whorehouse, but he never let on, any more than that. I didn't like his smile. I was worried for Dave. When Red Chaffee smiled it was like having a little cold wind blow on you out of nowhere, when the sun was shining and everything else looked good.

"You handy with a gun, kid?"

"I'm no gun-slinger, if that's what you mean," I said. "I killed me a Comanche at better'n three hundred yards with this carbine, though. That was down in Texas."

Chaffee was amused.

"I mean a handgun."

"I don't carry one," I said. "I like my carbine."

"Red," Dave said, "I'll get him a pair of Colts. I know a Mexican down by Little-Eye Springs that's got a pair of beautiful forty-four Colts with walnut grips. I'll fix him up with a pair of guns."

Chaffee got out a bottle and a cup from a drawer of the desk. He poured himself a drink and looked at me over the rim of the cup. He didn't offer either of us a drink. There was more to it than just lack of manners. He was drawing a line between the hired help and the boss.

"Dave," he said, "the kid don't seem too anxious."

Dave burst into laughter, loud laughter, and slapped me on the back. "It's just his way, Red. He's the cautious type."

"Cautious about what?" Chaffee asked.

Dave started to answer, but Chaffee waved him into silence.

"What are you cautious about, boy?"

"Well," I said, "what would I be doing if I worked for you? I'd have to know before I made up my mind, wouldn't I?"

Chaffee wiped his mouth and set the cup down.

"Your brother never was so nosy. I told him 'a hundred dollars a month', I said, 'an a chance to make a little money on the side'. He never batted an eye. Not him."

"All we do," Dave said, "we just work around, me and the boys. Red has something for us to do, we do it." He kept looking at Red Chaffee from the corner of his eye, like he wanted Red to explain. "There ain't nothin' to it."

Chaffee stood up, and I had forgotten how big and broad he was. There was the span of an axhandle across his shoulders, tight and black in the well-tailored broadcloth. He hooked his thumbs in his belt, sure and well-spoken like the Presbyterian minister back home.

"Kid, your brother ain't half the man I thought he was when I took him on. Look at him—right now he ain't got sand enough to put a name to what he's doing! All right, I'll tell you. I didn't get where I am by chewing my words too fine. I own a lot of property in Tucson. I own cattle, and grazing land, and a mine or two. There's some that'll tell you I don't have title to 'em. You'll find folks that say I stole 'em, or murdered for 'em, or claptrap like that. Now certain people can cause a man trouble. They're trouble-makers, that's what they are, and they have to be hushed up sometimes. That's what I keep gun hands like Dave Boston for. A man gives me trouble about a title or a piece of paper like that, I send Dave to have a talk with him. Kind of an agent, you might say. Yes, that's it." He was pleased with the neat sound of it. "Dave's my chief agent, that's all."

I looked at Dave. His face was red, and I don't know whether it was from anger at the way Red Chaffee was talking him down, or shame at Chaffee calling him a hired gunman.

"Mr. Chaffee," I said, "I reckon I don't want any job from you, sir. I'll just get along back to the Wells and plant potatoes and hoe weeds and be my own man. Thank you kindly."

Chaffee ran a big white hand over his curls. "Chiricahua Wells?"

"We changed the name. We call it Boston Wells, now."

He sat on the edge of the desk, a booted foot swinging. "Boston Wells, eh?" He started to laugh, a hearty deep laugh. "You hear that, Dave? Ain't that a caution? Boston Wells!"

It was like he and Dave shared some secret, but Dave didn't laugh. He flung out a hand and said, "Shut up, Red!"

Red Chaffee's heavy chuckling slacked and he looked sharply at Dave, not liking that, but not saying anything either.

Dave took me by the elbow and opened the door. "Come on, Joey," he said.

Out on the balcony I could still hear the low drum-like rumble of Red Chaffee's amusement. Dave kept his grip on my elbow, and steered me down the stairs, past the bartender with his toothpick and the motionless man with the bottle, pushing me ahead of him through the swinging doors.

"You get out of here." He kept his head down, like a small brown bull, and didn't look at me. "Go on, get out of here and don't never come back. This ain't no place for you, you hear?"

"Why not?" I said. "Now look, Dave. There's no call for you to act like that. I reckon if you want to work for Mr. Chaffee, well, that's your business. I'm obliged to you for wanting to get a job for me, but if I was to want to work for Mr. Chaffee too, well, that'd be up to me."

To tell the truth, I didn't know what to make of it, Dave first pushing me in there, and then pulling me out again. But Dave just shook his head. His mouth was set and hard. I'd never seen him like this before, but one thing was sure, he was mad clear through. I didn't know if it was me he was mad at, or Chaffee, or both. When I looked into his face, trying to make him see me, he still wouldn't look at me straight.

"Dave," I said, "I'm your brother, ain't I? I'm Joey. You don't have to be ashamed to me."

He swore some then, and looked at me hard. "You get away from here," he said, "I ain't got time to waste on you." "Dave," I said, "this isn't right. What's the matter with you? You can't make me just go away like this. I haven't even seen you for almost two years!" I grabbed the front of his shirt but he pushed my hand away. I saw him blink his eyes, and if it had been anyone but Dave I'd have thought he was crying.

"*Will* you go?" he said in a tight voice. "I told you I'm busy—I got work to do." He turned on his heel and went back into the Paradise Bar.

I stood there for a long time, the carbine under my arm, feeling people jostle me, stare at me, and not caring much. I'd found my brother Dave, and I'd lost him again, all in an afternoon. But as I went away, knowing in a dim unhappy way that now I had to hitch up the wagon and the mules and go back to the Wells again, I began to see what had caused it all. It was Red Chaffee. He'd done this to my brother Dave. And someday I'd have a reckoning with Red Chaffee. He could laugh all he wanted to, and pat his pretty red hair, and own all the whorehouses in the Arizona Territory, but some day I'd catch up with him and he'd be sorry.

CHAPTER SIX

I'd promised a Mexican boy a 'dobe dollar to watch the empty wagon and my team while I went to look for Dave. It was still there, all right, with both the mules, and I handed over the dollar as a fair transaction. But what else I got was a bargain. Someone flew into my arms, soft and happy against me, squealing with delight. As soon as I could pry her loose, I saw it was Eda. Eda Boston.

"Joey!" she panted, brushing the loose hair back from her forehead. "Oh, I'm so glad to see you!" She hugged me again, happy as a boy with a speckled pup. I liked it all right, but it was so public, right out there in the Military Plaza, with everybody gawking. I didn't know exactly what to say, but I didn't need to worry. Eda did all the talking.

"I heard you were in town, and then I found the wagon, and the boy said he didn't know when you'd be back. He wouldn't even let me sit down—he said he was guarding the wagon for the *caballero* and the *caballero* might not like to have ladies on the seat while he was gone." She squeezed my arm. "My, but you've grown, Joey! And you look so—so rough! Don't you ever cut your hair?"

I took her by the hand and pulled her around behind the wagon. There was a little knot of soldiers congregating and soldiers get kind of raucous.

"Why, Joey!" Leaning against the wagon, looking at me through half-closed eyes, she smiled. "You're not afraid you'll compromise me, are you? Not in broad daylight!"

"It's getting on into the afternoon," I mumbled. It was, too.

"I know all of those men, anyway." Her voice had a bright birdlike quality to it, and it stung me, like cutting yourself with a razor when you're shaving. "Sergeant Heacock—that's the one with the buck teeth—he's the sergeant-major, and he—"

I put my hand over her mouth. It was warm and wet against my palm, and her blue eyes looked at me, puzzled. Then she bit me, a short sharp nip.

I looked down at the neat line of tooth-marks in my hand. An edging of red was around one of the dents. "Don't talk that way, Eda. Don't talk about the soldiers."

"I'll talk about soldiers all I like, I guess. They're friends. That's something I haven't had too much of."

She tossed her head, and I marveled at the way she'd changed. Not that I blamed her. No, it wasn't that. I guess we'd all changed since we'd been out here in the Territory. But with Eda it was different. I wanted to remember her the way she'd been in Saul's wagon—warm and breathless and almost child-like, not knowing sin was in the world. But she wasn't that way any more. There was a hard edge to her, like something that's been tempered in a fire. Most of the respectable women in Tucson wore hats of some kind—maybe only a sunbonnet, but it was a badge of respectability. Eda's red hair sparkled in the late sun, caught back in a bright green ribbon, and her skirt was shorter than the fashion. She showed her ankles as easy as a man does, and didn't think anything more about it. She was reckless and hard, and maybe there was something to what Ike had said about her. Sometimes Ike was right.

I wiped my hand on the seat of my jeans. "You talk about soldiers all you like, Eda. I guess it ain't any of my business."

She caught at my hand and examined it "My goodness! I didn't mean to hurt you." She dabbed at it with a wisp of cambric, and I was aware that the Mexican child was staring at us with round eyes like buttons. "Joey, I've got to mind my temper, that's all. I've just got to."

I felt low. It didn't look like I had any legitimate place in this world. The whole surface of the globe, from Maine to Madagascar, was dank and unfriendly. Even the sun disappeared behind a low bank of clouds, and a chill came into the air. Down the street I saw a lamp wink on in a window, behind a lace curtain, and I felt lost and friendless.

"Well," I said, "I've got to go."

She tied the handkerchief around my knuckles, and gave the back of my hand a friendly pat "Go where?"

I remembered I hadn't said anything about Saul and me, or the Wells. But I was damned if I was going to. A woman that bites can't expect many confidences. "Oh," I said, "back home."

She sighed. "It was good to see kin again." Then she reddened. "Not really kin, I don't mean." Looking down at the dusty toe of her shoe, she kept her eyes turned away. "Anyway, I'm glad to have seen you, Joey."

Something seemed to break in me, like a fiddlestring pulled up too tight. I knew if I didn't step out bold right then, I'd never know her again. I might see her once in a while as I passed, but we wouldn't ever do more than wave, or nod. And that wasn't right.

"Eda," I said, "I've got to talk to you."

She didn't look at me, only stared down at her toe making circles in the dirt.

"I'm not going away from you like this." I grabbed her by the shoulders and shook her. I didn't care if she did bite me. "We came all the way out here from Columbus together, and I don't care what's happened. We can be friends, can't we?"

Her voice was uncertain. "Are—are you sure you want to be friends with *me?*"

"I guess," I said, "You're about the only true friend I've got anymore. You and Ike Coogan, only I don't see him much."

I was glad it was dusk, and we were in the lee of the wagon. She took my hand and pressed it to her lips, holding on with a grip that almost hurt. "Joey, you can't know what it means to me just to *see* you."

I swallowed hard. Ike said she was a whore. "Eda," I said, "what—what are you doing now?"

"I'm staying with a family named Landry. I board there." She looked up, her eyes gay and eager. "Joey, you haven't got anywhere else to go. Come to the Landrys with me for supper. We can talk and talk and talk. That's what I want to do. Talk to someone!"

"Well," I said, "I don't know if I ought to."

Her face fell.

"But," I said, "I got to eat *someplace,* don't I?"

One thing I can say about Tucson, there never was a dull moment. I'd no sooner tossed the *nino* another *peso* and moved off with Eda than I saw that old pimp and the dark girl that stole my eight hundred dollars. Maybe there was a more refined way to do it, but I dropped Eda's arm and took out after them, yelling and cussing. The Plaza was crowded with soldiers and cockfights and a bunch of people in the torchlight listening to a man sell Dixon's Electric Oil for the Lungs. The girl saw me blundering through the crowd and they turned and ran, the man way ahead and the girl with her long skirts lifted and making mighty good time. I came to a narrow dark street and looked in after them but it was like the inside of a cow, and I didn't want a knife in my ribs. Ten minutes before, it would have seemed a grand and tragic end, but now it was different. I wanted to be with Eda. I backed out of the shadows and stood there, scratching my head. That was when a corporal in high troop-boots shoved me, spoiling for a fight.

"By God, who give you leave to run up my back?"

He looked bigger than a Percheron, and he had a blue-steel knife with a thumbguard stuck in his belt. It looked long as a saber.

"That girl and that man," I said. "They stole my money." I remembered all of a sudden that I'd left my carbine in the wagon.

"I was just chasing them, that's all. "I didn't mean to bang into you."

A crowd began to gather, grinning faces turned up in the torchlight.

"You never had any money, I'll bet." The corporal hooked big thumbs in his belt. "You look like a dime's worth of cat-meat to me, bub." He looked around him, winking. "Now you just git down and dust off my boots where you tracked all over 'em."

I felt my neck get hot and prickly. "I told you I didn't go to do it." I tried to push away, but someone grabbed my arm and sent me spinning back into the circle of faces.

"My, ain't you the little rooster!" the corporal said. He put one big hand on the horn butt of the knife. "I tell you what, boy. A rooster's got to fight out here, or they slit his throat and make fricassee out of him."

He started to come for me but before we could clinch, someone came between us in a flutter of skirts. I saw a flash of red hair, and the corporal bellowed in amazement as Eda slapped him across his red face.

"Hank Schrader!" She pushed him so hard in the chest he almost sprawled over the delighted spectators at his back. "My goodness, don't you two know each other?" She stood between us, hands on her hips. "Joey, this is Henry Schrader, from B Company. Hank, I'd like to make you acquainted with Joey Boston. Joey and I are old friends, from back in Columbus."

Corporal Schrader was thunderstruck.

"Say you're glad to meet him, Hank."

The cavalryman shook his head as if dazed. "If'n you're a friend of Eda's—" He held out a hand like a quarter of beef.

"It don't make no difference whose friend I am," I said. "I'll fight you. All you got to do is find us a place where there ain't any damned women to interfere, and—"

"Shake hands," Eda insisted.

A man in a flowered vest slapped me on the back. "You done all right, sonny. Shake Hank's hand."

I shook hands, and Schrader made a rumbling bull-like sound and went away, the crowd stringing after him, talking and laughing.

"Goddamit," I said, "you didn't have to do that. I don't need no women to take care of me."

Eda laughed. She leaned against me in the shadows, burying her face against my shoulder, and laughed until I thought she'd choke.

"I don't see what's so funny."

She took a deep breath, with a catch in it. "I didn't mean to laugh at you, Joey. I—I—sometimes it's hard to tell whether to laugh or cry, anymore."

The way it looked, I never would understand women. But I understood one thing only too well. She was what Ike Coogan said. It made an ache inside me, right in the middle of my chest.

"You shouldn't have done that," I said. "You shouldn't have interfered between me and that B Company man. I can take care of myself."

"Joey," she said, "let's not talk anymore about it There—is that a bargain?"

She slipped her hand into mine.

"All right." I shook her hand.

Eda was living with a family right next to the San Agustin church. Mr. Landry was a clerk in Jimmie Lee's flour mill on the Santa Cruz a mile or so south of town, and Mrs. Landry was a narrow bony woman in black, with a starched lace collar. They didn't have much money, but they had a lot of children. I remembered what Ike Coogan said once—"a lean hound for a race and a poor man for children." They were glad to have a boarder like Eda, I guess, to help out, but I wondered if they knew much about her.

"Pleased to meet you, sir," Mr. Landry said, pumping my hand. He was a fat man with a dusty face and a gray floury look to him. "We'd be honored to have you take a bite with us. Fifty cents is all, and you can't do better at the Shoofly."

"I'll pay for it," Eda whispered in my ear.

"You will not!"

Mrs. Landry smiled a bony smile. "Pork is so dear, you know, Mr. Boston, and flour—" She rolled her eyes up. "Eighteen cents a pound. Now you know that ain't right!"

When they got the grub on the table, and all the little ones lined up on benches holding their spoons like they were daggers, Mr. Landry crinkled his eyes shut and said the Grace:

"Mush is rough, mush is tough.
Thank thee, Lord, we've got enough."

That was it, too, for the most part Mush in bowls, with a pitcher of molasses and a pot of coffee. There was some fried side meat, but Mr. Landry got most of that.

Mrs. Landry leaned toward me, wiping her mouth with the fringe of her lace collar. I'd wondered why it was kind of yellowish. "And what kind of work do you do, Mr. Boston?"

It was hard to talk over the clatter of the kids and their spoons in the mush-bowls.

"I'm a farmer, ma'am. Me and my brother. Down in the Sulphur Springs Valley. We been raising beans and melons and stuff for the soldiers at Military Plaza."

She whacked one of the louder kids with her knuckles. "And how did you and our Miss Gorman here become acquainted?"

That had been Eda's name before she married Saul. "Oh," I said, "we—I knew her back East. In Columbus. We were kids there."

Eda flashed me a look of gratitude, and Mrs. Landry seemed satisfied. Mr. Landry opened his mouth to say something, but the bell at San Agustin boomed the hour, and he bustled up, herding children before him.

"My land!" Mrs. Landry made a clucking noise. "Wherever does the time go?" She got into a rusty black coat and a big hat with a plume on it, and black gloves. "Now me and the mister will be at prayer meeting till nine, Eda, dear. You just red up the dishes, and see the children says their prayers, and then you and your young gentleman may sit on the bench out in front till we come home." Her voice turned suddenly iron-hard. "Not inside, you understand. There's too many might misunderstand. If Luther gets the croup, you come in and give him a spoonful of that turpentine. But you wait outside, Mr. Boston." She grimaced in what passed for a smile. "We have to be very careful, you know. Mr. Landry is a deacon in the church."

"Yes, ma'am," I said.

After they were gone and Eda had the kids all bedded down, we sat on the bench out front and felt the dusk settle around us. The church was big and white in the rising moon, and a flowering vine smelled like a lady's perfume. Tucson quieted down at supper time, but before long all hell would break loose around the Plaza. There'd be a few knifings among the Mexicans, and someone would get shot in the giblets and they'd take him into Ochoa's store to bleed a while on the yard goods, and everyone would be drunk and most of them would go to sleep in the street to the plink of a mandolin and a high-pitched Mexican voice singing about *mi corazon*. It was pleasant to be away from it, sitting here with Eda. Of course, that didn't change my opinion of her any.

"Joey," she said, "I think I'm going to cry."

I blinked at her, sitting straight and stiff on the edge of the bench, hands clasped tight in her lap.

"Cry? Whatever for?"

"I expect you'll think it's silly, and the only thing I can say is that I haven't cried once since I've been in the Arizona Territory. That's all the excuse I have. No matter what's happened to me, I couldn't cry before strangers. But you're different."

She looked at me, and I didn't say anything, and her face drooped. "I know what you're thinking. All right, you're not really kin to me. Not anymore."

"No," I said. "I guess not."

"Listen to me." Her voice was soft and quiet, but there was something in it that cut like a piece of grass on edge. Something that stung all the more because you weren't expecting it. "Joey, I want you to understand. I don't care what anyone else thinks, because there isn't anybody makes any difference to me any more. I haven't got any folks to go to." She twisted halfway round on the bench, her body pressing against me in eagerness, but still not looking right at me. "What happened that night at the Wells—I never got to tell my side of it to anyone. You've got to understand the way it was, Joey. I wasn't anything but a child then. Saul wanted me, and he was big and strong and had money, and I loved him. At least, I thought I did. But he didn't love me. Not really. He wanted a woman to take to the Territory and I was handy. That was all there was to it. Afterwards, he found out I wasn't much to cook and wash and carry water, and he got kind of disgusted. Oh, I don't blame him for that! I can look back now and see how sorry a wife I was. But it wasn't because I meant to be. I just didn't know any better, Joey. All I could do was sit on a silk pillow and sing to my dulcimer."

I remembered Saul and the dulcimer that night when I caught him with it, and the angry proud way he threw it from him, and the tinkling sound it made. "Maybe he loved you more than you knew."

"And still shame me the way he did that night, before all those people? The Galloways and the Thorpes and the Oggs? People that knew me back in Columbus?"

"Now don't yell at me," I said. "After all, what was he to think? You and Dave, off in the bushes together."

The bell of San Agustin boomed again, and with each stroke she seemed to shrink smaller and smaller, pulling away from me, the knuckles of her hands whitening where they gripped each other in her lap.

"I couldn't help it, Joey. As God is my judge, I couldn't. Dave came on me, and me naked as a baby. He put his arms around me and said things into my ear—Saul was a brute and he knew what I was going through and things like that. I fought him, at first. But Saul hadn't touched me. He was too busy. He always said 'Let's wait till we get to California'. And—Dave had his way with me. I didn't want to, Joey. Honestly, I didn't!"

Well, what did I care? This was all ancient history. What was done was done. I told her so. It was hard lines, but we've all got our lumps to take. I guess I sounded pretty gruff about it, but the truth of the matter was, she scared me a little bit. I was flustered to hear a pretty woman talk about things like that, and be so moved by them. All I knew so far—a woman was a soft attractive desirable thing, and when they were married they were supposed to wash and iron and cook and bear children and stay out of the way when important things came up. Now Eda was beginning to seem like a real person, and I didn't want to think of her that way. It didn't fit in with my plans.

"After that, there wasn't much left for me but to go to Tucson with Dave. Even that was a mistake. He didn't love me either. He wanted a woman to—to come to every two or three days. He was willing to keep me that way, but I didn't want to do it. I left him then and went to work."

Yes, I thought. *You know a lot of soldiers for a respectable working woman.*

"I got a job doing laundry for the soldiers at the Plaza." She showed me her fingers, rough and yellow and chapped. "That's all there is to it. That's the story of my life. I don't know what's beyond it. I—sometimes I don't want to think."

In sudden fright she clung to me, putting her arms around my neck. I could feel her heart beating against mine. "Joey, did

I do wrong? I never meant to harm anybody. Doesn't that go for anything?"

I was glad we were around the big white shoulder of the church, half-hidden from the street by the tangle of vines.

"Listen," I said. I was moved, without wanting to be. "You and I are kin, Eda, whether we want to be or not."

I told her about Saul and me—how we'd stuck it out at the Wells, and how Saul was getting farther and farther apart from me all the time, how he was quiet and brooding mad. I told her how losing her, and losing Dave, too, had turned him in on himself, and how he'd bet all his body and brain and what money he had against the country, how he was going to make himself rich and powerful in spite of anyone or anything. And I told her, too, about Dave, and about Red Chaffee, and how I feared for Dave, even after he'd run me off the way he did.

"I guess we're both kind of orphans. No one wants either of us, Eda. So we got to stick together, you and me. We're all the other of us has got."

She started to cry, then, and the tears came out like spring water from a crack in the rocks. It was the way she said—she'd saved them for her kin, and I was the kin. I could feel her breast heaving against me, and she hung to me like a sobbing child, panicky and frightened. But gradually the sobs lessened, and she lay against me longer and longer, arms still around my neck and her cheek against my shoulder.

"There." Her voice was ashamed. "I guess I got it all out of me. I'll be all right now."

That damned Luther had to pick this time to get the croup. I heard him squalling, and Eda sat up straight, patting her hair.

"I'll have to go in and give him some turpentine."

"Give him some rat poison," I suggested.

She laughed, and patted my cheek. For an instant, she was the same old Eda—gay and funny and friendly.

"Now don't make such a long face, Joey. I'll be back directly."

She was gone in a rustle of skirts. I leaned back on the bench and stared at the moon, wondering whether that pleasant smell was Eda or the twisted vine that groped upward on the white wall of the church. I felt at ease, in a way I hadn't known for a long time. Saul didn't bother me so much, and even Dave's brown merry face seemed to fade away. All I could think of was Eda. Eda Gorman, now. The roaring crazy sounds of Tucson at night came to me like they were filtered through cotton wool—faraway and thin and unimportant.

After a while Luther's bawling stopped. I knew why. With a mouthful of turpentine, the croup doesn't seem like much of a problem. Anyway, in a minute or so Eda came back, and she had a big pair of shears in one hand and a coal-oil lamp in the other.

"We've just got to get that hair cut, Joey." She made clicking sounds with the shears. "I declare, you look like a bear or something."

"Not here!" I said. "Not out here in the street, practically."

"Well," she said, "there's a grape arbor out in back, with a kind of a bench Mr. Landry made under it. I could do it there."

"My hair don't need cutting, anyway," I said. "It keeps me from getting sunstroke." But she wouldn't have it any other way, so I ended up under the grape arbor, spitting out seeds while she whacked her way around my ears, talking as much as any barber.

"I'll have to work fast. Mr. Landry says coal oil is eight dollars a gallon now, and he keeps track of how much is in each lamp." The scissors whack-whacked, and she chattered on. "Guess who I saw the other day."

"Mmmmm?"

"Old Mr. Coogan. You remember Mr. Coogan, that was with our party."

"I thought he was in Santa Fe or someplace."

"No, he was right here in Tucson. He was terribly drunk. He tried to pick a fight in Mr. Chaffee's saloon—what is it called? Oh, yes, the Paradise. Anyway, Mr. Chaffee's bartender threw him out. Old Mr. Coogan stood there for a long time howling at them and offering to lick anyone that would fight fair. He's not very well, I don't think. Poor old man—he was coughing and wheezing something awful."

I picked a bunch of grapes and held them up in the yellow light.

"Dave's working for Chaffee," I said. "I guess you knew."

The clack of the shears slowed for a moment, and then hurried on. "Dave tried to get him to go away but Mr. Coogan just yelled obscene things at him. You know how Mr. Coogan used to brag so about being up in Oregon with some explorer or somebody."

"Parkman," I said. "Maybe he was."

"Well, Mr. Coogan finally got tired, I guess. He said there wasn't any good men in Tucson like he used to know in Oregon, and he went away."

"Where?"

"I don't know."

I felt her hip press against my shoulder. It was warm and firm, with a delicious yield to it. I chewed faster on the grapes, and spit the seeds clear across the yard.

"There," she said, stepping back and holding up the lamp. "Now you look almost human, Joey."

I was human, too, I guess. I felt hot and crazy and a little dizzy but I reached out and pulled her to me. The lamp fell to the ground and broke and we were all alone in the moonlight under that damned grape arbor.

"Eda," I mumbled, pressing my lips against her cheek. A hand was fumbling around her hips, and I realized with a start that it was mine. I remember stepping on a piece of the broken glass chimney and the splintering sound was loud in the silence. "Eda, Eda!"

She pushed against me with her hands, and her voice was puzzled and hurt. "Joey, stop it! You're acting like an animal!"

I didn't stop. I couldn't. I should have.

"Joey, stop! Do you hear me?"

How white and smooth her knees were that day in the wagon when she stepped out into my arms! She'd been Saul's, then, but now he didn't have any claim on her. She'd been Dave's, too, but that had been a mistake. Now she was mine.

"Joey!"

In sudden fury she lashed out at me, her fingers curved like cat's claws. She ripped at my cheek and I felt the gashes, each one cold and clean and stinging.

"Keep away from me!"

Blinking, I dropped my arms and stood there, staring at her. Something hadn't gone right. Wasn't I as good as any of those soldiers at the Plaza? Or maybe—just maybe—

"You Bostons are all alike." There was scorn in her voice, a scorn that overlaid the panting and trembling. "You think a woman is just a—a convenience. Even you, Joey." She shook her head, and her long hair rippled in the pale moon. "Even you, Joey." She began to cry, and it was the sound of a child lost in a dark place. "I never thought you—"

I felt like someone had thrown a bucket of spring water over my head. Everything seemed to come out clear and sharp, and I understood a lot of things.

"Eda," I said, "I'm sorry. I didn't think—I mean I—"

There wasn't much to say, so I shut up. Already I'd got my hand bit and my face scratched.

"Where are you going?" she asked.

"Back to the Wells."

She hurried after me. "I didn't mean to hurt you." She brushed her fingers over my cheek. "Oh, I've made such a mess of things, Joey. Now I've done something to you, too. And we were such good friends!"

"Never mind about me. Whatever I got, I deserved, I guess." I fumbled in my pocket and handed her the Apache necklace I carried around with me. "Here, take this."

"What is it?"

"I took it off'n an Apache," I said. "You don't see many of them around. It's some kind of a medicine necklace." I swallowed hard. I'd put a lot of store by that necklace. "It'll bring you good luck."

She looked at it in the palm of her hand. "Why, thank you, Joey. I—I need good luck."

At the gate I paused. "I think I hear Luther bawling again. Give him some more of that damned turpentine."

I went away, walking fast as I could, blundering into the creepers of the vine on the church and almost falling. I knew she was standing there, watching me go, and I had to get away quick.

When I got back to my wagon, the *muchacho* was sitting on the seat in the moonlight, wrapped in a blanket, my carbine over his shoulder. The San Agustin bell tolled ten.

"Senor," he said.

I tossed him another dollar and he giggled softly.

"Did you see a woman tonight, *senor?*"

"You go to hell," I said.

CHAPTER SEVEN

All the way back to the Wells, I had a feeling someone was following me. The minute I left the Camino Real, I began to worry. I craned my neck around all the time, without seeing anything but the baked burned grass, and the only sound was the hiss of the wheels on the plain. The sun was fierce, like someone laying a brass hand on your head, and the mules breathed hard and lathered even pulling the empty wagon. The Dragoons were a chocolate jumble to the east, shimmering red and brown in the haze, and once I saw a single bright wink, like a diamond, that might have been a signal of some kind with a mirror. I picked up my carbine and held it in the crook of my arm while I drove. Near as I was to Tucson with its flour mill and ice house and all the modern conveniences, this was *Apacheria*—Apache land. This was where Cut Finger hung out.

That night I holed up in the same *barranca,* wishing the moon wasn't so bright. It was like a big gas mantle hanging up there, and I felt like a fly crawling around on a white tablecloth. Someone had a flyswatter, sure, and I was the one that was going to be squashed. But in spite of my edginess, the night passed and nothing happened. When sunrise came, I chewed a mouthful of jerky from my hip pocket and hitched up the mules again. I flogged them good for a while to get the wagon rolling. In a way, I was anxious to get back to the Wells and show Saul how good I'd done—twenty-five dollars from that captain for the truck, less three dollars for the Clubhouse Gin I'd bought for Dave—that made twenty-two dollars. I patted the bundle pinned in my shirt pocket, feeling real good. But it was more than the money. I wanted to get back to the Wells. Not Saul, particularly—he didn't have anything to do with it—it was more like the Wells was beginning to be home. Tucson was a real gay place, yet I couldn't help feel a kind of contempt for the shopkeepers and merchants and laborers there. What did they know about the Territory—the real Territory? About Cut Finger and building a house that was like a fort, with slits for guns, and running water into it, and scratching out a living come Apaches or high water or whatever it might be? No, Tucson was for old ladies and children. It wasn't for me. If a man was going to live in Tucson, he might as well never have left Columbus, Ohio, that was the way I figured.

When I heaved up out of the *playa* and saw the low green smudge of the Wells—Boston Wells—I felt a kind of tightening in my chest. "G'lang, there!" I yelled at the mules. "Git along there, you black devils!" If I could have sung, I'd have done it, but I never did have any voice for music. I liked it, but I couldn't sing. It took Dave to sing.

I wasn't prepared to have anyone shoot at me from our Texas house. I saw the puff of smoke first, and then something like a bumblebee went past my ear and sizzed off into the distance. After that came the low rolling boom, and I sawed back so hard on the reins the mules sat down on their haunches. For a second I just sat there on the seat of the empty wagon, the reins in my fists and a scared feeling tickling my backbone. Who was in our house? Had Cut Finger gotten Saul while I was gone? But that sounded like Saul's old fifty. Still, it could be an Apache on the other end of it. But they wouldn't pull anything like that. If they had the house and saw me and the mules coming, they'd suck me in first and then rush me. All these things floundered through my mind, including that feeling I'd had of eyes on me all the way back. I was just ready to jump down and take cover behind the wagon when I saw Saul come out of the house, waving to me. I let my whole breath whoosh out of me in relief.

When I got there, I'd forgotten my scare, and I was mad.

"What the hell you shooting at *me* for?" I tied the mules and slapped dust off me, glowering at him. "You ever see an Apache driving a team of mules and a Moline wagon?"

"I dunno." He blinked at me, scratching his chin. "I been pretty jumpy lately, Joey. There's been Apaches all around the Wells for the last three days, like bees at a bucket of sugar water."

I took a closer look at him and I was sorry I spoke so sharp. Saul was a big man, but he looked drawn thin and tight and his eyes were red-rimmed and bleary. I hadn't been gone long, and I expect a lot of the change was there before I left, but being to Tucson seemed to have given me a new look for things. I even noticed a sprig of gray at his temple that hadn't been there before, for sure. At least I never remembered it.

"I made us twenty-two dollars," I said.

He picked at the stubble on his chin, not seeming to hear me.

"All I saw was the dust, and I squeezed off a shot into the middle of it. I didn't know what it was."

He didn't offer to help me feed and water the mules—just stood there picking at his chin and talking. Talking about Apaches. "You see any of Cut Finger's people?"

"On the way in they jumped me, but I drove away from 'em."

He looked around, kind of sniffing. "I tell you, something's bound to break. I can feel it in my bones. They been playin' with me for the last three days, like puss in the corner. I see one of 'em on his pony a thousand yards out on the *playa,* and then he's gone and two more are sitting out by that gully to the east, just sitting there and looking at me." He ran the heel of his hand along the barrel of the Sharps, slow and deliberate. "I'll never leave here. They can't scare me out. I come here to stay."

There was something funny in the careful way he talked. It was almost like he was in a daze. But then I remembered he probably hadn't had any real sleep since I'd been gone, and he probably hadn't eaten much, either.

"I tell you what," I said. "I'll go in and fry us up some meat and boil a little coffee."

"There ain't been any soldiers by here for weeks," he said in the same dry slow voice. "Looks like we can't expect any help from them. A man's got to sink or swim."

"We'll swim, all right," I said. "You wait and see."

The house was like a boar's nest. Saul never believed in wasting time on domestic details, and it was mostly up to me to keep things straightened up. There was a trail of ants as thick as your arm leading to a spilled jug of molasses, and mama's old blue and white comforter was on the dirt floor and there was boot prints across it. I stamped out the ants and cleaned up as best I could, not able to be too put out about it. After all, Saul had put up with a lot while I was on the town.

I sliced chunks off a slab of salt side meat and put a handful of our precious coffee in the old smoky pot. But the meat wasn't even curled at the edges when they hit us. I hadn't been wrong about eyes being on me. Cut Finger and his Apaches. Later I didn't count more than twenty-five of them, but in that brief instant when they boiled in the open door, it looked like a swarm of gnats. I don't know before God where they came from.

I threw the skillet at one of them and it hit him in the nose but somebody grabbed me from behind and it was like an iron clamp pinching down. I couldn't even breathe. I remember wondering where Saul was, and why he hadn't been able to get off even one shot to warn me. The funniest thing was the silence. That many men, overrunning us like I'd stamped out those ants, and yet there wasn't a screech or a hoot or a yell. They knew what they were doing, and they went about it fast and easy—no fuss, no waste motion.

After that first shock, I began to get scared and sweat. I didn't do what I was scared I'd do—I was thankful for that. They dragged me out into the dog-trot and threw me down beside Saul. No one made any effort to tie us up. I guess there wasn't any need to. They had our guns, and any way we looked there was Apaches three deep. And right in front of us, squatting on his haunches in the shade of the dog-trot, was Cut Finger. Somehow or other I knew it was him, without even looking at the greasy stumps of his first two fingers.

He was short and stocky, even for an Apache, and his hide glistened with some kind of oil. Black smears of paint outlined the ridges of his cheeks, and his forehead, but he didn't wear the usual band of colored cloth around his temples. Instead, his hair was long and braided, and the braids hung down over his chest. He had a tanned skin of some small animal wrapped around his loins, and the thigh-length moccasins they all wore, but none of the claptrap like sacred beads or strings of shells. His dress was simpler than any of the bucks, and yet you could see he was an important man, someone to be reckoned with.

I knew what they'd most likely do. They'd tie us spreadeagled to the wheels of our old wagon, and pile brush on it, and set fire to it. That is, that's what they'd do if we were lucky. I'd heard about other things from Ike Coogan, like burying you to your neck and spreading honey all over your face. They'd leave you that way, to wait for the ants.

"I'll talk to him," I said to Saul. "I know some Apache."

"A lot of good that'll do."

At Cut Finger's right was his medicine man, a bony whiplike man with a catamount skin over his shoulders. He had a dusty-eyed rattler in a grass cage, and every once in a while he'd poke it out at Saul, trying to get him to rare back. But Saul sat there like he was made out of stone, and the medicine man made an angry noise.

"Now it's coming," Saul said.

Cut Finger began to speak, still holding up his fingers. I didn't catch much of it at first, but I understood enough to know that something very special was being planned for us.

"Saul," I said, "I'm sorry if I ever said anything mean to you. I didn't mean it, if I did. I forgive you, and you forgive me."

He didn't say anything, just sitting there and looking at the rattler in the grass cage.

"I think you ought to forgive Dave, too," I said. "And Eda. Saul, it was just the way things happen. I guess no one was really to blame. It doesn't make any difference, now, anyway. What counts, we ought to make our peace with God."

I saw Saul's chest rise and fall under his torn shirt. He still didn't look at me. The snake seemed to fascinate him. I closed my eyes and tried to think of a prayer of some kind. Saul was more religious than I was, but he seemed paralyzed.

"The Lord is my shepherd—"

Saul stirred a little, and the rattler jerked its heavy body together and struck at the grass bars of the cage. Even the medicine man drew back a little, and then took his medicine stick and poked at the cage. Cut Finger droned on and on, eyes half-closed, weaving from side to side as he squatted, still holding up his maimed fingers.

"Joey," Saul said, "can you tell him I've got some pretty good medicine myself?"

I blinked in surprise. "Tell him what?"

So quickly that the circle of Apaches didn't have time to move, Saul snatched the grass cage and ripped open the top. He grabbed the snake by the thick fat body, just back of the head.

"Tell 'em I've got some medicine of my own. Damn you, tell him, quick!"

Someone raised a lance, a long pole with a piece of red gingham tied to the blade, and held it against Saul's chest. But there wasn't the push home I'd expected, the sudden slice and gush of red. Instead the man looked at Cut Finger, waiting.

"Tell 'em," Saul said, the lance point pricking his chest. "Tell 'em I don't fear Ostin Snake. I've got bigger medicine than Ostin Snake. Tell 'em that."

The Apaches feared snakes. The reason they were scared of fish was because a fish has scales like a snake. Cut Finger's medicine man must have been a powerful figure even to carry one around in a wicker cage. But a snake in a cage and a snake in a man's hand are two different things. They all drew back, muttering and taking side-long glances at Cut Finger. The chief sat with legs crossed, unmoving, his bead-like eyes sharp and black as rock.

When I started to speak, fumbling along in the strange Apache tongue, no one looked at me. They heard me, I know, but their eyes were fixed on Saul, standing spread-legged in the shade of the dog-trot, the snake's muscular body coiling and whipping around his bare forearm. It was hot and still—there wasn't a puff of wind—and it seemed like I was in a dream, a terrible dream. Snake—what was the word for snake? *Tzintzin,* or something like that? Or was that the word for a kind of lizard?

When I finished, Cut Finger pulled a clump of grass out of the hard-packed earth and ground it into dust with his fingers. "Talk, all talk," he said, making a sign for talk, too.

I told Saul.

"All right," he said. He looked down at the flat triangular head of the snake. "I'll show 'em. No more talk."

Up till then I hadn't any idea of what Saul was proposing to do. I thought it was all a stall, a sham—a clever way to buy time. Right now time was precious. Our last minutes on earth were running out, and minutes are years to a man about to die. But it suddenly came to me what he was going to do. I knew. It was exactly what he would do, the stubborn hopeless thing Saul always had a fondness for. And as I cried out, he held his free hand up, palm out, and shifted his grip on the snake, waiting for it to strike. For a long minute, while my yell died away in the silence, the ugly head hung motionless, a ripe berry on a thick dusty vine. Then it struck, a lightning-fast blur and recovery, and poised again, the little forked tongue darting in and out.

"Tell 'em Ostin Snake can't harm me," Saul said in a husky voice. He looked down at the two little slashes in the palm of his hand. Then he dropped the snake into the basket and closed the lid. "Tell 'em they're monkeying around with pretty big medicine when they lay hands on me."

They all stared at him, and then a babble of voices broke out. Ostin Snake's medicine was well known, and Saul Boston, standing there among them, began to take on some of the attributes of a man already dead; a ghost, and the Apaches feared ghosts. The buck with the lance put an awestruck hand over his mouth. Saul jerked a blanket away from another Apache, who did not protest, and sat down crosslegged opposite Cut Finger and the medicine man, draping it across his shoulders. All the time he kept his gaze fixed on Cut Finger, and the chief stared stonily back at him. Perhaps that was why Cut Finger didn't see the madstone. I saw it. It was the one Mina Ogg had thrown at Saul's feet, almost two years ago, that day the wagon train pulled out and left him at the Wells.

"Saul," I said, "you danged fool!"

He'd slipped it out of the nankeen sack it was in and clenched it in his fist, holding it tight against the wound in his palm. For just a fraction of a second I saw it, small, gray, and squarish, with rounded corners. Then it was folded in his palm.

"Tell 'em!" Saul growled.

I told them. I put it into Apache words as best I could.

"Tell 'em this, too," Saul said. His face was already gray and dotted with little beads of sweat "Tell 'em I'm going to sit right here and wrestle it out with old Ostin Snake's poison. Tell 'em I'll be sitting here till my medicine works, and when it does, there better not be any Apaches around here, because I'll turn my medicine loose on the whole damned tribe, and they'll all sicken and die, men, women, and children, and fish will eat them and cast their bones in the rivers and lakes and into the sea. Tell 'em that!"

I did. If Apaches ever turned white, these did. I think the mention of fish did it. I'll give Cut Finger credit, though. He was quite a man. He reached up and pulled his nose in a deliberate gesture, and then motioned to the medicine man. They talked behind cupped hands but I followed most of it.

"He will die," the medicine man said.

"Probably."

"Ostin Snake is death."

Cut Finger nodded. "This is true."

"How can a man have a medicine that is stronger than Ostin Snake?"

"I do not know."

The medicine man jabbed at Saul with a painted medicine stick. "Already he looks sick."

Cut Finger rubbed his nose. "Well, let us see."

The medicine man was impatient. "He will die!"

Cut Finger's lean features hardened, and an edge came in his voice. "If you are wrong, Tahsay, there are many others to carry your medicine stick. If I am wrong, my people will die, and be eaten by fish." He looked around at the gathering clouds, and the sun starting its way down into the west. "Put out strong patrols. I will sit with this man and see. I will see myself."

I crept close to Saul, squatting motionless under the blanket. "How do you feel?"

"Hand's numb. My arm tingles a little."

Presently the Apaches quit staring and went about the business of getting a meal. One of them had our mule Gomorrah by the bridle. He reared his head back, snorting in alarm, but the Indian slashed his throat and Gomorrah collapsed like a balloon with a hole in it, all the life spilling out in a red fountain that pumped hard, and then less hard, and slowed to a trickle. They sliced off thick hairy steaks and seared them over a brushwood fire. But they all ate in silence, looking out of the corners of their eyes at the white man huddled under the blanket.

"Saul," I said, "can I get you a—a drink of water or something?"

He shook his head, and I squatted beside him, feeling the twilight cold begin to soak into me. Try as I would, I couldn't imagine Dave pulling a stunt like this. Or me either. Dave, now—he'd have jumped on them like a tiger, and gone down with a lance in him, quick and clean. But I'd be dead, too. It was Saul's doing that I was alive now. I owed him that. I worked with my fingers at a hole in my boot, listening to his breathing, deep and painful.

"I think it's working," he said.

I looked up, trying to figure whether he was just saying that to make me feel good. "How do you know?"

"It's sticking to my hand. Like a leech. It's sucking, that's what it's doing."

"How does your arm feel?"

Saul pulled a flap of the blanket over his head. "Like a board. But that's all right. I don't mind my arm. Just so it don't get into my chest."

Around us the Apaches lounged at their small fires, keeping a troubled eye on Cut Finger and Saul. The medicine man hovered behind Cut Finger, watching too. Once he stepped forward and threw powder from a little sack at Saul's hunched form, and made a couple of furious passes with his little stick.

"Go away," Cut Finger said. "Take your medicine and go away. This is between this man and me."

That night was a thousand years long. I squatted beside Saul, hoping that just being there would lend him some strength. Once he swayed under the blanket, and I pushed quickly against him and propped him up. I didn't know whether Cut Finger saw me or not. In the dark, with only the flickering small fires, all I could see of his eyes were two dark hollows.

"I'm sick," Saul said. He swallowed painfully, and the sound seemed loud enough to wake them all.

"I'll get you some water."

He shook his head.

"My throat's swelling. I—I don't think I can swallow anything."

I tried to keep my voice steady. "It'll work. Mina Ogg said it saved her uncle from a mad dog bite, and they're worse than a rattler anyday."

"Don't be scared," Saul said. "The Lord's hand is over us."

"I ain't scared."

I wasn't, either. After a while all the scaredness gets drained out of you. You can't be scared anymore. When I thought of the Apaches all around us, and what was going to happen if Saul didn't pull through, it seemed faraway and distant, like an earthquake in a foreign land. It would happen—all right, it would happen. I couldn't be scared any more. But I did feel an ache inside me when I thought of Eda, all by herself in Tucson. She's never see me any more, and I'd never see her. I tried to think of her the way she was that night when she scratched me, and I felt at the scratchy welts on my cheek where she'd raked me. She deserved better than she'd got at the hands of the Boston brothers. Maybe it was destiny, the way things were going. Everyone got what he deserved.

"Joey," Saul said in a strange voice, "I can't feel my hand anymore. I don't know whether the madstone's still in my hand or not." His voice broke in panic, and Cut Finger leaned forward, staring at him.

"It's all right," I said. "I know it's all right."

"I can't tell."

"You wait," I whispered. "Wait till they settle down again and I'll feel in your hand and see."

When they quieted down again, I managed to get my hand in under the blanket. It scared me when I touched his fist, closed tight around the madstone. His hand was cold, like a chunk of marble, and swollen and sweaty with an icy sprinkling on it But as far as I could tell, he still had the madstone.

"It's all right," I said. For the first time, I had a glimmer of hope. I'd heard a lot about madstones, and Mina Ogg's was supposed to be one of the best. Maybe—just maybe—

"I don't know," Saul said faintly. "I just don't know."

"Know what?"

He waited a long time before he spoke. "What you ought to do—" He paused again, swallowing painfully. "After it sucks for a while, it ought to be taken off and soaked in warm water to draw out the poison. Then it'd be fresh."

For some crazy reason, I thought of a grammar teacher I'd had in Columbus once. Miss Waters. She always was hard on me. Once she cracked me with a ruler and like to split my head open. She'd be sorry when she heard the Apaches got me.

"Maybe I can go in and—"

"No," Saul said. "They'd think it was funny. We can't take a chance. All we got is the madstone. If we was to lose that—" His voice trailed away, and he took a corner of the blanket in his teeth and bit down hard on it.

The clouds boiled and turned over our heads, and there was a fresh cold smell. The same clouds were probably over Tucson. Maybe Eda was looking up at the same one I was, and wondering if it would rain. *Eda,* I thought, *we wronged you. All of us.* I thought again and again of Dave and her, how they'd hear of Saul and me dying, and maybe that would bring them together. Dave wasn't half bad if you got at him right.

Suddenly Saul began to sing. It was a quiet mournful sound at first, almost like a whimper. Then it got louder and louder, like a man in a delirium:

"It happened in Jacksboro, the spring of sixty-three.
A man by the name of Crego come stepping up to me."

It was that song Eda used to sing. It was funny—I'd never heard Saul sing before. He wasn't the kind to sing. His voice had a queer childlike ring to it, pure and true.

"How do you do, young fellow, and would you like to go

And spend a summer pleasantly on the range of the buffalo?"

The Apaches stirred uneasily at that. Singing was a kind of ceremony to them, something not done lightly. The white man was singing to his gods, I guess they thought. Old Tahsay, or whatever his name was, shuffled forward, making a sniffing sound like a hound dog, turning his head this way and that, waving the stick.

Before we left Columbus, all of us, we used to sing that song together, and talk about California, and all the money we were going to make out there. Even Saul would get excited, and coax Eda to sing some more. That was a long time ago—such a long time ago.

Now he went on and on in that high-pitched wavering voice, letter-perfect, and when he finished he slumped down, head on his chest. I thought for one terrible curdling moment that he was dead. Ostin Snake had won. Cut Finger reached out his arms and planted his knuckles against the ground beside him, ready to get up. But Saul went on babbling stuff that didn't make sense. He talked to Eda, and to Dave. He went over our trip, and he counted the money out time and time over, and he gee-hawed at the mules and scolded and fumed and gave orders to people that weren't there any more. And then, he and Dave quarreled all over again, and Eda left him, and it wrenched a deep shuddering sound from him, and then he was silent.

"He will die," Tahsay said again. He knelt beside Cut Finger, but there was respect in his voice as he looked at Saul. "He will die," he said again. "This is ghost talk that comes before a man dies."

Cut Finger put the stumps of his fingers to his lips and rubbed at them. His eyes were two shiny winks in the firelight.

"Let us see."

Sometime during the night I went to sleep. I hadn't slept for two days. Still, I guess you couldn't really call it sleep. It was more a kind of daze. It seemed like my body was still there, glued to the ground alongside my brother Saul, but my mind went floating up and up, till I was over Tucson. I remember squinting hard, looking at all the flat roofs and into all the lighted windows, looking for somebody. Who was I looking for? It didn't seem clear to me. Eda? Was that who it was?

I saw her, then, the lamplight sparkling on her hair. She stepped forward, hands outstretched toward me, and then the light changed and it was Dave's face—a face that was smiling with a kind of terrible joke to it. He pulled off his hat, and there were thousands of tiny twisted red curls under it, Red Chaffee's curls, and I screamed and fell into nothingness.

I guess I made a noise of some kind, because when I opened my eyes Cut Finger was on his feet, his body shiny and sleek-looking. The gray morning light lit the high ridges of his cheeks, and Tahsay stood beside him, with the rest of the Apaches crowding up to look. *Morning,* I thought. *The whole night's gone by.* Beside me, Saul stirred under the shelter of the blanket.

"He did not die," Cut Finger said.

Carefully, like a hunter stalking a deer, the chief stepped forward and caught the blanket between thumb and forefinger. He tore it off, then, and all of the watchers made a crazy frightened sound in their throats. Slowly, with a terrible controlled slowness, Saul got to his feet. His face in that gray light was like death, and his eyes rolled in his head. But he was alive, and standing on his feet. Like some awful mechanical toy, he raised his clenched hands over his head.

He couldn't talk, not with his throat so swollen, but he shook his fists at them and made a harsh croaking sound, and it was enough. They all understood. His medicine had licked Ostin Snake. It was something to go down in Apache legend, a story to be told to children, along with the famous ones about Coyote, and White Painted Lady, and the rest.

Suddenly the heavens seemed to open, and sheets of cold water drenched us. Lightning split the dark clouds, and the water fell on the small fires of Cut Finger's band and turned them into hissing blackened piles of scorched wood. Nervous and scared, the Apaches fled, jumping onto their ponies and flogging them away into the rain. Anywhere, everywhere; wanting only to be free of this new and strong magic. The hoofs of their flying ponies, shod in deerskin, sucked and plunged into the wet earth. In a moment they were gone, swallowed up in the gray sheets of rain, leaving behind them the drowned fires and the slaughtered carcass of our mule.

All of them, that is, except Cut Finger. He stood there in the rain, the black paint on his cheeks melting and running and his long deerskin moccasins soggy and wilted. He stared at Saul for a long time, and then he turned and walked away, head down. He got on his pony like a tired old man, and it walked away with him. That was all. That was the last we ever saw of him, or of his Apaches.

"You beat 'em." My voice cracked. "Saul, you beat 'em! They'll never bother us again."

We owed our lives to the madstone. I wasn't forgetting that. But there was more to it than the madstone. The main thing, Saul had made up his mind a snakebite couldn't kill him, not right then, and it didn't The madstone helped, that was all you could say. The main thing was Saul.

I grabbed his hand and pried it open. Inside, clamped like in a vise, was the madstone. It had been small and gray before, and hard, like porcelain. Now it was swollen and bloated-looking—greenish, and soft

"It worked!" I yelled.

He followed me like a dumb animal, eyes glazed, as I led him into the house and pushed him down on the straw. I got water boiling and dumped a box of salts into it to draw the poison, and got him to hold his hand in the basin while I made coffee.

"You're all right," I said. "You're going to be fine! I guess there ain't anything that can lick us after this. No siree bob—there ain't anything!" I pointed out the open door. "Look at that rain come down! You can see the grass getting green already. You know what? We ought to get us a lot of beef cattle and feed them up on our range! The Government's buying all the beef cattle they can get in Tucson. How about it, Saul?"

I held the coffee to his lips, but he couldn't get it down. His throat was swollen almost shut. He kept shaking his head and pointing to his neck, and then holding his hands up in the air, like he was praying. I couldn't understand at first—then I did. He wanted me to give thanks for our deliverance.

I never was much good at out-loud praying, and I tried to talk him out of it. "The Lord knows we're grateful. Just think it, that's all we have to do."

But he wasn't satisfied. I had to say it. So I got down on my prayer bones and tried. "Lord, you know we're grateful. We'll stick on here and try to make a go of it in your name. I guess that's all now."

It didn't sound very churchy but it seemed to satisfy Saul and after a while he went to sleep.

How he ever got on his feet that morning and outfaced Cut Finger, I'll never know, because it took another three days before he could walk and talk again. But he did it, and the Wells was ours for good now.

CHAPTER EIGHT

In the months that followed, I got to know that Tucson road real well. Our old Moline wagon began to make a pair of ruts in the trail, piled high with com and beans and melons, with once in a while a load of cheeses, or maybe good sweet hay. After the rains, the grassland turned lush and green for miles. For a short spell the land didn't look much different from the country around Columbus. It wouldn't last too long; the sun would scorch everything parched and brown again, but for a while it was nice. I put our money in the bank in Tucson, and what with the thousand or more that Saul had from the farm, and what we made off the Army, we had a big enough stake to think about buying beef cattle and running them on our land. We'd come through a long dry spell our first three years there, but that was unusual. Maybe there'd be more rain, enough to keep the grass going for cattle. Anyway, it was worth trying.

Saul was against it. He didn't want to take a chance.

"But it's our main chance," I said. "Aside from the Wells what's this country good for? Nothing but grassland. We get a few more good rains and it's prime for cattle. There isn't enough water for a lot of little farms like around Columbus and Delaware and Springfield. It's going to take hundreds of acres for one man to make a go of it, and that means cattle."

He rubbed his hand where the snake had bit. After the swelling had gone down, he said it still hurt, and it got kind of stiff and stayed that way.

"Well, I don't know."

"Look at it this way," I said, getting excited. "If we buy cattle and—"

"I don't know!" he blurted. "Damn it, Joey, I told you I don't know! I got to think about something like that. I don't want to go rushing into anything till I think it over. Now be quiet, will you?" He went into the house and sat there, rubbing his hand.

That worry I felt about him stirred in me again. Up till we'd had that scene with Cut Finger, the time Saul let the snake bite him, he'd been driving himself, and me too. He was always busy, pushing, driving, never still for a minute. Everything he did had meaning and purpose behind it. He was going to make a go of the Wells in spite of hell or high water or Apaches or whatever. And here we were, sitting on top of the world. But Saul had hit his peak that day with Cut Finger, and ever since he'd been sliding downhill. Not fast—a little here and a little there. His hand hurt him, and I did most of the hoeing and irrigating and cutting hay and watering the mules and slopping the pigs. Saul took to walking alone, out on the bluff that overlooked the *playa*. Sometimes he wouldn't speak for days, just sit in the house and stare at the wall. It made me pretty mad, but I knew I had him to thank for having a whole skin, and I couldn't object. Still, I was glad to get away to Tucson every once in a while with a load of produce. At least, I could see Eda and have someone to talk to. She and I had long talks together. I rented a buggy from the livery stable and we'd drive out to Little-Eye Springs in the evening and sit and talk, or maybe under the willows along the Santa Cruz south of town. After that night under the grape arbor at Landry's, I never touched her, though. She was like a sister to me. It was a point of honor, with me, anyway.

"Joey," she asked one night, "what's going to become of us?"

I was rolling me a cigarette, and the frogs were chunking in the swampy land along the creek. "What do you mean?"

She looked up at the stars, grains of sugar dusted around the sky. "Sometimes all this seems like a dream to me. I want to know what I'm doing out here. I want to know what I'm here for, how I fit into things. A person can't just *be* here. Everybody's here for a reason. It might not be a *good* reason, I understand that. But what am I doing, when I do laundry for the soldiers at the Plaza? How does that fit in?"

When she talked that way, I always had a leery feeling. The few women I'd known never talked like that. They were too busy to worry about faraway things. But after a while I got to like it. It made you think.

"I expect it all fits in," I said. "Look at it this way. You do the laundry, the soldiers get their clothes clean, you're really helping the Territory grow, if you go back far enough to figure it out."

She smiled. It was a stiff little smile, as though she wasn't used to smiling often. "How do you fit in?"

I sucked deep on the cigarette, and it glowed high and went down again. "That's easy. Saul and me—we're hacking out a place for people to live some day. The world's getting crowded. There's over sixty million people in the United States today, do you realize that? They've got children, their children will have children. There's got to be some place for them to go, and food for them to eat, room to settle where they can make a living. Someday there'll be a town at the Wells, with a school and a drygoods store and a Baptist church and everything else. And it'll be built on what me and Saul have done. They'll owe us something—not that we mean to ask for any reward—but it'll be a good feeling to know that we did something for the lives of people that aren't even born yet."

Her voice was thoughtful. "Somehow that doesn't sound like Saul."

She was right. It wasn't. Saul never cared for people very much, except when he could boss them and get something out of them. He never trusted anyone. The only reason he wanted people at the Wells was to make his own holdings secure. But I didn't want to say it.

"Well," I said, "it's the way I feel." Then I felt embarrassed, talking about things like that, and I changed the subject. "How about you? Do you want to do things for people?"

"I used to. Now I don't know. Sometimes it seems like a person has all she can do to look out for herself."

"I guess it's our fault you're out here in the Territory," I said. "Saul's and Dave's and mine. I don't think any of us is proud of what we've done." For a minute I stopped, not knowing how to put into words what I wanted to say. I didn't even want to say it, knowing she might agree. And yet I had to say it. "Eda, Saul and I have got quite a bit of money in the bank here in Tucson. If you wanted to go back to Columbus—"

"No." Her voice was quick. "No, I couldn't. There's no one there to go back to anyway. My aunt—that's all. Anyway, I couldn't go back. Not this way." She leaned her head back on the seat of the buggy, hands clasped behind her head. "This is my home, I guess. From now on. Only—"

"Only what?"

She swallowed. "If I only knew what it was all for. What it meant. If I had a feeling there was more to my life than just *being* here, just holding on till I get to be an old woman. Tub after tub of dirty clothes—" She looked down at her fingers, and then laughed. "It's clean work, anyhow. Honorable work."

"You'll never get to be old," I said. The thought hurt me. "Not you."

She stared at me, a straight hard look. Then she looked away, toward where the white tower of Bac stood, high and ghostly. Her voice was so quiet I could hardly hear. "That's the nicest thing anyone ever said to me, Joey."

I felt nervous at the turn the conversation was taking, so I clucked at the mules and they lifted their ears and shambled toward town. I let her out at the Landrys, and wished her goodnight.

"I've still got that Apache necklace you gave me," she said. Then she went into the house without looking back.

The word about the Wells spread fast through Tucson. One day a man stopped me in front of Lord and Williams's. He had a wagon load of barrels of sweet water from the Bishop's farm, where they had a good spring. He was selling it for a dollar a barrel.

"You that feller from Chiricahua Wells?"

"Boston Wells," I said.

He was a short thick man in a woolen undershirt, a wide straw hat jammed down over his ears. He scratched his chin with the butt of his whip and looked me over.

"Name's Mowry. Come out here from Rutland, Vermont. Intended to make a fortune. Didn't have much luck." He waved the whip at the water wagon. "It's a living, but I don't eat very high on anybody's hog." He went on, talking through his nose in short clipped sentences. "Heard there was right good land down there, around the Wells. Heard you and your brother run the Apaches right off'n it."

"Well," I said, "they haven't bothered us for quite a spell."

He pursued his lips. "Used to farm in Vermont. After I busted two plowshares in one afternoon, I took out for new land. Saw Tucson, looked around for a job. Hell, there ain't nothin' here. Put all my money in this here water wagon. Been workin' like a dog ever since." He frowned at me, eyes shrewd. "Think a man could make a living down there?"

"There's water," I said. "Plenty of water. The land'll raise anything if you run water to it. Melons as big as your head, com, beans—we've got a good stand of grass now, and we're planning on running cattle, too." I tried hard not to sound too excited about it. I didn't want to scare him off. "A man that wants to work can do real well."

He scratched his chin again, slow and thoughtful. "You and your brother file on the best land, I suppose?"

I always left the legal stuff to Saul. "We claimed it all, I guess," I said. "But I reckon he'd be glad to make you a good price on a few acres."

"With water?"

"There's plenty of water, even in the summer. It comes out of a spring back in the rocks. You don't have to worry about water."

Mowry looked with distaste at his mules. "Damned hammer-headed brutes. Don't know if they'd pull a plow or not." He spat, and wiped his mouth. "Well, we'll see." He waved the whip at me, and trudged on beside the water wagon.

Others stopped me in the street, too, asking about the Wells, what I thought of their chances there. They were mostly emigrants like Mowry—farmers from Missouri and Ohio and Kentucky who'd had rough sledding back home and just pulled stakes for the West. No place in particular, it seemed—there was just something magic about the word, and most of them had a pretty shaky idea of geography. With all of them it was the same; a passel of kids needing mush and pinafores and shoes and jeans, a wife with a sharp tongue, no money coming in. Some of them found jobs as swampers or livery-stable hands or clerks in Fish and Collingwood's store; sometimes the women got laundry to do up from the private residences of the well-to-do, people like the Carillos and Sam Hughes and Hiram Stevens. One skinny man with spectacles was a reporter on the Tucson *Arizonian,* but it folded up and left him stranded. He'd never done anything but sharpen pencils and keep books and fill inkwells all his life, but he was sure he could make a go of it at the Wells, now the Apaches were licked. The story was the same, though; "I got to get out of this godforsaken hole and make me a decent living." And I gave them all the same answer; "Come down to Boston Wells. There's plenty of water and the soil's good." After a while, I had to be cautious about saying even that much, because if everyone came that was thinking about it, the springs at the Wells would run dry. But if even half of them came, Saul would be pleased. It would be the beginning of the town he wanted.

When I got back to the Wells after that trip, a strange wagon was there—a sagging John Deere, each wheel pointing in a different direction, and a team of the sorriest swaybacked nags I ever saw. Saul was talking to the man, and I tied the mules at the watering-trough and went over.

"Yes, sir," Saul was saying, "mighty glad to have neighbors, Mr. Frisk." He'd made a rough map of the Wells and the land around, and he pointed out a plot about a half-mile from our house, where Boston Creek wound through a thicket of willows. "Now that's a pretty piece of land. Level as a table—water practically piped to your door. I can let you have it for a hundred dollars cash."

Mr. Frisk was a big man with sweeping black mustachios and his arm in a sling. He had an Indian wife on the seat beside him, a stocky little woman in calico, with a face that looked like it was carved out of a juniper stump with an axe. When he took off his hat his head was bald as a doorknob, and I remembered him from someplace.

"Well," Mr. Frisk said, "that's a powerful lot of money." He gestured with his bandaged arm. "Used to drive oxen for Tully and Ochoa, up from Sonora, but last trip we tangled with a mess of Yaquis and they shot hell out of my arm. Dunno if it'll ever be right again. Ain't no good for driving six span of critters any more, but I figgered I might get us a little place and raise us enough grub to live on."

"Say," I said, "didn't I meet up with you someplace, Mr. Frisk?" Then I remembered. "Sure—it was down on the Camino Real a while back. Cut Finger and his gang was chasing me, and I caught up with your train and they let me alone. Remember—I give you some lettuce and some cheese. When we got to Tucson you bought me a drink at that place on Camp Street."

Mr. Frisk slapped his thigh, and nudged his wife. "Why, sure enough!" He beamed through the thicket of his mustache.

"Sweetheart, this here is the young gentleman I told you about that time. The one that give me that hunk of cheese. And mighty good cheese it was, too." He shook hands with me, his left hand. "Just call me Jim, youngster. Jim Frisk, that's what I answer to."

Saul cleared his throat and rattled the paper. "A hundred dollars, take it or leave it. That's valuable land. I filed on it a year ago."

Jim Frisk put his hat back on and looked at his wife. She stared straight ahead, her face blank, and finally with a sigh he fumbled in a tattered wallet and drew out the money.

"Done," Saul said. He scribbled him a receipt. "There, That makes it legal."

Frisk stuck the paper in his shirt pocket and waved us a cheery goodbye. After I got the team rubbed down and grained, I went out in the dusk and looked down that way. I could see a fat little yellow spark in the willows, and it felt good to have neighbors, even if Mrs. Sweetheart Frisk wasn't too talkative. Tomorrow, I figured, I'd go down and give them a hand. I'd cut some wood—with his lame arm Jim Frisk couldn't do too much—and maybe give them some pointers on building a Texas house. There wasn't anything to compare with a Texas house.

There were more came after that; not everyone that asked about the Wells, but enough to make a pretty fair sized little settlement. Mowry came, his water barrels still on his cart, and a grim-faced female on the seat. "Figgered I'd hang on to them barrels. Might come in handy. Mebbe make me a little com whisky." But his wife turned a ferocious look on him and he quieted down. There was a family named Turner, in a Shuttler wagon garnished with ragged children, and a Mr. and Mrs. Casey in an old Army ambulance. There were the Everetts, that had a little rosewood organ they'd carried all the way from New York State, and the aristocrats from Virginia—the Morgans, with four span of oxen and two wagons and a dark-haired daughter that smiled at me. Things weren't looking—no, not much!

I was busy as a hog on ice, helping them all get settled. Old Nacho and his brood came back, once Cut Finger cleared out, and I put them to work, making 'dobe bricks, dragging the land with a harrow we made out of an old wagon tongue and fire-sharpened sticks. We even got a kind of *acequia* started—a shallow rocklined ditch to bring water down from the Wells into the fields. None of us had much money—nobody but Saul, anyway—but we traded among ourselves, a wagon jack for a day's plowing, a water-bucket for a peck of seed-grain, a Rochester brass lamp with a red glass shade for one of the milk goats the Caseys brought in their ambulance. It was like one big family, and at night we'd get together down by the willows and build a roaring fire out of greasewood and sing.

All except Saul, that is. From the start, he let it be known he was the squire on the hill. He never even helped me with the chores anymore—just sat in the house, laying out more maps and counting the money and thinking. One night I came back from a walk along the creek with Betty Morgan, and he was sitting in the dog-trot in the rocking chair he'd bought from the Turners.

"Kind of late, ain't you?"

"Well," I said, "I was helping the Turners get their roof on. Afterwards they invited me to have a bite to eat with them."

He snorted. "Those Turners are trash. Pure trash."

"Now wait a minute," I said. "How do you know anything about the Turners? You've never been down there. John Turner's a good man—he's just had a little hard luck, that's all. And Mrs. Turner's been doing the Morgans' washing to make a little cash. You can't hardly call them shiftless."

Saul seemed to have aged. He'd kind of shrunk, I guess you'd call it, in more ways than one. He'd always been a big man—big body, big talk, big ways. People stayed out of his path. But he'd changed. Slumped in the rocking chair, he looked bitter and spent.

"They're shiftless, all right," he said. "I know the kind. There was plenty of them down south of Columbus in the hills—ridge-runners, we used to call 'em." He got up, stooped and almost bony. He hadn't bothered to trim his beard for a long time, and he didn't look much like the strapping big man that led our wagon train to the Wells three years ago. "Let 'em go," he said. "I ain't their keeper, am I?"

He went in the house and got his tin box. He kept it hidden someplace, and he was always careful nobody was watching him when he went to the hiding place. He brought the Argand lamp out with him, too, and set the box and the lamp down on the table.

"What do you think of that?" In the box was a thick sheaf of bills. "I done pretty good so far. Twelve hundred dollars. With what we got in the bank in Tucson—"

"There's over a thousand."

He shook his head, and rubbed at his nose. "Not enough yet."

"Not enough for what?"

He put the money back in the box and locked it with the key he carried on a string around his neck. "Just not enough, that's all."

"There's enough to buy us some cattle down in Sonora," I said. "The grass is showing green around the Wells. We could start off with maybe fifty head or so and see how that goes. This is cattle country around here."

He shook his head. "Don't want to risk it on cattle."

"What do you want to do with it, then?"

He looked at me hard from under his shaggy brows. "Don't have to do anything with it. Let it build up. The way I'm making money, selling land and supplying the soldiers in Tucson, I'll be the biggest man in the Territory before long. It takes money to make money, that's what the fellow said. I believe him."

"Land isn't just something to sell," I said.

"It is to me."

Maybe I shouldn't have brought it up, because if it hadn't been for him I wouldn't even be here. But I was a little mad;

I'd been working like a horse, and Saul didn't even give me any credit for it.

"You'd ought to remember," I said, "that part of that money belongs to me. Aren't we in this together?"

For a minute he didn't say anything. Then he passed a hand over his forehead, blinking in the glow of the lamp. "Yes, that's right." He seemed truly sorry. "Of course that's right, Joey. Half of it's yours, by rights." He shook his head in a puzzled way. "My mind don't work so good anymore, seems like. I forget things. Well—" He put the box under his arm and picked up the lamp. "Goodnight, Joey."

"Goodnight," I said.

The next morning, I was helping Jim Frisk irrigate the beans he'd planted when who should show up but Ike Coogan. I was naked to the waist, sweating like a Turk. When I dropped the shovel to wipe the sweat off my face, there was old man Coogan sitting his paint pony. He had the Hawken rifle across his pommel—I think it grew there—and a disgusted look on his face.

"Ike!" I said. "Where in hell did you come from?"

He smacked his lips like there was a bad taste in his mouth, and looked around at the plowed fields, the green tips of the crops, the water foaming along in our *acequia.*

"There's too dod-dummed many people in this country," he said. I moved to give him a hand down, but he squawked at me like a wet rooster, and I let him alone. "Used to be, a man could ride through this country and not lay eye to a soul." He wiped his mouth. "Not counting Apaches, that is. They ain't got no souls." He eyed Jim Frisk. "What in the hell did you say your name was?"

Jim got mad, and blew out his mustaches. "I'm damned if I remember saying."

Wait a minute," I said. "Ike, this is Jim Frisk. Used to drive a freight wagon for Tully and Ochoa. Jim, this is old man Coogan. He led our party out here from Santa Fe three years ago."

They shook hands, and Ike said gloomily, "That's all right, Mr. Frisk. Just so you ain't one of these hayseed farmers that's been cluttering up the Territory." He looked again at the dark furrows and the rills of water, and shook his head. "Where's Saul?"

"Up at the house." I put on my shirt. "Come along, Ike. Saul'll be glad to see you."

Maybe he was and maybe he wasn't. Saul's greeting to Ike Coogan was cool. He hunkered on his hauches in the shade of the dogtrot, puffing on his pipe and saying nothing after the handshake. Old man Coogan took it as long as he could, and then he blew up.

"Dod-dum it!" His whiskers stood out like a porcupine. "Ain't you even gonna offer me a cup of coffee?" He slapped the butt of the Hawken down close to the toe of Saul's boot. "Or do you drink tea in this la-de-da potato patch nowadays?" His voice was scalding.

"You're drunk," Saul said.

"Sure I am," Ike said cheerfully. "That's the only way to be anymore. Keeps me from throwing up when I look around and see what's happening to this country. Too dod-dum many people."

Saul hitched up his pants and went to heat up the coffee pot. Ike Coogan watched him go, and then he spoke to me out of the corner of his mouth. "He sick or something?"

"Why?"

Ike shook his head. "He don't look well to me. Kind of ganted in the haunch. Got a wild look in his eye."

I motioned to him, and he shambled after me around the corner of the house. "He isn't well, Ike. Something's eating him up from the inside, like a worm in an ear of corn."

Ike sniffed. "Don't know why he should have a burr under his tail. I heered in Tucson that he was getting to be a mighty prosperous man. Ain't that a fact?"

"He's got a lot of money," I said. "That's all. I'm worried about him, Ike. I don't know what to do."

"Sho," Ike said. "You was always the one to worry about things. Now Dave never was one to worry about anything."

"Have you seen Dave?"

"From a distance. Dave's too good fer an old bastard like me anymore." He spat, drowning a wasp in a brown thread of tobacco juice. "Him and his fancy vest and his two guns! Now that he's Red Chaffee's chief butt-licker, he ain't about to run with the likes of me no more. Oh, my, no!"

"That's a damned lie," I said. "Dave wouldn't lick any man's butt, and you know it."

Ike sighed.

"I guess I just got a case of the uglies today." He cuffed me on the back. "Well, you got more brains than the whole both of 'em, Joey." He looked at me sharp under his bushy eyebrows. "That puts an obligation on you. You got to look out for the two of 'em, seein' they ain't got sense enough to do it for themselves."

I didn't say anything. There wasn't anything to say. It was true, and I knew it. I'd felt it drawing over me like a cloud for a long time. Tucson was only fifty miles away.

"Eda said to say howdy to you." Ike scratched at the ring of dirt on his wrist. The wind veered a little, and he smelled just the same as always. But I didn't mind. It was a kind of homey smell. "That's a good girl, that Eda. I miscalled her onct, and you took me up on it. But you was right." He put a hand to his mouth and bellowed. "Saul, you growin' that coffee in there?"

"Ike," I said, "sometimes I think I ought to pull stakes and head for Sacramento. Carl Ogg offered me a job anytime I wanted to come."

He scratched his chin. "Hell, you got to make up a better lie than that. You know you ain't got any business in Sacramento. You belong right here, right at the Wells. I can see it in your eye, hoss. This is home, ain't it?"

I tried to spit, too, but my mouth was dry.

"Besides," Ike said, "I got a little piece of news that might interest you. It ain't none of Saul's business, but I reckon I better tell you. You're a growed man, and you got a level head on you." He looked around, and then he put his whiskered mouth close to my ear. "Travelin' out here from Tucson, I cut sign all the way. Three riders. They was ahead of me, no more'n an hour or so. But when they came to the *playa,* they circled around behind the Wells for a look-see."

"Cut Finger?" I said, feeling a hand close round my windpipe.

Ike shook his head. "These ponies was shod. And I ain't never yet knowed an Injun had the price of the good stogies these three was smokin'." He shaded his eyes with his hand and stared at the high-piled rocks back of the Wells. "Good gin, too—there was an empty bottle at their last camp. Wa'n't nothing left in it, though."

"Well," I said, "it's a free country. I guess a man's permitted to ride around if he wants to."

"Three men," Ike said.

Saul came out then with the coffee pot and some tin cups. He poured Ike's full and handed it to him. "Ike," he said, "I'm glad you're here."

It sounded like it was going to kill him to get it out, and he glared at Ike while he was saying it. But Ike whooped with laughter and pounded him on the back till he spilled his coffee.

"Dod-dum it!" He grinned a snaggle-toothed grin. "That's the ticket, old hoss. Fer a while I didn't even know if I was welcome!"

He winked at me, but it wasn't just a wink. There was meaning in it.

CHAPTER NINE

I left Coogan talking to Saul and saddled up Buster. My hands shook as I cinched the girth, and Buster rolled his eyes, smelling the nervousness in me. Of course, it might not be Dave. And then Coogan had said *three* men. Could be it was just a party of hunters, or soldiers on their way to Fort Bowie. But why did they skirt around the Wells instead of coming in and filling their canteens and having a cup of coffee? The Wells was the only settlement between Tucson and Fort Bowie.

I spurred Buster along a narrow hard-packed trail that the deer ran to come down to water. The scrub was thick, and it tore at my clothes. I had to keep one hand in front of my face. But the trail got me high in the rocks above the Wells, and got me there fast. I broke out on a flat rubble-strewn mesa just as the sun was sliding down into a sea of streaky purple clouds, edged with gold. The air was already chill, and there was a gray haze lying in the hollows of the rocks below me. It was going to be a cold night.

It didn't take me long to find them. Off to the north, still higher in the rocky slopes, a blue ribbon of smoke curled up, and then flattened out like it had hit a ceiling, and spread out. Whoever it was, they were staying clean away from the Wells. It was a good five miles. But here the trail was so narrow and overgrown with juniper and manzanita that I had to get down and lead Buster. And that was the way I walked in on the three strangers.

"Howdy," I said.

Two of them were rolled in blankets around a fire glowing in a shallow cup of rocks. The third was a small thin man in a tight-buttoned black coat, holding out his hands to the blaze. They hadn't heard me, I guess, because when I spoke the small man made a sharp convulsive jerk and he was covering me with his gun. He didn't say anything—just stood spraddle-legged, looking at me with the palest eyes I ever saw on a man. They were so pale they didn't seem to have any pupils—just two pale holes in his face.

"Drop that carbine at your feet, kid," he said.

The men in the blankets rolled out, and one of them was Dave. He saw me standing there, still holding the carbine, and he started to laugh. He slapped his thigh, and went over to the pale-eyed man and shoved the gun aside. "It's all right, Scudder."

When the man still held the gun on me, Dave slapped his hand aside, hard. "It's my brother Joe, you damned fool. I told you about him."

Scudder dropped the gun back in his holster and squatted down at the fire again, warming his hands. They looked almost transparent in the glow.

"Joey, goddam you!" Dave said. He grabbed my arm and pinched so hard it hurt. "Old Joe Boston!" He stood off a piece and looked me up and down. "Gettin' to be a big one, ain't you?"

The other man came up behind Dave and looked at me hard, scratching his chin. He was a squat stocky man in an old cavalry greatcoat, and he needed a shave. I remembered him. The last time I'd seen him he was sitting in Red Chaffee's Paradise saloon, just him and a bottle. He kept on staring at me under heavy-lidded eyes, and sucking on his cigar.

"This is Joey," Dave said. "Bluejaw, meet my brother Joe."

Bluejaw kept on scratching his chin. "I remember him. Come into Red's one day. Looking for you."

"That's right," Dave said, pleased. "You'd remember him anywhere." He took the carbine away from me and stood it against a tree. "Ain't I told you not to come barging into places carrying that mean little old gun?"

They had coffee on, and a chunk of deer meat sizzling over the coals. Scudder didn't take coffee, I noticed. He had a tin teapot off to itself.

Dave squatted down over the fire and hacked me a piece of venison. "Travelin' light." He poured me coffee into a tin can. "Hell, I never was one to eat much. Bluejaw, here—he's a pig. Ain't you, Bluejaw?"

Bluejaw didn't say anything.

"Eats like a pig," Dave said. "Never happy 'less he's got his belly full. Or unless he can gun somebody. Ain't that so?"

Bluejaw turned his heavy eyes on Dave. "You talk too damned much. That's what Red always said about you. He said 'that fool's tongue is long enough to cut his throat'. That's what he said."

Dave chuckled, and sipped at his coffee.

"You knew I was coming," I said. "How?"

"That damned Ike Coogan. The old jaybird! We saw him once, on a ridge behind us. He's gettin' too damned old and feeble to mix in things that ain't none of his concern." His face got dark and somber. "He'll get a ball in his skinny old ribs if he ain't careful. He's been warned." Dave sloshed the grounds out of his cup, and the fire sputtered and hissed. "Anyway, I knew he was headed for the Wells, bustin' to tell everything he knew. It was just a matter of time till you showed up."

"I guess that's right," I said. "It always took me to keep the peace between you and Saul."

Scudder poured himself a cup of black tea and sat hunched like a cat in the shadows.

"Dave," I said, "isn't there someplace we can talk?"

Scudder coughed, and looked down into the dregs of his tea. Bluejaw broke a handful of sticks over his knees and said, "Ain't got any secrets from us, have you, Dave?" He didn't look at Dave—just threw the sticks into the crackling fire, and watched them catch.

Dave ignored Bluejaw's question. He looked up at me, his pointed face grave. He sat his tin cup down on a flat rock beside the fire. "Sure, Joey." He got up, shoving his hands into the pockets on his lean hips, looking up at the dying sky. "Sho, it does a man good to get away from town once in a while. Well—" He took me by the arm and pulled me away with him, back down the trail. High as we were, we could see the last rays of the sun painting the tips of the rocks with fire.

We found a niche in the rocks, a hundred yards or so away from their camp. Dave lay down, hands behind his head. I sat down beside him, feeling the warmth from the rocks. A little animal skittered across the ledge with a rustling sound, and the air was dry and cold.

"Dave," I said, "what in the hell do you want out here?"

He broke a sprig of dry grass and put it between his lips. "Well," he said, "I guess you got to know sooner or later." He chewed on the grass. "You and me always been friends, Joey."

"Not the last time we met," I said.

He frowned.

"Hell—you know I didn't mean anything by it. I—well, I just didn't want you hanging around Red's place. That's all. It ain't no place for a kid like you."

"Or for you."

He was silent for a moment. Then he said, "I can get along. Don't worry about me."

"I don't like the friends you keep," I said. "Those two hardcases back there."

"Like I said," Dave went on, "you got to know sooner or later. Well, I'll tell you. Red Chaffee's had his eye on Chiricahua Wells for a long time. Red's got an eye for a good thing. Now he's bought himself a thousand head of Mexican beef, down in Sonora, and he needs grass to fatten 'em up. The Wells is made for it. Plenty water, rich grass. Red sent me out here to look it over and make Saul an offer."

I felt like someone had hit me in the nape of the neck with a billyclub.

I shook my head. "Saul won't sell."

Dave sat up, cross-legged. "Look at it this way." His voice had an edge to it. "Red don't have to pay anything. Saul ain't got any legal rights to that land. He filed on it, sure, but the government's too damned slow and bogged down with papers for that to mean anything. It's just a piece of paper, that's all. Red knows how to handle papers. Saul ain't anything but a nester, to Red. Hell, the only reason he ain't moved in here and run the whole kit and kaboodle out of there is because I'm Saul's brother. Red thought it was a good joke to send me down to make him an offer." Dave reached in his shirt pocket and brought out a bundle of bills tied with string. "There ain't nothin' cheap about Red. He'll give Saul a thousand dollars to clear out."

I didn't say anything. I had an awful feeling. I had to look out for both of them.

"Ain't that a fair offer?" Dave asked.

"Part of the Wells is mine," I said. "I guess I own half of it. I won't sell either."

Dave gave me a little shove, chuckling. "You ain't gonna give me any trouble, are you, Joey? All I got to do is give the word to Red, and you get a nice little stake too. Red's fair, I'll say that for him. He always offers to pay people before he gets rough."

I swallowed, my throat tight and painful. "What about all of those people down there? What about their crops, and houses and all? What's to become of them? The Morgans and the Turners and the rest?"

Dave shrugged. "They're nesters, the whole lot of 'em. They never should have taken up land down there! That's cattle country. Anyone can see that."

"You mean you'd just run them out of there? After all the work they put in? The *acequia* and the crops and—their homes?"

He shoved his hat far back on his head, very patient with me. "Now, Joey, you got to understand this thing. You feel for those people—sure. But they ain't got any rights there, any more than Red Chaffee has got. Someone's got to get hurt, that's the way things are. You and Saul get your back scratched, don't you? Well, then—why worry your head about a lot of no-good drifters? They'll get along—there's plenty of land out here for everybody. All they got to do is be reasonable."

I thought of John Turner, a meager rackety man with a hoe in his hands. That was the way he seemed to live, with a hoe grown tight to his fists, chopping away at the weeds that choked his little patch. And Jim Frisk with his bunged-up arm, and Mrs. Sweetheart Frisk. The Morgans. All the rest of them. And I thought of Scudder, the pale-eyed Scudder and Bluejaw's heavy stare.

"You mean you'd just run 'em out of the Wells?"

Dave grinned. "I wouldn't call it by that name, exactly. But after a thousand head of them Sonora longhorns pass by, there won't be much left. If any of 'em plan on staying, the cattle'll take care of that. A steer likes to wallow in a plowed field. Scratches his back, gets rid of the bugs."

I stood up and dusted my hands. They weren't dirty, but I had a feeling I had to get something off them. "You call it anything you like," I said, "but there's only one name for it. Stealing. Just plain stealing." I put my hands in my pockets. It was cold up there. The dry air sucked off the daytime heat like a sponge picks up water. "Dave," I said, "how did you ever get into a thing like this? Remember that Ketteman boy at home—the one with the buck teeth, the one that was always shoving people and getting them down and twisting their arms? You went after him one day when he picked on Horace Windom, and you beat the tar out of him. You used to get mad as hops when someone picked on somebody littler than them. And that's what this is. Red Chaffee is picking on the people at the Wells. A thousand dollars don't make it no different."

A dry twig cracked, and I saw a man's bulk tower over us. Bluejaw's voice was heavy and sarcastic. "Excuse me, Dave. I figgered maybe you and your kid brother run off and left us."

Dave got to his feet. He looked taller in the starlight than I remembered. "Get the hell out," he said. "If I wanted you around I'd have called you. Now fade away."

Bluejaw stood there for a long moment. It was calculated to the tenth of a second—just enough to let Dave know he wasn't impressed. Then he turned and shambled down the trail. I heard his boots scuffing on the rocks.

"I see how you stand," Dave said. "I'm sorry, Joey. I'm mighty sorry. But this is something I've got to do, Saul or no Saul, nesters or no nesters. This is the first big job Red's let me do. He's putting a lot of money in this cattle deal. They're already on their way up here. I can't let anything go wrong."

I saw what had happened to him. Dave always wanted to be a success but he didn't have the steadiness of Saul, or the capacity for hard work. He didn't care too much how he got to the top. But he always intended to get there, one way or the other. Now Red Chaffee, him and his damned curls and his big white hands—Red held out a shiny bauble to him and Dave was after it. He never stopped to get the right of anything. He was blinded by Red Chaffee and his big ways, and his promises. Red would use Dave, use him till he was used up, then get rid of him.

"Dave," I begged, "let me do this. Let me go down to Saul and spring this on him easy."

He reached in his pocket for a sack of tobacco and spilled some in a paper. Licking it with his tongue, he kept working at it with his fingers, and it was more care than I ever saw him take to a smoke. He stuck it between his lips and a match flared and in the sudden yellow light his face was hard and lined, like an Indian mask cut from a slab of wood.

"I told you I can't have any slip-ups. How do I know you won't go down there and spill the beans and have the whole place upset and excited?" He shook his head. "There's too much riding on this to take chances. Me and Bluejaw and Scudder—we'll ride down in the morning, casual-like, and talk it over with Saul. You stay with us."

I felt a great weight in my chest. I didn't want them to meet. Saul would kill him. Someone would get killed.

"I now what you're thinkin'." Dave took a deep drag on the smoke, and tossed it away. "What do you think I brought Bluejaw and Scudder along for? There won't be any trouble." He chuckled, a dry, tense sound. "Hell, everyone in the Territory knows Scudder! He's about the meanest one gunslinger around. Nobody ain't going to give us trouble. And Bluejaw—he ain't quite as fast on the draw, but he's awful tough."

He touched me on the shoulder, rough affection in his voice. "We're not kids anymore, Joey. I ain't, and you ain't. Saul ain't. We're growed up, and life is hard lines. You take what you can get, and that's a fact." He turned and walked down the trail toward the camp. I followed him, sick at heart.

When I reached for my carbine Dave had propped against the tree, it was gone.

"Someone took my gun," I said.

Scudder looked up at me. He was always cold, and always hunched over the fire, his thin hands spread out. "I put it away for you, sonny," he said. "Don't fret about it."

I looked at Dave. He turned his face away from me and rolled up in his blanket.

The word had gotten around without my help. I don't know who spread it around—probably old man Coogan, when I disappeared and didn't come back. When the four of us rode out of the rocks and reined in front of the Texas house, there was quite a crowd. None of them had guns; they were carrying their rakes and hoes. Ike Coogan was just getting ready to leave, maybe to look for me. Anyway, he was sitting his bony old paint, the Hawken across his pommel, watching us ride in. Saul stood before the house, his face pale and grim, the clothes hanging on him so they fluttered a little in the stiff breeze.

Ike pinched his nose with his two fingers and blew over his horse's ears. "Just about to take a look for you, Joey." He nodded to Dave, curt. "Howdy, Dave."

Dave threw a leg over the saddle and climbed down, wiping his hands on the seat of his breeches. He knotted the reins to a post, jerking hard at them, his back to Saul. Saul didn't look at him.

"Where you been, Joey?" Saul asked.

I nodded toward Dave. "With him. I heard he was up there—him and Scudder and Bluejaw—I went up to see what they wanted.

Coogan leaned forward, deliberately, and spat. It hit almost at Dave's feet.

Saul stood like he was grown fast to the dirt, and the skin was stretched tight over his cheekbones. "I told you, Dave," he said. "I told you if you ever came back here, I'd kill you."

Dave's eyes flickered over him. "You ain't got any gun. You don't look dangerous to me." He looked around at Bluejaw and Scudder. "Don't any of you farmers look danrerous to me." Standing between the settlers and Saul, he put his hands on his hips, a solid matter-of-fact gesture. "Now I'll tell you folks what. You take them firearms and go back to your bean patches. I got a matter of business to talk over with my brother here."

John Turner had more grit to him than I gave him credit for. He stepped forward, his rabbity face pale. "Mister, we hear what you got to say concerns us."

"Whatever you got to say," Saul said, "you can say it right here. Or maybe you ain't used to talking out in God's sunlight, Dave. Maybe you got to crawl into a slimy hole in the rocks someplace, where sunlight don't reach!"

Dave flushed. "All right. If you want it that way. I'll tell you right off." He stood a dozen paces from Saul, and the air between them was stretched tight like India rubber. Scudder and Bluejaw nudged their mounts up and sat in the saddle behind Dave. Scudder's pale eyes flicked around, settling on one face, and then another, trying to remember them all. Bluejaw scratched his chin, and seemed half-dozing.

"Red Chaffee needs the Wells. He's got a thousand head of cattle need fattening. The Wells has got the grass, now, and plenty water. Red's offering you a thousand dollars for your stake here, Saul. You taking it, or you leaving it?"

They day seemed suddenly still. Saul's face was gray, and he rubbed at the knuckles of his bad hand. Jim Frisk muttered something and stepped forward, but Scudder slipped a hand in his coatfront and pulled out a gun. Jim stopped.

"What about us?" John Turner demanded. "You buying and selling us like we was cattle, too?"

There was a sudden uproar, heads vigorously shaken, all of them demanding at once to be heard. But Bluejaw leaned across his saddle and hit Turner with the barrel for his gun, and Turner went down, the old musket toppling with him.

"There's your answer," he said. "Any more trouble-makers?"

They all looked to Saul. Saul's face was terrible—the color of ashes—and his mouth worked. But he didn't say anything.

"Well?" Dave measured him with his eyes. "Do you want the money, or do you want our cattle to romp across the Wells and stamp this mangy outfit right into the ground?"

Saul bit his lip. The sweat stood out on his forehead. They looked to him, waiting for him to speak, to say something—anything. Finally, in a voice that was as thin and gray as his face, he said, "You can't buffalo me. I was here first. I filed on this land."

Dave laughed, watching John Turner pull himself away into the crowd like a wounded animal. Turner's daughter bent over him, wiping the blood from his face with the hem of her skirt.

"That's paper. Just paper. I'm talking about the land. The land and the water. I'm giving you a chance to make a piece of money. You've worked hard—I hear you gave the Apaches what for, too. Now you've got a chance to take your stake and clear out. Go back to Columbus and live comfortable. You've earned it."

"You go to hell," Saul said.

It was a weak thing to say. It didn't carry any conviction with it. Someone sighed in the crowd, a long shuddering sound.

"You go to hell," Saul again, almost as if he hoped to make something out of it by saying it twice. Then he turned on his heel and went into the house.

Dave shrugged, and unknotted the reins. "Well, I did my best." In the saddle, he looked down at the settlers. "You folks heard what I said. In about two weeks them cattle'll be along. A cow can be hurt bad falling into one of them sloughs of yours, or hanging up on a fence. Ain't none of you got any business here. This is cattle country. Get off'n it before the cattle comes."

Jim Frisk clenched a big fist and shook it. "We paid out good money for this land. It's ours."

Scudder was near him, and I saw the pale-eyed man heft the gun in his hand, getting a balance on it to strike Frisk down. But Ike Coogan spoke up in his nasal drawl. The Hawken rifle swiveled around, still resting on the pommel, but it looked unwinking at the buttons of Scudder's coat.

"Put the gun away," Ike said mildly.

Scudder blinked at him.

"I said put it away."

The pale face sagged, disappointed. Slowly, Scudder tucked the gun into its holster, but continued to look at Ike with his flat eyes. Ike sat like a graven image, one finger curled around the trigger. "That's better."

"We've said our say," Dave murmured. He handed my carbine back to me and jerked his head at Scudder and Bluejaw. They followed him on the rocky trail. They rounded an outcropping in the trail, and then they disappeared. But they'd be back. With a thousand head of cattle.

There was silence when they left. Jim Frisk got Turner by the shoulders and half-dragged, half-carried him to the 'dobe shack he'd built for him and his kids. Some of the people looked toward the Texas house, and there was bitterness in the faces. Tom Morgan slammed his hoe to the ground and looked at it. Even Nacho and his brood were stunned. They'd watched the whole thing from the shelter of their wickiup, and now they stared out with round frightened eyes.

"Tom," I said, "I—I"

I don't know what I mean to say. Something. Anything. Tom looked up at me, anger in his face. Then the face got all loose, like melting putty, purposeless and beaten. I knew what he was thinking. I'd been one of the Wells people, worked with them, eaten their bread. I was Saul's brother, too. If Saul didn't stick up for them, maybe it was for me to speak up. But I hadn't. I'd let my tongue stick in my mouth, and just watched.

I went into the house. It was dark and cold. Saul huddled in a chair, biting his knuckles.

"That was a hell of a performance," I said. "We both laid down and let him walk over us. Over everyone else, too."

Saul gnawed at his hand. "What can I do?" He shook his head. "There wasn't anything I could do."

I remembered the first day I came back from Tucson to find Saul holed up by Cut Finger's gang. I remembered the boom of the old fifty, and the way he'd looked down at the dead Apache and then stove his head in like an eggshell with the butt of the Sharps. And he'd stuck out his hand to that rattlesnake. No man could have done more, or been braver and tougher in adversity. Now it was all come to this.

"Saul," I said, "we owe those people out there something. They came here to settle. We told them what a fine place this was, how much water there was, the land was fertile and all that. They depended on us, and we let them down."

"What can I do?"

"Those people—"

"The hell with those people!" He looked up at me with a wild look in his eye. "The hell with them! I'm not worried about them. They took their chance, they lost! But I got to hold on here. I need money. I need—"

"What you need," I said, "is a whole new insides." He was gone inside, eaten out. This country had burned him out like a hollow log. And his own damned pig-headedness helped too. "Eda never was unfaithful to you," I said, "and you ruined her life, too."

He looked up. "What the hell do you know about it?"

"I know."

He hitched his shoulders, scowling. "That's all over now. That hasn't got anything to do with it, anyway. How'm I going to hang on here now? That Scudder—I've heard of him. And I've heard of people that tried to buck Chaffee. It isn't right, to take from a man what he's earned."

He didn't give a damn about Eda—I could see that. I don't think he ever did; it was his pride that hurt him. And now that he didn't even have that anymore, he was a pretty sorry specimen. I took a deep breath.

"It's up to me, I guess."

He grabbed at my pants leg, suddenly hopeful. "What can we do, Joey? You got an idea?"

I pulled away from him and went to the door. Ike Coogan was still sitting his paint, and chewing. He pursed his lips and plastered a hill of ants dead center. I walked past him, and walked faster and faster, and then I broke into a dead run toward the pole corral. Buster was chomping hay, and his ears pricked up when I ran into the corral. Old man Coogan was right behind me on the paint.

"Now where in damnation are you goin'?"

I levered the action of my carbine once, and then stuck it in the saddle boot. "To Tucson."

His jaws worked on the cud. "Think you're man enough?"

"You're damned right," I yelled.

He blinked at me, his face somehow pleased. "Sure you ain't makin' a mistake?"

I shook my head. "Dave isn't important. Chaffee's just using him. It's Red Chaffee I've got to see."

I dug my heels into Buster's ribs and he gathered his haunches under him, scared at the rough treatment. He plunged away like a locomotive, and it was all I could do to hang on. I let him have his head. Out on the *playa* I looked back over my shoulder. Ike still sat his paint, the Hawken over his saddle. He might have been grinning, but I didn't have time to spend on him. I had to get to Tucson before Dave got back there.

CHAPTER TEN

When I got to Tucson, I left Buster at the livery stable and went looking for Red Chaffee. I pushed my way through the crowds hardly seeing the people, or feeling them in my way, or hearing the noise and confusion, thinking only that it was the same. Tucson was always the same, its hordes of Indians, Mexican dandies smoking their brown paper *cigarillos,* the flicker of torchlight, the smell of unwashed bodies and burning mesquite and powder-like dust. The "Quartz Rock," the "Golden West," the "Hanging Wall"—all the same, the clink of chips, the smell of stale beer and cigar smoke. And I remember even a mild exasperation that it was always the same. A town had to change in appearance to grow, and to become great. But Tucson was always the same, unless there was some kind of yeast working in it I didn't see.

The Paradise was empty, except for the bartender leaning his black sleeveguards on the bar, sucking at a cigar and staring out at the street. He hardly looked up when I pushed aside the slatted doors.

"I'm looking for Red Chaffee," I said.

He turned his head on his fat neck, slow. "Ain't here."

"Where can I find him?"

The man looked at me with careful bright eyes. "Might try Congress Hall. Said something about going down there to close a deal for more cattle."

I went to Congress Hall. It was bright and garish. Poker games were going under the smoking lamps, and bankers in eyeshades dealt cards from faro boxes, or spun balls into the trough of roulette wheels. A game called *chusas* was popular, and a little man with hairy ears said to me, "Make your bet, young gentleman. The game's made and the ball's arolling."

Red Chaffee sat at a table half-hidden behind a beaded curtain. In earnest conversation with him was a burly Mexican in a vest heavy with silverwork, and a pair of boots with big-roweled Mexican spurs. The wide hat on his knees was sweatstained and dusty. I edged up beside them and cleared my throat. Chaffee looked up. I don't think he remembered me. Not then.

"Well?"

"I want to see you," I said. "Begging this gentleman's pardon, I'm in a hurry, Mr. Chaffee. It's important."

He chewed hard on his cigar. "What's on your mind, sonny?"

"I can't talk about it here." I nodded to the door. "Come outside."

He took another look at me. Then I think it came to him. "Ain't you—"

"It's about Dave," I said. "Dave Boston. My brother."

Under the lamplight his hair seemed to shine like crinkly brass. He gave it a pat and pulled on his hat, shoving back his chair. "*Senor,* I regret the interruption. An important business matter—"

The Mexican turned dark somber eyes on me, and then shrugged, slapping the dusty hat across his knee. "I wait, *senor.*"

Outside, Red took me by the arm in a grip that made me wince, pulling me alongside him. I wrenched away, mad. "All I want to do, I want to talk to you. About Dave. He—"

Chaffee swore. He bit angrily at the cigar and then tossed the butt away, and a dozen small brown urchins scrambled for it. "This ain't no place to talk over private business. Not out in the goddam street." He looked around him, and I became aware that even in this noisy good-humored crowd there were listening ears, and unfriendly ones—ears anxious to know the details of Red Chaffee's business. I shifted the carbine to my other hand.

"Come along to the Paradise," he said.

I followed his broad well-tailored back. The throng seemed to part silently before him, like the waters of the Red Sea in the Bible, and I hurried along before they flowed back. The chatter and the joking stopped before him, and resumed after we passed. But Chaffee wasn't carrying a gun. The coat fitted tight and sleek, without a bulge. A man as important as Red Chaffee didn't have to carry a gun.

In the Paradise, the bartender's gaze followed us up the stairs, along the balcony. Red pulled the door to behind him and lit a match to the wick of the lamp. Then he went over and pulled down the window and the sounds below died away, cut off like a knife. The dingy curtains settled to rest.

"Well?"

"It's about Dave." I felt my palms sweating. I didn't know exactly how to begin. I stumbled on. "You've got to call him off, Mr. Chaffee."

He sat down at the roll-top desk. "Call him off? Why?"

"He and two gunmen named Scudder and Bluejaw rode into the Wells and told us to get off. All of us—the settlers and Saul and me. And it isn't Dave's idea. I don't think he'd ever harm us. But he's working for you. Dave said you'd bought a lot of Sonora cattle, and wanted to pasture 'em on the grass at the Wells."

Chaffee's face was half-shaded, but I saw his full lips roll out in a pleased pout. "Hell, the way you come bustin' in, I figured something was wrong." He laughed his booming laugh, and lit up another cigar. A fine long cigar, from a humidor on the desk. "I didn't hardly think a kid of a boy and a broke-down hulk like your big brother—" He blew out the smoke, looking with approval at the slender cigar. "What's his name?"

"Saul."

"That's right." He chuckled. "I didn't hardly think you and Saul and that sorry bunch of nesters could buffalo Dave. Now Dave's an easy-goin' man. He likes his licker and his women, and he don't hardly never give me no trouble if I keep them in stock, but sometimes he's mean as a sidewinder. No, I didn't think you was going to run Dave Boston. Not Dave."

My fist gripped the stock of the carbine till it must have left fingerprints in the walnut stock. But I couldn't get mad. I had an obligation. "Mr. Chaffee," I said, "there's been an awful lot of trouble and grief at the Wells. People died there. Saul and me has fought Apaches thick as flies, and went hungry and cold, and sweated to raise our crops. But we've won through, and it's our land. We'll fight for it. We won't let anyone throw us off what's rightfully ours. The only thing I'm asking you—don't push Dave into a dirty business like this. It isn't right for him to fight his own brother. And Dave wouldn't do it if you wasn't pushing him."

Chaffee licked a loose flap of tobacco back into place.

"A man's got to prove himself, don't he? I've paid Dave Boston's way for a long time now, waiting for a good chance to use him. He's as anxious as I am to run you people out of there—he's got to show I didn't misplace my confidence, don't he?"

"Confidence?" I asked. "What kind of confidence?"

Chaffee was annoyed. "This is business, that's all. Hell, I know how you people feel! I offered a thousand dollars for the Wells, didn't I?"

I couldn't speak. My tongue seemed dry, and stuck to the roof of my mouth. But Red Chaffee got the wrong impression. He leaned forward, and took the cigar carefully from between his teeth.

"He did offer you the money, didn't he? I gave him a thousand dollars in bills."

"Yes," I said. "He—he offered us the money."

He settled back, chuckling. "Had me worried there for a minute. I'm a pretty good judge of men, and I didn't hardly see Dave as a petty thief. No, not Dave. On something *big*, now, he might double-cross me. But not for no thousand dollars. That's dirt to what we stand to make on this cattle deal! And I'll take care of Dave. He knows I will."

His manner changed. The interview over, he got to his feet, buttoning the coat around his big chest. He turned his back to me, looking into the mirror hanging over the desk. "I've give you enough time, sonny. Now you just light a shuck out of here, and go back home and pack up your things. I don't want trouble no more than you do, but there's going to be thunder and lightning stewed down to a fine poison if you and your brother don't get out of Chiricahua Wells before I bring my cattle in." He turned to me, indignant. "You can ruin a steer gettin' hung up on a fence or something! You people never had no right movin' in there and puttin' up fences, anyhow."

I couldn't make him see it was wrong. He didn't know any more about right and wrong than a pig knows about Sunday. When he moved toward the door, I knew I'd been beat. I'd lost. But maybe—just maybe—

"Hey!" he said. He stopped in his tracks, big legs planted wide apart. "Put that damn popgun down, you! Don't point that thing at me!"

I had to find out if he'd spook. So far, he'd always had his paid hands around. That was what he paid them for, to do his dirty business. Now there was no one but the two of us.

"Sit down," I said.

He backed up, slow, till he felt the edge of the desk against his thigh. Then, eyes small and hard, he moved around the desk and sat down.

"Put your hands flat on the desk."

He did, still watching me. But he wasn't scared. No more scared than a red bull in prime pasture. "You can't get away with anything like this." The diamond rings winked in the furry growth on the backs of his hands. "All I got to do is yell for Smoky downstairs, and he'll come runnin' with his shotgun."

I remembered the dark fat barman with the lick of hair plastered over his eye. I had a dog named Smoky once. "That won't help you," I said.

His beefy face paled, but his voice was steady. "Look, kid, you're into something that's over your head. Put that gun down and get out. I won't prefer no charges against you. I'm human—I know how you feel." He reached into his pocket, and my finger tightened around the trigger. But he only brought out a thick wad of bills. "Here—take this. Tell Dave I said to give you the other thousand, too. That's a fair price. Two thousand—almost three."

I shook my head. "There isn't any amount of money can buy the Wells."

"What do you want then?"

I said the words slow and clear, so he couldn't mistake. "I got to look out for my brothers. So what I want you to do, I want you to call Dave off. Him and Scudder and Bluejaw are on their way here now. When he comes, I want you to call the whole thing off."

Chaffee's eyelids flickered. "How do you know I'll do it?"

I moved over to a curtained alcove where Red Chaffee's suits hung, and shiny boots lined up on the floor. "I'll stay right here, and I'll have my carbine on you. You speak up and tell Dave you made a mistake. You tell him to leave the Wells alone. You tell him to go up toward Phoenix and look around for grazing land."

Chaffee's face got red, dark red with the blood in it. "You tellin' me what to do, you sassy whelp?"

I waved the muzzle of the carbine. "I'm telling you. You know I'm not fooling."

So quick I hardly saw it, too quick for a big man like that to move, he pulled open a drawer of the desk and his hand came out with a gun. I think we shot at the same time because a sheet of yellow flame, like a flower, sprang out around his hand and I felt a blow in my hip as if someone had swatted me with a board. I pulled the trigger at the same instant, and for a minute we stood there, staring at each other. I thought I'd missed. Chaffee rose, one hand fumbling under his coat, the other planted on the desk among the bills and papers, holding his trick body up.

A kind of dark pressure was building up behind my eyeballs, spreading and growing. It was the same as that time the Apaches jumped us at the Wells. After it was over I'd felt the same way. Faint… dizzy. Something wet and warm ran down my side into my boot.

Slowly, hitching himself along the desk, Red Chaffee came toward me. He picked up the pistol, his hand fumbling, and pulled himself along. I closed my eyes and felt myself swaying. I couldn't hold myself up. I couldn't raise the carbine, small and light as it was.

He didn't speak, only tottered on in that sick broken way, and when he got to the edge of the desk, he tried to raise the gun. But it fell out of his hands. He slumped to his knees, one hand still searching inside his coat. Then he fell over, his arms outspread, and he was dead, staring up at the lamp with sightless eyes.

I felt a blast of cold air at my back, and Smoky said, "Drop that gun, boy. I got this shotgun pointing at the small of your back. Drop it."

I dropped it, fighting hard to keep that filmy blackness out of my head. But it was coming on, and spreading. Smoky moved in front of me, and his hand flicked up under my clothes, patted my hip, looking for another gun.

"All right." He jerked his head toward the open door. "Get going. Out on the balcony. Down the stairs."

I turned, almost falling, trying to hold up arms that were made of lead. At the door I paused, feeling giddy. I smelled something. Something just beyond the door. I guess I was delirious. I smelled old man Coogan.

"Move," Smoky said. He nudged me with the muzzle of the shotgun, and I staggered through the door, not daring to look around me. I could see the railing, and over the railing the dim lamp-lit smoky cavern of the Paradise. And I could smell Ike Coogan. I knew I smelled him.

"Turn," Smoky said. "Down the stairs."

I stumbled on, feeling the blood soaking in my boot. The smashing shock of that first blow was wearing off, and my whole side burned like fire. I stopped again, feeling a bitter nausea back in my throat, and leaned against the wall. I couldn't go any farther. And that was when I heard, through the haze that was creeping over me, a dull meatlike whacking sound. Like someone chopping meat with a cleaver. Propping myself against the wall, I managed to look around, over my shoulder. Smoky was flat on his back on the balcony, and Ike Coogan stood over him, holding the Hawken rifle by the barrel like it was a club.

"A bartender," he said, "ought to stick to tending his damned bar."

Satisfied, he hooked the rifle under his arm and put a hand under my shoulder. It was a skinny and bony hand, but there was a toughness and strength in it that surprised me.

"Amachoors," he said, and spat. "They ain't any real hardcases around anymore." His skinny shoulder digging into my arm-pit, he half-lifted, half-dragged me down the stairs, through the empty bar.

"Ike," I wheezed, "I killed him. I killed Red Chaffee. He pulled a gun out of the drawer, and I killed him."

"I know," Ike said.

He dumped me against the bar, and went to look through the slatted doors. Then he came back and hoisted me again.

"Dave—" I said through clenched teeth.

He chuckled. "Now, hoss, don't you worry about Dave. I spooked his camp real good on the way in. They're probably still lookin' for their ponies. I cut the picket line and slapped 'em on the rump."

I managed to get a hand down inside my belt. When I pulled it away it was smeared red, and the blood dripped off my fingers.

I think I fainted then. The last thing I remembered was Ike Coogan saying in a fierce annoyed way, "Now what the hell did you do that for?"

I don't know how he got me across Tucson and to the Landrys' house by the San Agustin church. I had a dim recollection of the moon shining, and a lot of dark alleys, and once of a man speaking Spanish, and a jolting two-wheel *carreta* that made me almost scream with pain every time a flat place in the wheel came round. Finally it hurt too much to faint, and I gritted my teeth and looked up at the stars and felt some measure of rationality come back to me. When the cart ground to a halt in a deserted back alley, I asked Ike, "Where are you taking me?"

He and the Spanish man got me between them and dragged me through a dusty yard and under a grape arbor. I remembered the grape arbor, and for a moment all I could think of was Mrs. Landry, grim and mustached, and I didn't want to go there, and fought them weakly. But Ike said, "This here is where Eda lives, hoss. Good old Eda'll take care of you." and I thought dimly *that's right—this is where Eda lives.* I was suddenly docile, although my head ached and there was an awful verdigrease taste in my mouth. I started dreaming crazy dreams and I was floating up and down, up and down, on a sea of green grass, and there were cattle swimming all over the ocean, bellowing and roaring, and I put my hand down to touch one of them but the roaring was in my own ears. And after that there was the smell of sweet hay, a dusty spice-like smell, and when I opened my eyes the rays of a lamp stung them and I put my hand across my eyes.

"He'll do," Ike said.

I was in the haymow of the Landrys' barn. Eda was there, kneeling beside me, holding my hand, and a grizzled man in a stiff white shirt-front rolled down his sleeves. Ike Coogan threw a basin of bloody water through the window and came back to stand beside me, leaning on the long rifle.

"Give him one of these powders in a glass of water three times a day," the grizzled man said, taking an envelope from his little black valise. "It's a clean wound in the hip—probably heal quick. Tore him up a little, but didn't hit any bone, and that's a blessing."

Ike handed him a crumpled bill. "You ain't one to talk, are you, doc?"

The doctor folded the bill and stuffed it in his wallet. "It isn't any of my business how people get hurt. I just patch 'em up, that's all. If I pried into all the shootings I clean up after, I'd have precious little time to practice medicine. That's the way I look at it."

"That's right," Ike said.

"He's got to have someone handy," the doctor said. "He can't move much for two, three days."

Eda put her cheek against mine. 'I'll take care of him."

I tried to struggle up, but she pushed me back.

"Will the Landrys—"

"Hush." She patted my hand. "The Landrys are away at church. Mr. Landry doesn't even use this old barn. He says a horse costs too much to keep. He and Mrs. Landry walk wherever they go."

The doctor buttoned his coat and climbed carefully down the ladder, and then I heard the door slam and he was gone. Ike blew out the lantern, and we were all three alone in the dark, the star-shine sifting through the warped boards and curled shingles of the roof. I felt drowsy, and comfortable. The doctor must have given me something: I had a faint recollection of a large bitter pill.

"Well," Ike said, "I guess I done all the damage I can do." He paused at the ladder. "You stick tight, Joey, and I'll rustle up some grub."

He heard the sound when I did—the thump of boots in the yard below, the clink of spurs, the low whispers. We froze, silent and watchful, and someone said in a heavy voice, "They ain't home. Nobody ain't home." And then Dave's voice, sharp and urgent. "Spread around. Take a look."

Ike Coogan fumbled with the Hawken rifle, but Eda put a hand on his arm and whispered, "No, Ike. Not that way."

"What the hell other way is there?" he asked sourly.

Around the house, someone knocked on the Landry door. The sound was hard and hollow. After a while a voice said, "There ain't no one home, I told you." Boots scuffed in the yard, and a horse nickered and pawed the dirt.

"I'll go down to them," Eda said.

"No you won't." I clutched at her sleeve but a great ripping pain shuddered up and down my side and I fell back, gasping as quiet as I could. "Don't go."

She touched her finger to my lips. It smelled of soap. "I'll slip out the back way and then come around to the front, like I'd been out someplace. I'll tell them something. I don't know what. But I'll handle them."

Before I could protest, she rustled away in her stiff skirts and was gone down the ladder. In the new silence, Ike Coogan whispered, "Now that's a woman, Joey. If I ever had me a chance at one like that, I'd be a dod-dum fool not to take it."

We waited. The San Agustin bell boomed ten long strokes overhead, and the flimsy stringers of the barn seemed to shake with the heavy blows. Then, in the thin metallic after-whispering, I heard Eda, bright and airy.

"Well! Dave Boston! And his helpers!" Her voice was scornful. "What gives you the right to break into Mr. Landry's home and tramp through his vegetables?"

Silence. Then Dave's voice, careful and deliberate. "Where you been?"

"None of your business." She must have tossed her head at him. "But I can tell you this—you'd better get out of here before I call for help and—"

"Get along," Dave said to someone, and then Bluejaw's heavy stubborn voice said, "We ain't looked all around yet."

"I'll handle this," Dave said.

There was a long silence, and then the creak of saddle-leather, and the hoofs of horses plodding away in the dust.

"Eda," Dave sad, "I'm looking for Joey."

"Oh?"

"There's a very serious charge against him. He and Ike Coogan shot up Red Chaffee's Paradise. They killed Chaffee, and Smoky's at the Army hospital with a knot on his head the size of a melon. They can't get any sense out of him, but someone saw Ike running away from the Paradise dragging Joey. Red's gun had one shell fired, and from the bloodstairs down the stairs I figure Joey got hit. What I want to know—have you seen Joey?"

Ike Coogan hissed in my ear. "Don't give a damn about *me*."

I punched him with my free hand, and he kept quiet.

"No," Eda said, "I haven't seen him, Dave. Why would he come here?"

"Where you been?" Dave asked again.

"Why—why—" She hesitated a moment, and I felt my stomach turn over. Then she said, "A gentleman friend and I were together."

"I believe you," Dave said dryly.

"I used to walk with you," she said in a low voice.

"That was a long time ago." I could hear him pacing back and forth in the dust below. "Eda, this is a very serious business. I want to be sure you're not shielding someone. It will go very hard with you if you are. Mr. Chaffee was an important man, with a lot of friends."

Her voice was faintly mocking. "Are you afraid someone will bame you?"

He laughed, a short bitter laugh. "No. Hardly that. I'm Red's heir-apparent, I guess you'd call me. I take over now. Only—"

"Only what?"

He was silent for a moment. A match flared and the sagging beams over our head bloomed with light and then were dark again.

"Only now I got to go through with it I got to run Saul and Joey off'n the Wells. And after that I got to deal with them for the murder Joey pulled off tonight."

"He's only a boy," Eda said.

"Red Chaffee's just as dead. No, that won't wash." The pacing stopped, and I imagine they confronted each other. "Eda," Dave said, "I got to look around. What does Landry keep in that old barn?"

Her voice changed subtly. There was a lazy and languid tone to it, and I stiffened. "Nothing but hay."

He was silent, and I could hear heavy breathing.

"Nothing but hay," Eda repeated. She sighed—a long soft sound. "Doesn't it smell good tonight, Dave? Like perfume. That's the jasmine vine on the church."

"That's you," Dave said. "You smell good. You used to put perfume on all the time. I remember."

"I used to," she said. "I used to, all the time. For you. But I don't any more."

They talked in low tones, while I lay stretched full length in the hay only a long reach over their heads, my nails biting into my palms. The pain in my thigh was nothing compared to the new wound in my heart. Once Eda laughed, a low delicious laugh, and Dave whispered something I couldn't hear into her ear, and then she laughed again. I couldn't stand it. Ike Coogan knew how I was feeling, because he squatted beside me, saying nothing.

Finally Eda said, "Tonight?" in a queer astonished way, and Dave said "Yes." There was silence—a long rending silence. I got on my elbow and managed to put my head to the window. Below the yard was bare in the starlight. No one was there. They were both gone. I wished Red Chaffee had killed me.

"Dod-dum it," Ike said.

I lay down again, on my face this time. I wept, grinding my fist into the blanket that covered the straw.

CHAPTER ELEVEN

When I began to feel a little better, life in that hayloft got boring. The days came and the days went. Eda brought me food smuggled from the Landrys' kitchen leanto, and that was quite an accomplishment, seeing how stingy and sharp they were. Ike slipped in at night like a bony ghost to tell me he'd seen Scudder down at Little-Eye Springs inquiring about me, or Bluejaw leaning all day against a wall at Military Plaza, looking—just looking.

"Have you seen Dave?" I asked.

"Nope." He shook his head. "He's probably too busy goin' through all Red Chaffee's stuff. Dave just kind of moved into a vacuum, you might say. Red was always the big boss, didn't trust nobody. Now that he's out of the way, Dave's making hay, and he don't intend to let it rain while he's at it."

My heart was heavy. Bluejaw and Scudder didn't bother me. It was Dave. Dave sent them after me. My own brother Dave. We were blood brothers once.

"Now I'll tell you," Ike said. He shifted the wad of tobacco in his cheek and spit out the window. "I know it gits mighty teejus cooped up in this crackerbox, but it minds me of something happened to me and young Parkman up at Chimbly Rock, back in forty-seven. It was on the Dry River, right near a passel of Sioux that was havin' a dance on account of they just slaughtered a horse they run off from some dem settler." He settled down, one skinny buckskin leg cocked over the other, and spit out the window again, wiping his brushy mouth with the back of his sleeve.

"Young Parkman was a scrawny kind of man—had to stand twice to make a shadder. But he had sand, I'll say that."

The San Agustin bell boomed seven. It was almost dark in the loft. Eda should come soon. She'd bring food, and some coffee. But I wasn't hungry. That is, not for food. I wanted Eda to be there, that was all. The bell went on tolling, and the brassy shivering sound made the loft quiver and vibrate. Old man Coogan went right on talking. I could see his lips move but I couldn't hear anything. Then the last stroke pealed out, and it died away with a tinny rustling sound, and Ike Coogan's voice came out clear and nasal.

"... and nothin' would do but what he'd smoke some of this here Sioux tobacco. It wasn't exactly tobacco, I wouldn't call it They'd buy themselves a little poke of store tobacco, and then mix it with shaved-up bits of bark—*shongshasha,* they called it. Kind of a willow tree they got it from, a red willow it was. Anyway, they was this buck they called The Horse, see? And when young Francis went to light up his pipe, this Horse come over and wanted to borry a light."

Ike slapped his knee and guffawed at the memories of thirty years ago. While I wished Eda would come, he maundered on and on. I knew he wanted to cheer me up, make the time pass a little faster. But my hip was itching—I guess that was a good sign, maybe meant it was healing—and I found my mind wandering far afield.

"... and them damn Sioux kept us shet up in that tepee for three days," Ike said. "Wouldn't let no one come near us, 'cept an old woman to bring us a hump-rib, maybe, or a piece of liver." He sniffed, smelling broiling buffalo across the years. "Well, anyway, I—"

"Hush," I said. I got up on my elbows, listening. A door pulled to below, a slight scraping sound. Ike flattened himself against the wall, the Hawken ready. But it was only the doctor, carrying his little black bag. He poked his bald head through the trapdoor, and saw Ike covering him with the rifle.

"Put that damned thing away," he said.

"Sure, doc," Ike apologized. "Didn't mean no harm."

The doctor rolled me over on my stomach and pulled the dressing off the wound.

"Hmmmm," he said. I never knew a doctor to say anything any different. They learn to say "hmmmm" at medical school. He poked and prodded, and I jerked away from his finger.

"Little tender, eh?"

"You're damned right it's tender," I said.

He rolled down his sleeves, unfolding them just so, and worked at the cuff-links.

"Is he all right, doc?" Ike asked.

The doctor nodded.

"Be mighty inconvenient for him to sit, at least till that scab firms up a little more. But I'd say he can travel in another day or so. Not sit a horse, mind you! But maybe lie down in a wagon bed."

Wagon bed! I didn't have any wagon.

"And now that I think of it," the doctor went on, "it might not be a bad idea to get him out of here. I don't inquire into the private lives of my patients. It's against medical ethics. But it's no secret around town that someone shot Red Chaffee to death the other night over the Paradise Bar. A lot of people are looking for the man that did it. Mostly unsavory characters, looks like to me, but they're narrowing things down, and it wouldn't surprise me if they'd come by this barn soon. I don't like to waste my time patching up a man if he's going to get shot to hell all over again."

"Yeah," Ike said. He scratched his chin. "Well—"

He offered the doc another bill. I didn't want him to do it but I didn't have any choice. I'd come away from the Wells without a penny in my jeans. But I kept track of all he spent, and I'd pay Ike back every cent.

"No," the doctor said. He pushed the money back into Ike's hands. "This one is on me. Tucson's better off rid of Red Chaffee.

A lot of us didn't have the guts to stand up to him. The least we can do now is show we're glad someone else did."

He climbed down the narrow stairs, and the room was dark and silent again. Good and dark now. There was a faint patch of silvery light on the sagging floor. A narrow sliver of moon was in the sky.

"You know, hoss," Ike said, "he's right. We been stretchin' our luck for quite a spell. How Eda kept the Landrys from knowin', I dunno. But maybe if I can get us a wagon—"

"Get us a wagon!" I snorted. "That's all we need—you driving a wagon and a pair of mules up here and loading me in. You might as well set up a circus tent and invite Bluejaw and Scudder, too."

Ike bit off a fresh chew. He didn't say anything—just stood by the window, thinking and chewing.

Eda came in after while, slipping up the stairs quiet as a bird. She had a plate of stew, and fresh-baked bread. She was nervous.

"Joey, I'm so scared! I was in the leanto, slicing bread for Mr. Landry's supper, and Mrs. Landry came in, and she said 'My land, but you don't get many slices out of a loaf bread anymore, Eda!' And when I left, she was measuring the slices to see how thick they were, and how many should come out of a loaf."

She tried to help me eat, but I was feeling feisty, and I pushed her hand away, thinking of what the doc had said. And now the damned Landrys were spooking, too. I'd have to get out of here. Get out quick.

"Eda," I said, "I left Buster at the livery stable down on Camp Street. Do you think you—"

"I'll wool lightning out'n you if you try to ride a horse," Ike said. "Eda, the doctor told him—"

"You be quiet," I said. "This is *my* skin I'm worried about. If I don't get out of here quick, it won't make any difference how I go. Probably in a pine box with handles to it. I guess I ought to know what I can do."

We'd been jawing so we didn't hear the shuffling on the steps below. The door opened, and there was Mr. Landry holding a lantern, his floury face gray and bug-eyed. Behind in a night-cap and wrapper was Mrs. Landry.

"Well!" the miller said. He held the lantern higher, and looked from one of us to the other. "Ain't this a nice little teet-a-teet now!"

Eda put a hand over her mouth and made a smothered little cry, but Ike just spit out the window.

"Evenin', folks." He held the muzzle of the Hawken on them. "Now you jist sashay right on up and visit for a while." When they hesitated, he jerked the muzzle sharply, and Mr. and Mrs. Landry skittered up the stairs and stood like a pair of nervous birds, their eyes rolling.

"I'd like to know what's going on here," Landry shouted. "Who's this man in bed here?"

Eda took a deep breath. "Ike, it's no use. We can't hold Mr. and Mrs. Landry prisoners in their own barn."

"I can if it'll help Joey."

Eda shook her head, and spoke to the Landrys. "This is my friend Joey. Joseph Boston. He—he and Mr. Chaffee had a fight. Joey killed him, and he was hurt. They brought him here because Mr. Chaffee's toughs were after him. That's all there is."

Landry's lips made a soundless O. But Mrs. Landry was shrill and angry.

"You mean to tell me you been feeding that man with our hard-bought food? Well, I never! Snatching the bread right out of our mouths, without a how-de-do or please Mrs. Landry!"

Eda sighed. "I didn't want to tell you. There were so many men looking for him, and he was so weak."

Landry put a hand on his wife's arm. His face looked even grayer.

"You mean to tell me this is the man they're looking for? The man that killed Red Chaffee the other night? Oh, my God!"

He got out a handkerchief and dabbed at his forehead with it. "They'll blame us! That Scudder—" He shuddered. "They'll think I had something to do with it. Why, my life won't be worth a weevil!" He stared at his wife, and she burst out crying in a wail that cut your ears like a handsaw.

"I'm sorry," Eda said. "I did what I thought was best." She advanced on them. "Now stop, Mrs. Landry! Stop that noise." She clenched her fist, and stamped her foot. "Now stop! Listen to me, both of you."

The Landrys watched her like frightened chickens watching a hawk.

"I—I'll get him away from here, somehow. You just go back in the house and be quiet. Don't say anything to anybody, because if you do I'll—I'll do something awful to you."

Ike cleared his throat. "I believe she would."

"All you've got to do," Eda said, in a terrible and yet patient voice, "is to go inside and—and read or sew or mend or something, Mrs. Landry. Mr. Landry, you just sit and be quiet. Do you hear me?"

They nodded dazedly.

"I'll get him out of here in an hour. No more. And there'll be no one to connect you with him at all. No one will ever know, if you don't talk. Is that clear?"

They nodded again, together, like a pair of mechanical toys, and closed the door above them and disappeared. Eda watched them go, fists clenched and breast rising fast and falling. She looked like an avenging angel. I wouldn't have wanted to tangle with her then. Not me. I was glad she was on my side.

"You got an idee?" Ike asked.

"I don't trust them," she said. "They're little people, both of them. The kind that would sell you out for cash any day in the week." She dropped to her knees beside me. "Joey, you've got to trust me. Promise you won't move till I come back with help."

I managed to struggle up to a sitting position, but there was an awful stitch in my side.

"I'll be all right," I said. "Just give me my pants and I'll get out of here right now. If someone will just get Buster for me, I'll get out of here and won't be any trouble to anyone."

"No you won't!" She put her hand flat on my chest to keep me down. "Ike, see that he doesn't move!"

"I'll take keer o' him," Ike promised. "But—"

She faced him fiercely. "But what?"

"I think you ought to take me into your confidence," Ike said mildly. "What you got in mind?"

Eda shook her head. "I don't know if it will work or not. But Corporal Schrader might help. The Army has wagons going to Fort Bowie all the time. They take supplies and ammunition and forage and everything. If he can get you into one of their wagons without anyone knowing about it, you can go right to the Wells. No one will stop you. They won't know you're in the wagon. I'm going to see Hank and see will he help me."

I remembered Corporal Schrader and the time he was going to lick me until Eda interfered. Now I was in debt to her again. Here I was in bed, weak as a chicken, and bounden to a woman. I tried to get up but she appealed to Ike and he squatted beside me, one skinny knee on my chest.

"You just sit tight, hoss. Ram around the way you're doin' and you'll bust that scab. Then where'll you be, bleedin' like a stuck hog!"

It was hard to breathe. "All right," I said. "Take your knee off my chest."

"That's better," Eda said. She bent over me, the long silky red hair falling into my face in a sweet-smelling torrent. Her breast touched softly on my bare chest, and the brush of it sent a tingling through me. Maybe I wasn't as sick as they thought.

"Joey," she said, her voice low so Ike couldn't hear. "I love you so much."

Then she was gone like a slim red cat, quick and silent. The door shut again and Ike and I were alone, waiting for Corporal Schrader and the wagon. If she could arrange it, that is. But Eda could do anything. I knew that.

Ike kept an eye on the house. He was silent for longer than I'd ever known him to be quiet. He stood at the open window, leaning on his rifle, staring down at the yard below.

"The Landys got a lamp burning," he said. " 'Course, that don't mean much. They could 'a slipped out and blabbed. God damn such chinchy people!"

The San Agustin bell boomed ten. No longer did we hear the little sounds of the evening—the faint calls and greetings, the thud of hooves, the sound of a far-off mandolin, a faint pop of a gun in some saloon. The silence seemed to press in on us when the bell stopped its tolling and shivered away into silence. The air in the loft was stifling, thick with dust. Eda had been gone—how long? An hour? Two hours?

"We got to trust her," Ike said.

If she'd been gone this long, something must have gone wrong. She'd know by now whether she could arrange the wagon, and she should have been back.

"Come to think of it," Ike said, "I don't know anyone I'd ruther trust. She's a blue-white little lady. Hard, maybe, and shiny, but they ain't anything can scratch her. No, not my Edy."

He began to sing *The Buffalo Hunters*, very softly, and off key, in a kind of a melancholy whine. Then he wiped his nose with the back of his hand and said, "Too many people. Too goddam many people. This here was a fine place to be a long time ago. But it wasn't ever made for folks to live in, with gas lights and rocky-chairs and claptrap such as that. Hell, this ain't no place for paper collars and pretty vests and church on Sunday."

"Ike," I said, "I won't ever forget what you did for me."

He broke off the whine, listening, a hand to his ear. "Do you hear something?"

He shuffled forward to the window, his moccasins making a rustling sound on the floor. He put a finger to his lips, and peered down. He kept his head very still, for a long time, and then he pulled it in, like a skinny old bird.

"I dunno." He shook his head. "Seems to me I heered something. Just a leetle stirring sound below. 'Twasn't much. But 'twasn't the kind of a noise ought to be down there this time of night."

"A lizard?" I whispered.

"Lizards don't frisk around at night."

We waited in silence, straining our ears so it was almost painful. A woman shrieked some distance away—in pain or delight I couldn't tell—but the shrill noise made me jump.

"Now I hear it again," Ike said. He slunk to the window, keeping away from the patch of moon. Suddenly he stiffened, and I saw his hand clench the barrel of the Hawken. "They's someone down there."

"Maybe it's the Landrys," I said.

"No." He put the rifle in the crook of his arm. "It ain't likely them sorry birds. They're probably shiverin' in their damned parlor, wishin' Eda'd come back just as hard as we are."

He tried to pitch his voice low, but it was so cracked and hoarse I was sure the person below heard him.

"Hand me my carbine," I said. "They went and told, that's what they did. Hand me that damned carbine."

He handed it to me. "I think I know who it is. It's that mangy Scudder. Someone tipped him off." Ike crawled to the window again and looked out, then came scuttling back like a crab. "That's exactly who it is. That mean little sidewinder of a Scudder."

I remembered Scudder and his pale eyes, so flat and thin there was no light in them at all. The thin fleshless look of his hands, holding them out to the flame that night in the hills above the Wells. I remembered, too, the way Ike threw down on him when Scudder was going to pistol-whip Jim Frisk. Scudder had trembled that day with the caged-up anger that was in him.

"Ike," I said, "get out of here. Now, while you've got time! If Scudder wants me, he's got to come up here to get me. I can shoot from here. And I don't miss, not as far away as from here to that trapdoor."

He chuckled. "You ain't afeared for me, are you, Joey?"

"Go now," I said. "Slip out the back way."

"Now if that ain't a hell of way to treat an old friend," Ike said. "Tell him to leave by the back door." He snickered again. Then he was serious. "Edy'll be back any time with that wagon. I know it And we can't have Scudder hangin' around then, can we, old hoss?"

I swallowed hard. I hadn't thought of that And Eda—suppose she stumbled onto Scudder, stalking us in the yard below! Suppose he thought she was me, or something, trying to get away. My mind was mixed up and panicky.

"Sho, now," Ike said. He punched me in the shoulder. "I tell you what! I'll just play a lettle game of puss-in-the-corner with that ornery sneak. I seen the Sioux do that a hundred times or more, I reckon. Soldiers get too close to a Sioux camp—why, them Injuns jest set up a hell of a rookus somewheres else and draw the soldiers away till they can light out. That's an old Sioux trick."

"I don't give a damn what kind of a trick it is," I said. "You stay here. I've caused enough people trouble as it is. I don't intend to cause any more. This is my fight." Somehow I managed to get up on my knees, and then to my feet. I felt light-headed and queer, and my knees were made of water. But I propped myself against the wall and hung on tight to the carbine.

"Don't hear nothin' now," Ike whispered. "What'll you bet that critter's sittin' down there hunched up like a owl, battin' his yeller eyes, jest awaitin' for us to move?"

I knew Scudder was there. Something told me. My fist gripped the cold barrel hard, thinking of him sitting down there in the shadow like an evil bird. He knew we were there. And he knew that we knew. He wasn't in any hurry. He was just waiting.

"Well," Ike said, "I got to go, hoss." He put out his hand and shook mine. "Now you jest sit tight and don't worry. Hell, I handled meaner critters than Scudder before. Onct on the Big Nemaha, I—" He lifted the trapdoor, and looked down into the dark hole. "The way I look at it, you got to trust people. Took me a long time to learn that. That was Saul's main trouble. He didn't ever trust nobody, except Saul, and that wasn't enough." Then he was gone, a buckskinned ghost flitting away with the rustle of hide moccasins.

That's right, I thought. *I should have trusted Eda, too.* I'd done her an injustice, but maybe I could make up for it someday. I leaned against the wall, biting my lip at the hot scratchy feel in my side, like a cat with fiery claws was raking me. I thought of Ike Coogan, too, and how mangy he looked to me that first time I ever saw him. At Mesquite Springs, it was, a long time ago. Now I'd trusted him with my life, and he took that trust like it was only fair, and no questions asked.

In a minute, I heard his voice below. He called to Scudder, somewhere in the black shadows of the yard.

"Scudder? You polecat—where are you?"

At first there was no sound, and then Ike yelled again.

"Scudder? You hidin' from me, you beauty? Come out in the open where I can get a clean shot at you!"

A muffled curse came from the blackness, and a shuffling sound. Then Ike Coogan's voice again, taunting and nasal.

"Skeered o' me, Scudder? A old man with the rheumatiz, and a rusty gun?"

This time the voice was farther away, and faint, but there was no mistaking the jeering to it. I heard running feet, and when I looked out Scudder was standing below me in the moonlight, feet planted solid, swiveling this way and then that, gun out and searching the shadows. He shouldn't have moved into the moon that way. I guess it showed Ike Coogan was getting under his skin. I raised the carbine. I didn't care what happened, not to me, anyway. All I could think of was Ike Coogan, dodging around down there in the dark. He couldn't even walk without his joints hurting. I cramped my finger around the trigger.

"Scudder!" Ike's voice was nearer. "God damn you, you ugly little bastard! You gone home, Scudder?"

The voice seemed to come from one side of the yard, then the other. It was all around, quavering from the grape-arbor, the well-sweep, the kitchen leanto where a light burned. I squinted down the barrel, seeing Scudder's dark form swimming over the front sight. But then, in a flurry of motion, he darted back into the shadows and was gone. Coogan shouted to him again, and the voice came from away toward town. Again Scudder cursed, and he ran toward the front of the house, seeking his tormentor. The yard was clean and washed-looking in the light of the moon. Scudder was gone. Ike was gone, too.

No more than five minutes later I heard the rumble of wheels in the yard, and the stamp and snuffle of mules. A Dougherty wagon was down there, with two span of big fat black mules. Eda came flying up the stairs with Corporal Henry Schrader behind her.

"Joey!" Her voice was scared in the dark, but then she caught sight of me standing by the window. "I looked to the bed," she said, "but you weren't there. I looked at the bed first, but you weren't there."

Schrader still had that big blue-steel knife stuck in his belt, but now he looked good to me. He looked real good.

"Eda says we got to get you out of here," he grunted. "All right, sonny. You're lucky we got a train going to Fort Bowie tomorrow." He helped me get into my pants, and took my carbine in one big hand. "We'll just git on the road," he said, "and come mornin' we'll be a good fur piece from town. Won't nobody bother you, not in a blue Army wagon."

"You won't get in trouble?" I asked. "I mean—"

"In trouble? Me?" Schrader laughed. "Hell, boy, the corporals *runs* this army." He patted the big chevrons. "A sergeant's too damned important to get his hands dirty, and the shoulder-straps're too busy with women and liquor and blackjack. It's us corporals that keeps things rollin'."

"Where's Ike?" Eda asked.

I told her. I told her about Scudder, and about Ike. She didn't say anything, but stood pale and beautiful, holding one hand tight in the other like she didn't want them to tremble. Her head was high, and she said, "Hank, you take good care of him."

Hank helped me up in the wagon, and pulled the straps to let the curtains drop all around. The back of the Dougherty was filled with sacks of grain, and I let myself down easy. I stuck one hand out through the flap and Eda took it and held it tight.

"Goodbye, Joey," she said. "Thank you, Hank."

Corporal Schrader gathered the reins. "You're welcome, ma'am."

There was something rueful in the way he said it, and Eda put a foot on the nigh axle and pulled herself up to kiss him soundly on the cheek.

"Git!" Hank bawled, and the mules leaned into their collars and drew the wagon swiftly away. I looked out the back; Eda was standing there waving till the corner of the house cut her from view. When we swung around the front of the Landry house, two faces peered out, black silhouettes against the yellow glow. But I didn't care about the Landrys any more. I was going home. It was my home, and I intended to fight for it.

CHAPTER TWELVE

I slept that night, though not a great deal. The jolting and swaying of the wagon flung me this way and that, and it wasn't till early morning that I managed to wedge myself among the grain sacks in a way I couldn't be tossed around. The last thing I remembered was the sight of Corporal Schrader's broad back against the stars. Then I slept.

By dawn we were twenty miles out. We'd left the Santa Cruz behind, and the land was dry and barren again, in one of the quick violent changes of the country. The parched brown grass wasn't enough to hold the soil together, and the air filled with clouds of stinging yellow dust that got in your eyes and ears and made your nose itch. When the sun came up, Schrader turned to me, powdered with the fine stuff, and said, "Guess we better hole up here for a while. I'll make some coffee. The wagons left about two this morning. They'll catch up with us before long."

In the wind it was hard to make a fire, but Schrader finally got one going in a little oven of rocks. He took an old black can and dumped a handful of coffee into it and we sat in the lee of the wagon, shivering, thinking the coffee would never come to a boil. But it did, and the warmth of it took some of the chill from our bones. A weak sun strained through the sifting yellow clouds, and I began to feel better. I was out of Tucson, anyway.

"Now that Eda," the corporal said, cupping his hands around his coffee, "she ain't a girl to tell you much. No, she keeps her own counsel, I'd say. Didn't hardly tell me nothin' 'bout how you got in that hayloft, all shot up. Didn't even tell me what her stake was in it."

He paused, eyeing me over the rim of the cup. It was a clear invitation to explain myself.

"All right," I said. You had to trust people. I told him about the Wells, and about Red Chaffee and what he'd done to Dave, and how I tried to stop it and ended up shooting Chaffee and becoming a hunted man myself. "Now," I said, "I'm going back. I'm going to fight for what's ours. Nobody can take it away from me."

Schrader scratched his bristly chin. "Not even your own brother?"

It came to me in a blinding shock what was going to happen. Somehow or other, in all this confusion and violence, I'd kept a picture of Dave that was about the same. Oh, he'd gotten persuaded against his will to throw in with Chaffee, and he'd only done what he had to do. But now it came to me what all this really meant. I wasn't fighting Chaffee anymore. Chaffee was dead. I wasn't fighting Scudder, or Bluejaw, or any of the toughs that worked for Chaffee. They were only hired hands. What I was fighting now was Dave Boston, my own brother. My blood brother.

"Them's tough lines," Schrader said. "Mighty tough. But this never was no easy country. It's got a way of making people do things they never would 'a thought of doing in Utica, New York, or Birmingham or Indianapolis." He squatted on his heels and chewed on an unlighted cigar. "The territory's a damned big grindstone. It wears off the slick on the outside, and if you ain't got good hard insides, it just chews you up and throws you on the junk-heap."

About noon the wagons caught up with us, a dozen or more of them, dusty blue wagons creaking and groaning, the canvas flapping in the wind. A child lieutenant rode up to our Dougherty and dismounted. He was a slender little thing, slight as a girl, and he had a pencil-thin mustache that might have been dark, but now it was powdered blonde with dust.

"Where the hell have you been?" he asked Schrader.

The corporal got stiffly to his feet and saluted, a ragged salute, calculated, just the right amount of deference, and yet not quite enough.

"Sir, askin' the lieutenant's pardon, them mules was restless last night. I don't know what gets into a mule's mind, sometimes, but there just ain't no dealing with them when they get like that. Best thing to do is harness 'em up and run them ideas right out of their minds. Seein' how we was goin' to Fort Bowie in the morning anyway, I just got me a loaded wagon and tied them mules to it, and here we are!"

It was an outrageous story, and Schrader knew it. So did the child lieutenant. His face got red, even under the powdering of dust. He turned to me. "Who the hell are you?"

"I was restless, too," I said.

I thought he was going to swell and go up in the air like a hot-air balloon on the Fourth of July. "I'll see you in the guardhouse soon," he said to Schrader. Chewing at the thin mustache, he slapped his gauntlets into his palm, scowling. Then he turned in a trim about-face and stalked away.

"I swear," Schrader said mildly. "Them lieutenants gets younger and littler every day. Who do you reckon changes his didies?"

I giggled. The lieutenant looked back sharply, and I was taken with a fit of coughing.

"Well," Schrader said, "guess we better roll 'em again."

The lieutenant beckoned us to the front of the column, I guess where he could keep an eye on us to make sure our mules didn't get restless again. We rode that way across the valley and into the *playa*. That night we camped, and Schrader shared his beef and biscuits with me. I slept long but I dreamed of Dave.

"By God, you are restless," the corporal said the next morning. "Tossed and turned all night long. Sounded like you was tryin' to talk, but I never got the straight of it."

"My side hurt a little," I lied. As a matter of fact, it was feeling pretty good.

It was the next day, about noon, when we came up out of the *playa*. I could see the distant greenery of the Wells. We'd had rain since I was gone. The land was filmy with a green haze, tiny shoots of fresh grass. That wind a ways back had been the tail end of a storm, I figured, and it had dumped rain on our land.

"Look at that," I said to Schrader. "Isn't that beautiful? Just look at it."

I'd no sooner said it than a head popped over a hummock, and a rifle barrel. Then another head under a ragged straw hat. Schrader sawed on the reins and brought the mules back on their haunches.

"Did you see that?" the lieutenant yelled. "Corporal, who are those men?"

For a minute it seemed like we'd been tricked by a mirage. The plain was flat and empty ahead of us, and the wind riffled the grass. All around us the wagons of the train seemed deserted, the mules standing fat and patient, but you could see a rifle-barrel poking out here, another there, one under a wagon. These boys had been through it before, and they didn't stand on ceremony. They just took cover and waited.

Schrader pointed. "I see a feller along that rise there, comin' this way."

We watched the tiny figure approach, calling out hoarsely.

"Hold your fire, men!" the lieutenant bawled. "Keep him covered, but don't shoot till I tell you to!"

When he got closer I saw it was big Tom Morgan. His face was red and peeling, and he looked like he'd lost a little heft since I'd seen him last. He had his shotgun in one hand.

"What the hell is this?" the lieutenant murmured.

Schrader grinned. "Looks like everyone's restless today, lootenant."

"I know him," I said. "That's Tom Morgan. He's one of the settlers at the Wells."

Tom wiped his forehead with a bandana. "Lieutenant, we been keepin' an eye on this road. We been expectin' trouble to come from this way, and we aimed to be ready when it came."

"Sir," the lieutenant said, "are you aware you damned near got shot to hell? And what's all this cock and bull about trouble coming this way? Who do you people think you are, holding up United States Army wagons with weapons in your hands?"

"Now just hold off a minute," I said. "I know this man." Heads peered at us over the top of a dune on the right, and from another little rise on the left. I recognized Jim Frisk and John Turner and George Mowry and a few others, but I didn't see Saul. "Red Chaffee and some of his gunmen are trying to run them off their land. They're only trying to defend it, that's all."

"Chaffee's dead," the lieutenant said.

"I know. I killed him."

His eyes widened, and he fondled his mustache. When he spoke there was a kind of respect in his voice. "All right. If you vouch for them—"

"I do," I said.

"But as for you—" He looked at me hard. "I don't know but what I ought to put you under arrest. A lot of people in Tucson are looking for you, including the law."

Schrader cleared his throat. "Beggin' the lieutenant's pardon," he said. "Troops is not to take any part in civil matters unless specifically requested by a lawful constituted civil court. And if—"

"Shut up," the lieutenant said.

I didn't want to hang around while they decided the legal aspects of the case. I got down from the wagon and Tom Morgan threw his arms around me and hugged me. It hurt my side but I didn't let on.

"Joey! Where the hell you been? You didn't tell nobody where you was going." Suddenly he was sober. "Is this true—what we hear about Chaffee being dead?"

"It is," I said.

"Then we ain't got nothin' to worry about!" He threw his hat in the air, and waved his arm. "Fellers, come on up here! Chaffee's dead!"

"Wait a minute." I raised my hand. They crowded around me, all the old familiar faces, my neighbors. I didn't want to tell them this but I had to. "The fighting's just begun," I said. "I—my brother—I mean Dave, you all knew Dave—well, he's taken over from Chaffee. I'm afraid he's sticking to Chaffee's plan. He still intends to take the Wells away from us."

Tom Morgan went and got his hat again and stood looking down at it, like it was strange to him. John Turner put his hand on my arm and said, "Dave? Why, he's your own brother!"

I nodded.

"Well—" Morgan pulled his hat down over his eyes. "Let's get back to our posts, men."

The lieutenant still eyed me uncertainly.

"Lieutenant," I said, "bring your wagons into the Wells. There's plenty of water, and forage for the animals. We've got fresh meat, too, and cream for coffee. You're welcome to anything we've got."

He looked at me in perplexity. Then he took off his hat and scratched his head. He looked at Corporal Henry Schrader. "You damned guardhouse lawyer!" he said. But he was grinning this time, and Schrader winked at him, a broad cheerful wink.

I was home.

As soon as the soldiers left, we had a council of war in Tom Morgan's place. Betty Morgan made a pie out of dried apples, and we sat around and drank coffee. We'd left half of our men scattered around on picket duty; two on the Tucson road, another out toward the direction of Fort Bowie, one more in the hills north of the Wells. To the south it was all *playa.* They'd hardly be coming that way, and we could see them a long way off in the daytime. At night it was a different story. We'd have to put an outpost there, too. With only twelve men, we had our hands full with crops to plow and water to be let into the ditches and stock to be fed and watered.

"We ain't got much ammunition," John Turner said. He still wore a rag around his head from the beating Bluejaw gave him that day in front of our house. "I got plenty powder and ball for this old musket, but she don't hold on a target so good. Shoots low and to the right."

"Let's make a list of the firearms we've got," I said. "That way we can figure how we stand."

"That's the ticket," Jim Frisk said.

"Now up at the house Saul and I have got a fresh case of shells for Henry carbine. Jim, you've got a carbine. And how about that man you said moved in down south of you, by the stand of willows. Didn't he have a carbine, too?"

They didn't say anything, and then it came to me that they'd all froze up when I mentioned Saul's name. Saul wasn't here, either. No one had asked him. They probably didn't mean to.

"He ain't goin' to help us with no cartridges," John Turner said. "Day after you left, he come down here steppin' high like a rooster in deep mud. Said we couldn't hardly expect no help from him. Said this wasn't his fight, it was forced on him, and we'd better scatter while we had a chanct."

Betty filled my cup again from the big pot and I was glad for the few seconds it gave me to think. They accepted me as one of them—they always had. But they didn't like Saul.

"All right," I said. "We won't take him into our calculations. If we get any help from him, fine. If we don't—then we won't be any worse off. Anyway, I'll get that case of Henry ammunition."

We made up our list: three Sharps carbines, two Henrys, an old Maynard with a flintlock, Turner's musket, a '66 Winchester rimfire that was the latest we had, a few shotguns, a queer assortment of handguns. Plenty of black powder and ball, and the case of Henry ammunition.

"They won't be expecting us to fight," I said. "That's a big advantage to us." I drew a map on the dirt floor with a stick. "Here's the Wells, and here's the Tucson road." I laid out our plan, covering the approaches, arranging for signals, scheduling patrols, seeing that someone watered the stock. "And remember this," I said. "We can't defend the whole damned Wells. Some of you are going to have your corn trampled, maybe a roof set afire. They're mean, and they'll try to do all the damage they can. But if we surprise 'em on the road, we've got the initiative. We'll call on 'em to halt, and if they keep coming on, we'll make 'em scrap every inch of the way. I don't know how many of them there'll be, but my guess is Chaffee wouldn't have gone this far without planning pretty thorough."

"Chaffee's dead," Mowry said.

"I know. But what Chaffee stood for isn't. We've got to prepare for the worst." I pointed to the X on the floor that marked our Texas house. "We'll fall back, if we have to. We can't let 'em flank us. If worst comes to worst, we'll hole up in our place. There's water there, and slits to shoot through. The roof's rock slabs. No one's going to set fire to that. It's been tried before. Once they get us in there, they'll see it's like dragging a bobcat out of a hole in a rock. It's something you want to think about twice. If we pick off enough of them, maybe they'll give it up as a bad job."

"What about them Sonora cattle?" someone asked. "Lord, I don't want no thousand head of steers wallowing in my bottom land! Might as well give up now as let something like that happen. There wouldn't be anything left to save, anyhow."

"They figured two weeks for the cattle to get up here," I said. "A week's gone, or more. Let's hope the cattle don't show up till we've licked Chaffee's men. Then we can handle them."

"Chaffee's dead," John Turner said mildly. They all looked at me, something queer in their eyes.

"All right," I said. "My brother Dave, then. But it was never Dave's idea. It was Chaffee's idea. Dave's just got to carry through with it."

"Joey," Tom Morgan said, "we think a lot of you. You're mighty near a son to me. But I can't help thinkin' about it this way. You're Dave's brother. You sure you're in this with us? It's mighty hard to throw down on your own kin. When the time comes—"

"When the time comes, I'll throw down on him," I said. My face felt hot and burning. I slammed down my coffee cup and went away up the hill toward the Texas house.

The mules nosed up to the edge of the pole corral when I came by. They were thirsty, and the rock trough I'd made for them was bone-dry. The place looked run-down and sorry. The beans were full of weeds and the com looked like thin sticks, with little dried-up ears. I carried water for the mules from the ditch, and left them sucking it up with their big rubbery lips.

Saul was sitting in his rocker, smoking his pipe. The old trunk we'd brought all the way from Columbus was half-packed with things. It looked like he was going way. When he saw me he quit rocking and took the pipe out of his mouth. "Where the hell you been?"

"Tucson," I said.

"Ike Coogan with you?"

"He was." I pointed to the trunk. "You going someplace?"

Not looking at me after that first glance, he knocked the dottle of his pipe out on his bootheel. His big hands hung between his knees, and he looked old and tired. He wasn't more than forty but he looked like Methuselah. His voice was thin, without spirit or conviction. "I'm going back to Columbus."

"Where?" The name seemed strange and unfamiliar to me, like Timbuctoo, and only then did I realize how far away Columbus was to me anymore.

"Columbus. I should have gone back a long time ago."

"You mean—" I shook my head, not sure I'd heard him right. "You mean you're just pulling out, and leaving all this? Leaving the Wells? For good?"

He nodded, sucking at the empty pipe.

"It hasn't been an easy decision to make. But I know what I'm doing. If you had any sense, you'd come along too. I've got plenty of money. And Ohio's a state. They've got law and order there. You don't have to fight all the time for what's yours."

"You did fight for it, once."

He put his head in his hands. It was powdered thick with gray, and long in the back where it hadn't been cut for months. "I haven't got the stomach for it any more, Joey."

I felt a chill, a feeling like my stomach was filled with icewater. When you've had someone older for a long time, it comes as a shock to find you're suddenly standing on your own feet. Up till now, I'd always had someone to go to. It was easier, somehow, to make the Tucson trip knowing Saul would be at the Wells when I got back. He was crabby, and he was irritable, but he was family. All the family I had.

"Saul," I said, "you can't go. This is your land. You can't just walk out on something like that. Part of you is here. It'll always be here, no matter where you go."

He shook his head, staring down at the backs of his hands. "Sure, it was mine. I fought Indians and wind and dry spells and gullywashers and everything and everybody. You and me. We did her. We made it stick."

"Then how can you just go away and leave all this?"

"Leave me alone," he said. "I got to do what I got to do, that's all." He reached out and plucked at my pants leg. "You don't have to stay here, either. We got three thousand dollars cash on the barrelhead. That's a pretty good stake. We can load everything on the wagon and get the hell out of this place. In two hours we can be on the way back to Columbus, and live like gentlemen."

"I can't leave," I said, miserable.

He didn't seem to hear me. He swallowed like there was a lump in his throat, and his adams-apple bobbed up and down. "That'll buy a nice piece of land back there. Good black land—none of this godforsaken scrub and sand."

I grabbed him by the lapels and shook him. "You can't go! You can't just take your money and run out on all these people like a hound with your tail between your legs! Dave and Chaffee and Bluejaw and Scudder all put together never had half your spunk, and you know it! We can fight them. We can hole up in here and lick the tar out of them!"

He blinked at me. "Dave?"

I pushed him from me, sick.

"You'd fight Dave?"

"Of course I'd fight him. And anyone else that tried to take the Wells away from us! If you're not interested in it anymore, I am! It's mine, and Tom Morgan's, and John Turner's, and Jim and Sweetheart Frisk's. It belongs to all of us, and there ain't any bunch of hoodlums can take it away from us."

"You'd fight Dave," he said. "You'd fight Dave. Good Lord! That's what this country's done to all of us. You were a good boy once—a God-fearing boy. You had a duty to your folks, and when they were gone you had a duty to me, me being the eldest. You saw that duty, and you stood by it. Now you'd kill your own brother."

That was it. He'd said it. It was something I didn't want to think about. Maybe something would happen. Maybe Dave wouldn't come. Maybe he'd just send Scudder, and Bluejaw, and the rest of the gang. That would make it easier. When the time came, I didn't know if I could throw down on Dave. Not Dave.

"You told him once you'd kill him if you ever saw him again," I said.

He sighed, a long shuddering sound. "All that was a long time ago." Rubbing at his eyes, he stared at the ground. The rock trench was still there, water bubbling along in it, just like it had been that first day he'd dug it. In case of Apaches, it was. But I don't think he even saw it. His eyes looked clear through it, looking someplace where I couldn't go with him. It was like he was floating away from me, and I was trying to reach out and catch him but my hands found nothing but shreds of smoke.

"All right," I said. "You pack up. I'm damned if I'll help you. I've got work to do. You take everything, hear? Every damned thing—all the money, too."

For an instant he flared up. He was Saul again, proud and stubborn, and I hoped I'd gotten to him, somehow. But all he did was grab me by the sleeve, and say, "Don't talk to me like that, you young pup! By God, I've wet-nursed you and fed you and paddled you when you were sassy. And I'm damned if I'll let you stay here and dip your hands in blood!"

I pushed him away and said, "How you going to stop me?"

His bony face was almost purple. His mouth opened and closed without any words coming. He raised his fists high above his head, and then he sort of collapsed, slumping into the rocker, body shaking and his face buried in his hands.

"When you get that trunk packed," I said, "I'll get someone to help you put it in the wagon."

I went out into the sunlight, feeling my breath come hard and heavy. My heart hammered under my ribs like a steam-engine, and the palms of my hands were wet and sticky. I took deep breaths of the air, trying to clear my head. I think if I'd not had so much to do, I'd have bawled. But as I stood there, feeling the whole world was collapsing around my ears, I saw Ike Coogan come riding into the yard. It was the most beautiful sight I'd ever seen.

"Ike!" I said. "You old—you old—"

I didn't know what to call him. There weren't words.

"Howdy, Joey," he said.

He let himself down off the paint, slow and easy, and stood there for a minute, hanging on to the saddle horn with one hand. Then he straightened up, and banged the butt of the old Hawken rifle on the ground.

"Got some news few you." He screwed up his mouth and spit a ropy strand into the dust. "Dave's on his way here. Him and a dozen of Chaffee's varmints. I follered 'em most of the way from Tucson, and then I lit out and rode around 'em to bring the word."

"How soon?" I said.

He wiped his mouth on his sleeve.

"Hell, they ain't in no hurry! Ridin' in style, with plenty of liquor and tobaccy. Like a fox hunt, sort of."

"How soon?" I yelled.

He scratched his chin. "Maybe an hour. Two hours."

I went back in the Texas house. "Saul," I said, "if you're going, you better light a shuck. Dave's on his way here, with Chaffee's men. All hell's going to be popping."

Even then, I hoped he'd change his mind. We needed him. And he needed us. More than he knew. But he only stared at me with that kind of preoccupied look. Then he blinked his eyes, and said, "Thanks, Joey."

CHAPTER THIRTEEN

Saul took the money in an old valise. He took his clothes, and the Sharps rifle, and the Argand lamp. "That'll bring ten or fifteen dollars in Tucson." He hurried around the house, packing stuff in sacks, and I helped him carry it out to the wagon. "It's only fair," he said, "me leaving you my share of the Wells, the way I am." Finally he was loaded, and he hitched up the mules. Not till then, looking around at the stuff in the wagon, did he seem embarrassed. He hooked the reins around the brake and looked down at his hands, rubbing one of them with the other.

"Joey, I know it looks queer to you for me to run out this way. But I'm older'n you, and I got better judgment."

"There's nothing wrong with your judgment." I had a bitter taste in my mouth, and I cleared my throat and spit. "Your judgment's pretty good. There's going to be a hell of a battle around here in a little while, and you're getting out before then. No, I'd say your judgment was all right."

"What good would it do me, or anybody for that matter, to stay here and get killed? No, I figure it's better to run away and—how's it go? To live and fight another day." He nodded, thoughtful. "You better come, too."

I shook my head. "You won't fight any more, Saul. Not you. Not unless you can't get out of it." He didn't fool me talking the way he did. "You did a lot for me," I said. "You taught me how to hang on by the eyebrows when the going got rough. You taught me not to trust anybody, just to depend on yourself. You taught me how to work hard, and sweat, and how to scratch for a living where no one else had enough guts to. The only thing—"

He looked at me hard under the shaggy eyebrows.

"The only thing," I said, "I wish you'd taught me how to say goodbye to someone without choking up like this."

He bent his head under the wide straw hat and rubbed at the bridge of his nose, his eyes closed. The weariness had grown on him almost like moss. "Joey," he said, "right now you don't think much of me. I guess you don't think much of Dave, either. We both let you down, and I ain't asking any forgiveness for that. But it's a fact that people are what they are. The Lord made me the kind that likes to till the fields in peace, and say a grace for bread, and go my own way. I never wanted to fight Apaches and scrabble in the dust and fight this country with my bare hands. For a while I did it, but it wasn't my way. It—" His voice broke a little, and he opened his eyes. "It forced me to be something I never was cut out to be. And I'm doing something else I've got no stomach for, but I've seen death too many times to go looking for him now. Being loyal and brave and stuff like that is for young men. I ain't got the ginger for it anymore."

He reached down and touched me on the shoulder, an awkward kind of motion. I don't remember he ever did that before. "Don't judge me too hard. I always meant well. I just wasn't cut out for the long haul."

I blinked once or twice. "Well," I said, "good luck."

I wanted to tell him to write sometime, maybe, but we were both thinking the same thing. Maybe I wouldn't be around to get it.

"I'll ask you again," he said. "Will you come?"

I shook my head.

"You got your lights you go by," he said. "That's you, Joey, and I'm proud you got 'em. But I got to get on my way." He slapped the reins over the mules, and they leaned into the harness and drew the wagon swiftly away, toward the east. And I knew I'd never see him again.

Jim Frisk and I were wrestling cases of ammunition around, trying to get them up on Jim's wagon when I heard the first shots. We'd agreed on our signals, but this was no signal. There wasn't time for any signal. All it was, it was a quick spatter of shots, like rain tapping on a tin roof, a long way off. Jim dropped his end of the box and looked at me, mustache draggled with sweat. "You hear that?"

"I heard it." I ran for my carbine and threw a bridle on Buster. I didn't have time to bother with a saddle. Jim dropped far behind me on the spavined nag he was riding, and old man Coogan brought up the rear, easy and casual like there was all the time in the world. But I came out so fast into the rubble on the edge of the *playa* that I almost rode down Tom Morgan and the rest who were camped out there, watching.

"What is it?" I asked.

Tom pointed. "There's a dozen or more of Chaffee's men out there, behind that low ridge with the scrub on it. They were riding along like they were on a toot, all singing and laughing. I don't think they figured us to make a stand, but we cut loose at them and they scattered."

"They'll be back," I said. My hands were sweating and my collar seemed tight. I jerked it open and the button popped off.

Tom asked, "What do we do now?"

I looked at the wavy ripples of heat that lay over the land. Empty, and silent. That was the way this country always was just before it rared up and smacked you down. "Look to your guns," I said. "You all got plenty of ammunition?"

A sharp cry broke out from one of our lookouts on a high pinnacle. Tom Morgan pointed. "They're rallying—trying to get around behind us!"

Twisted and wavering in the heat, a group of mounted men flogged away toward the south, and more of them took off in the other direction, bending low over the horses' necks. Jim Frisk squeezed off a shot at them but the range was too long and the bullet kicked up dust a hundred yards short.

"Jim," I said, "get back to the Wells. Get all the women and children into our house."

Someone asked, "They won't harm our women and children, will they?"

"I don't know," I said. "They're capable of anything. If they can't get at us any other way, I think they would." I climbed up onto Buster. The cloud that had hung over me for so long was gone. I found myself thinking hard and fast, and right. I knew it was right. "Soon's you get them in the house, Jim, take off to that strong point in the rocks east of the house, where we cached the ammunition. Tom, you and Dick and Charlie stand fast here. Don't let them cut you off, though. Fight like the Apaches do—fire and fall back and make 'em sweat for every inch of ground."

"What happens if they bust clean through?" Tom asked.

"If you've got to give, then give," I said. "But fall back in order. We'll rally at the house. We can hold out forever in there. That's a fort, practically. That's the way Saul built it." I didn't any more than make it back to the house when the shooting broke out for fair. It sounded like an old-fashioned Fourth of July at home, all the popping and banging, and in a way it was exciting, too. Ike Coogan and I rode out to where Jim Frisk was. That was where most of the shooting came from. Sure enough, they'd tried to flank us and come in on that side. Jim was laying in a hollow in the rocks, his face black with powder already and drops of sweat running down his long black mustache. Even with the bunged-up arm, he could still rest his rifle on the rocks before him and bang away.

"About five or six of 'em," he said, pointing. "They rode through that little gully there and right up the sights of my gun. I got one of 'em, anyhow, and scared hell out of the rest."

As we watched, a hat poked up over a slab of gray rock. Jim squeezed off a shot and the hat spun into the air. There was a stick below it, that was all, and slowly the stick went down again.

"Wasted that one," Jim said.

Ike Coogan poured powder into the barrel of the Hawken and rammed a patch and a bullet down the bore. "Don't never shoot at a hat," he said. "A hat's often got a man's brain in it, and he ain't likely to take chances with a set of brains. A leg or an arm, now—" Squinting down the barrel, he squeezed off a shot. The Hawken roared and smoke bellied around us, and even in the sunlight we were half-blinded by the flash. A man stood up from behind a rock, cursing, and holding his hand up. Then he started running, stumbling and falling, and collapsed behind a pile of rubble where we couldn't get at him.

"He ain't got as many fingers on that hand anymore," Ike said, ramming a new charge of shot home. "Teach him to be a little more careful, I think."

We sweated in that shallow cup of rocks most of the afternoon. They rushed us once, three of them on one side and three on the other, but we'd picked a good spot. The land pinched into a shallow gully grown up with thickets of catsclaw, and they had to come right to us, up the gully. We beat them back, and laid there sweating and powderblack, but happy. I hoped Tom and Dick and the rest were doing as well. We could hear the shots behind us, and once in a while one would sail high over our heads, whizzing and singing, to splatter into the rocks.

"Reminds me of a time up on the Bijon Creek," Ike said. "Near St. Vrain's Fort, it was. There was this feller—"

A bullet spanged against a rock near us and sprayed us with needles of lead. From the angle it must have hit, this one didn't come from behind us. It was off at the side. I looked up, and there was a man in a red shirt standing high a point of rock off to our left, and he was shooting down at us.

"Let's get out of here!" I yelled. I shot at him with my carbine, but I missed, and we scrambled away, out of the line of fire, dodging and running low through the catsclaw, back toward the house again. I'd hoped we could find another place to hole up, but the man on the high place could see us all the way, and he kept shooting at us and we couldn't stop. One ball clipped a branch right in front of my nose, and it scratched me as it whipped by me, dangling.

Tom and Dick and the rest were at the house, taking cover behind Nacho's wickiup. The sun was low in the west, and it came to me with a shock that we'd been fighting for most of the afternoon.

"Joey," Tom said, "there's more than a dozen of them. There must be twenty at least. We got two or three of 'em, but John Turner got barked by some flying rock, and it got in his eyes and he can't see."

Even as I watched, a splinter of light pricked out of the dusk and left a little hole, like a pockmark, in the wall behind me. And another came, from the direction we'd just fallen back from, and then another. For the first time I began to get an idea of the size of the outfit we were fighting. The size, and the ugliness of it. Red Chaffee's outfit.

"All right." I said "We got our backs to the house now. That makes it easy. We're all here together, and they're going to have one hell of a time."

Bit by bit they ringed us. We had good men, all of them, and they never showed their heads, and never shot unless they had a target. The bitter fight went on and on, and there was never a full minute that didn't have a dozen shots to fill it in. Our men were beat back from the corral, from the barn, from the wickiup. I used my carbine till the barrel burned my hands, and it was shooting high and the left. They came at us in vicious rushes—two men at a time, and then three. They timed it so they all seemed to be moving at once, and it was confusing, seeing new targets spring up all over the circle of fire that ringed us. They were professionals at it, that much was sure. They went at it like butchers in a slaughterhouse, quiet, efficient, and silent. After the man that Coogan winged, I don't think we got any more of them. It sobered them. If they were drunk when they came, it wore off fast.

"Joey," Ike Coogan said, "we ain't gettin' anyplace out here. Mebbe we better get inside before it gets plumb dark." His chin whiskers waggled in the gloom. "Them sons are sneakin' up mighty clost."

I shot once more with the carbine at a shadowy figure skulking at the edge of the clearing. It might have been Dave. I pressed the trigger almost blind, hoping it would be, and yet wishing it wasn't. "All right," I said. I waved my arm. "Everybody inside! Quick, now!"

Ike and I covered them while they fell back. The moon was out, lighting the Wells with a filmy gray light, and that made it even harder to see. It was like shooting into a veil that twisted and turned and hid the people under it. But they knew where we were, all right.

As they passed into the house, grim and silent, I counted them. Seven, eight, nine—ten. As he dodged through the door, Tom Morgan got a ball through the back. It was high enough so it probably wouldn't be fatal, but it seemed like it broke his shoulder and he was stretched out on the floor inside with the women tending him. And Jim Frisk—I didn't see Jim.

"Jim?" I called out. In the dim lantern light inside, I looked around.

"Ain't seen him for the past hour," someone said.

I took one last look outside, standing to one side of the half-open door. All around us in the gathering dark those spiteful little flowers of red and yellow bloomed and died and bloomed again. It was like a garden. A garden of death. A ball spanged on the heavy wood of the door and drove a splinter into my cheek, and I dodged in and pulled the door to and bolted it.

Someone had a coat rigged over the lamp to keep the light shut away from the rifle slits in the wall. The shutters were pulled to and latched. Heavy and muffled now, filtering to us through a foot or more of dobe, the shots came to our ears. The air was foul with the smell of men sweating, and black powder, and the fresh sticky smell of blood. Tom Morgan laid on Saul's old pallet with a piece of a bedsheet wrapped around his chest and up over one shoulder.

"You all right, Tom?" I asked.

"I'm all right."

The children squatted in a corner of the house, playing in the dirt. One of the older boys had Tom's shotgun, and he held it over his shoulder like he was on parade, marching up and down. I took it away from him, and his mother rapped him over the head with her knuckles.

"We're all right," I said. "Everything's all right. We've got plenty of food and water. When they see how we 're holed up here, they'll think twice trying to root us out. It's like trying to pull a coon out of a chink in the rocks. You can get bit real bad."

The shooting stopped for a minute. In the quiet, the sound of the water purling through the room in the trench Saul dug was loud and clear. I looked through one of the slits. They'd made a strong point out of Nacho's wickiup, now, and a man darted out and ran to the shelter of a big boulder near the corral. They were carrying ammunition to the wickiup. Nacho and his brood were long gone. They had a nose for trouble. Long before the shooting started they'd packed everything on a swaybacked pony and lit out.

"Hey, in there!" a voice bawled at us. It sounded like Bluejaw. "You folks in there better give up while your hide's in one piece! Come on out, now, and we won't harm no one!"

The faces were smeared and dirty and sweaty in the glow of the lamp, but they were all set in the same stubborn cast. Ike Coogan squatted in the corner, chewing tobacco and looking daintily for a place to spit.

"Tell 'em to go to hell!" someone said.

I didn't say anything. There wasn't any need to. Then I heard Dave's voice, calling to me outside someplace.

"Joey?"

In my mind's eye I could see him, hunkered behind a rock, his pointed face anxious.

"That's Dave," Ike Coogan said.

"I'm here," I called.

His voice was thin and unreal, drifting to me out of the moon-smoked dark. "You tell those people to open that door and come out. You got a responsibility to see there ain't any more shooting. You got women and children in there. I can't be responsible any longer." He paused. "You hear me?"

I didn't answer. I didn't want to talk to him, not ever again. He could always talk me into anything.

After a while he yelled, "All right then. Be bullheaded if you want. But we got ways of smoking you out."

John Turner pulled at my sleeve. He had a handkerchief pressed to his eyes, and he still couldn't see.

"What does he mean?"

"Nothing," I said. "Just big talk."

Tom Morgan struggled up to one elbow, pushing his wife's hand away.

"Joey, you ain't got any call to stick it out with us here. You done everything you could. You ain't bound to fight your brother for us."

"You be quiet," I said. "I didn't ask your advice."

He sank down on his side again, and turned his face to the wall.

"Make some fresh coffee," I said to Betty Morgan. "It's going to be a long cold night."

When I said it, I realized all at once I wasn't hearing the water in the trench anymore. The shallow ditch was empty. The rock slabs lining it glistened damp in the rays of the lamp, but the water was gone. Already some of the rocks were white and dry, like bones, the water gone up into the thirsty dry air.

"They found the water," someone said in a quiet voice.

"They turned it aside."

It was my fault. I looked down at the empty coffee pot. That ditch was well-hid, twisting down from a rocky *tinaja* under the brush and rubble so no one would ever see it. Not even the Apaches ever found it. But Dave did.

"There's gallon or two in this jar," Ike said, holding up a clay *olla.* "It ain't gonna last long, though, the way it's seeping out."

It was my fault. I handed the coffee pot back. "All right. That makes it a little harder. But we're not licked. There's soldiers going past here every once in a while, to Fort Bowie and back. Isn't that so, Tom?"

He didn't say anything. No one did.

"They can't lick us," I said.

"No," Mrs. Morgan said quietly. "That's right. They can't drive us away from our homes."

I leaned against the wall, trying to think. You had to depend on yourself. That was what I'd learned. They'd do whatever I said, but it was a decision I didn't want to make. All along it seemed I didn't want to do the things I did, but it was a gathering noose that kept creeping in on me, forcing me toward the knot, and there was nothing I could do about it.

"Let's stick it out a while longer," I said. "Come morning we'll take stock and see how we stand."

The night wore on. There was no shooting, now, but the silence was worse, almost, than the rattle and bang. Chaffee's men must have had plenty of liquor, because I heard loud yells and laughing and a snatch or two of a drunken song. They were in no hurry; they had plenty of time to wait us out.

"I'll tell you," Ike Coogan said. "I'll tell you what I been thinkin', Joey. Now if I—"

"They're burning my house!" Casey said, unbelievingly. He was standing at a rifle slit, and he pointed. "They're burning my house!"

Everyone crowded around to look, each at a slit. The night was suddenly bright with flames. Casey had rigged him a wagon canvas for a roof, and the rotten stuff went up like a Roman candle, in leaping sheets of flame. In the fiery light shadowy horsemen wheeled and turned their mounts in Casey's garden patch, knocking down the corn, turning the carefully-tended plot into a sea of plowed-up dirt and broken greenery. I snatched up my carbine but before I could fire the light died and there was only the faint moon and the smell of smoke from Casey's ruined farm.

"That's the kind of people you're dealing with," I said.

The night wore on. Chaffee's men knew they had us wrapped up. It was only a matter of time, and not much time, either. One of the kids started to whimper, wanting a cup of water, and the mother snatched it up and cradled it in her arms, pressing her lips against its head and staring with wide shiny eyes into the flame of the lamp. Tom Morgan went a little out of his head, and Betty found enough dampness in the trench to wet a kerchief for him to suck on. We had to save the water in the *olla*. I'd been so smart.

I looked out the slit, not figuring to see anything, but wanting to look away from all those tired faces. Every time I turned around someone was staring at me with a weary intensity, as though I held the answer to a problem that vexed them. But I didn't. I didn't even know how to solve my own problems.

Across the *playa* a coyote howled, and the sound was like a fingernail scraped across a slate. Out in the darkness someone laughed, a heavy bellowing laugh. Scudder was out there, and Bluejaw. And Dave. Ike Coogan came up to stand beside me, and cleared his throat, saying, "What I was aiming to say a while ago—"

"What?"

He pulled at his whiskers. "Now Dave ain't really got nothing against *me*. Oh, I give you a hand with Chaffee, right enough, but that didn't hurt Dave none. It kicked him right into the driver's seat, so he shouldn't have nothing but love and admiration for me."

"What are you talking about?"

He grinned a snaggle-toothed grin. "I think mebbe I could go out there and palaver with them boys and work out a deal of some kind. Least I could do is get the women folks and childer away safe. And maybe I could—"

"You're crazy," I said. "They'd shoot you down on sight."

"Now I don't know," Ike said mildly. "I dealt with a lot of different kinds of men in my time. I reckon they're all about the same. If I was to go out there with a flag of truce, kind of—" He picked up a ripped sheet from the floor. "Ain't anybody don't respect a white flag. Even them Minneconjou Sioux up at Fort Laramie—*they* knew what I meant."

"Ike," I said, "You mean well. I'm glad you're trying to help us. But the men you knew—that was a long time ago. Men have changed. They don't understand things the way you old people did. I can't let you go out there."

"Dod-dum it, you can't hardly stop me, Joey."

He stepped to the door, trailing the dirty sheet. I grabbed for his arm but he jerked free of me and drew the bolt back. Before I could get to him he had slipped out like a skinny old ghost and the door slammed in my face.

"Hey, you fellers!" he yelled. "You fellers out there! This is Ike Coogan! I want to talk to you fellers!"

There was silence, a kind of stunned silence. I could imagine Scudder and Bluejaw and the rest of them creeping among the rocks, staring, listening, eyes roving the moonlit yard.

"Hey, Dave! It's me—Ike Coogan!"

Thinking of Scudder reminded me of that day in the yard when Ike Coogan threw down on the pale-eyed man, and the evil that glowed in Scudder's flat eyes. And I knew that Scudder must be sighting along a gunbarrel at Ike Coogan right now.

Something told me. I could see the mean cold flicker in his pale eyes, and I jerked the door open and yelled, "Ike!"

But it was too late. And more than just Scudder were shooting at the old man. As I stood there, frozen with horror, they mowed him down like a duck in a shooting gallery. His skinny body bucked and reeled under the shock of a dozen slugs, and it was like a crazy dance, the way he jerked back, flinging his arms up, and falling back against me.

"Ike!" I yelled again. "You god-damned fool!"

He still had one corner of the sheet clutched in a fist and it dragged after us as I pulled him and shut the door. I laid him down and someone brought a folded coat to put under his head, and someone else turned up the lamp a little and brought it over beside us.

"Ike," I said, "I told you not to."

It was funny—he was riddled with bullets, and yet there wasn't a drop of blood. They'd stitched him up and down the front, and the scummy buckskins were dotted with small black holes, each with a kind of burned black edge to it. But there was no blood. He was so old there wasn't any more juice in him. And he still had the edge of the torn sheet in his hand.

"Not even an Apache would do that," he said in a weak voice.

I tried to get the buckskin jacket open, but I think he was sewed up in it. It wouldn't come. And it wouldn't do any good if I did get it off. He was dying.

"Joey?" he said.

He was looking right at me, but his eyes didn't see me.

"Yes, Ike," I said.

He rolled his head a little on the folded coat, and there was regret on his leathery old face.

"Too many people," he said.

I leaned closer.

"Too many people," he said again. "Too—too many."

Then he was dead. For a minute I didn't realize it. I couldn't. Ike Coogan was indestructible. What was it he always said? He was nine years older than God. And then it came to me like a kick in the pit of the stomach. He was gone. He was gone for good. And I owed him money when he died. I still owed him for the doctor in Tucson.

"Ike," I said, "don't go."

But he was gone, gone back to old Fort Laramie with Parkman and Chatillon and the rest of the people he used to talk about. People who would never shoot any man under a white flag.

It was the darkest part of the night. John Turner came up and stood beside me at the slit. He'd got most of the rock slivers picked out of his eyes and he could see again, though not too good.

"You think we're doing the right thing, holding out like this?" He swallowed painfully. "I mean—well, I'm fer sticking out to the bitter end, myself. Don't make no difference what happens to me, I guess, but—" He jerked his head toward the corner where the children slept. "I got to feel I'm doing the right thing. I'll stick it out here till hell freezes over, but I got to be sure first."

"I don't know," I said. "I guess it's up to each one to decide for himself."

"I guess I had my share of hard knocks." He put up a hand and felt at the scar on his head where Bluejaw had cracked him that day. "Come to expect it, seems like. I don't care anymore—not for me, that is—but I got kids. I figgered mebbe the Wells was where I could make a stake for them, but mebbe not. If I could get out of here, now, I wouldn't have lost much. Just another chance, that's all. If I—"

I made up my mind. "Don't worry," I said. "I'll get you all out of this. I got you in, and I'll get you out."

He followed me. "Where you aimin' to go?"

I knelt down, looking at the hole in the wall where the *acequia* came through. I was skinny enough to get through there. If I could wriggle out, and somehow sneak past Chaffee's men,

I could get out on the *playa* and walk toward Tucson till I met a wagon train or some soldiers. That was our only chance.

"Hand me my carbine," I said.

Heads lifted, feet scuffled, people got up from the shapeless masses on the dirt floor and looked at me.

"Listen," I said. "We've got one chance. If I can get clear of the house and off into the brush, they'll never catch me. I'll run all the way to Tucson if I have to. But I'll meet someone on the road, I know it. I'll bring help back. All you have to do is sit tight."

There was a clutter of voices, everyone speaking at once. But I had my mind made up.

"Don't do anything foolish," I said. "Don't provoke them. They think they got us in a bottle here, and they'll probably just wait till we get good and thirsty. But by then I'll be back. You see if I don't."

Nobody thought I ought to, but I did. I squirmed down into the hole, feeling the rough rocks pick and snatch at me. It was cool and wet and muddy down there. The mud helped. It greased me, kind of, and I popped out back of the house like an eel. The brush was high and tangled there, and I squatted for a minute, breathing hard and trying to get my bearings. It was hard, with my head down the way I had to keep it. I couldn't see anything. But the first light of dawn was coming, and I had to move quick. I could hear a drunken snore from Nacho's wickiup, and I hoped they were all asleep. I stuck my head up slow and looked around. As the night lifted, the Wells looked ghostly and unreal. Casey's place still smoldered, and the fields were smashed and gutted. It was a ghost landscape.

They weren't all asleep, though. My brother Dave was standing at the corner of the wickiup, thumbs hooked in his belt, looking at me. The smoke from Casey's farm hung in thin layers around him, but through the veil his eyes looked at me with a kind of detachment.

CHAPTER FOURTEEN

"That you, Joey?"

Where Dave stood, he was out of the line of fire from the Texas house, but I could see him plain—short and wiry and confident-looking.

"It's me," I said.

The sun tipped over the edge of the mountains and the gray haze thinned where the fire of the sun touched it. All around us it was silent. From somewhere I could hear heavy breathing, and I knew people were watching. Chaffee's men were watching; maybe Scudder with his flat cat's eyes, and Bluejaw. In the Texas house, no matter how quiet we talked, I knew they were hearing us too.

"Saul lit out?" Dave asked.

"He went back to Columbus."

Dave hooked a bootheel on the wickiup wall. "That leaves just you and me, don't it?"

I didn't say anything. I still had my carbine in the crook of my arm, and I wondered whether to make a dash for it. But Dave's face was dry and brown, filled with a weary wisdom.

"Don't get any crazy ideas, kid."

My mouth was tight and dry but I said, "Dave, there's women and children in there."

He grinned. "Someone should have thought of that when they fired on us."

"Let the women and kids out," I said. "Just that. That's all."

The rising sun made a patch of shadow behind him. The shadow was long from the angle of the sun, and black.

"What happens then?" Dave asked.

"We'll fight you some more, I guess. We're not licked."

He spun himself a cigarette from brown paper and a bag of tobacco, and licked the flap shut. The silence seemed to press down, and the sun grew brighter. It was going to be a hot day. A fly buzzed around my neck, and stung, but I didn't slap at it. I just held on to my carbine.

"Joey," Dave said, "I'm glad I run into you this way. It's the kind of thing I knew you'd do—risk your neck for a bunch of nogood farmers. You always was one to do crazy things like that. Now me—I ain't built that way." He took a deep drag at the cigarette. "I always had an eye for the main chance." He chuckled. Almost, he seemed to be enjoying himself. "I'll tell you what," he said. "I can't let you go back in there with those people. I can't with a good conscience. And I'll tell you why. Joey, you're the glue that's been holding 'em together. Anyone can see that. I ain't about to let my only brother throw away his chances on a lousy bunch of clodhoppers."

I let him talk. Dave always liked to talk.

"So I'll tell you what, Joey. You throw down that mean little carbine. Just throw it on the ground in front of you there and walk slow toward me, with your hands in the air."

"No," I said.

He didn't hear me, or didn't want to. "Then me and the boys will give these farmers a good lesson. I can't have a bunch of plowboys thumbing their nose at my outfit. No, sir! The way I see it, I got to teach them a lesson they'll remember. Not only them, but any others that tries to get tough."

He blew smoke through his nose, and dropped the cigarette. "Throw that carbine down, quick!"

"No," I said again.

Furious, he ground the cigarette into the dirt with his heel. "Goddamit, Joey, I'm telling you this for your own good! I can't stand here and palaver all day. All you got to do is lay down that carbine and walk over here to me. That's all there is to it Do that, and you're a made man in the Territory. We go together, you and me, and there ain't anything can stop us from now on."

My hand was tight on the carbine. I had it tucked under my arm, and my hand was wrapped around it just forward of the trigger guard.

"Dave," I said, "don't ask me to do that."

"Why not?"

"Because these people are my people."

He was nervous. I could see his hand shake a little as he shoved his hat back on his head. "Hell, ain't I your brother? Ain't you got any obligation to me?"

I shook my head. Something was going out of my life—seeping away like water in the sand. "No," I said. "No obligation. Not any more."

All of a sudden his face changed. I could see what was going through his mind. I always knew what was in Dave's mind. He couldn't let me stand up and sass him this way, not in front of Scudder and Bluejaw and the rest of Chaffee's gang. His face changed, and I knew what it meant. There was just the two of us, and it would have to be settled now.

"I'm sorry," he said. "I never wanted it this way. I guess you know that. Only now—I got to tell you to throw that gun down. Before I count three."

Legs spread wide, hands hooked in his belt, he faced me. In the Texas house a woman screamed, and the sound was bitten off short like someone had put a hand over her mouth.

"All right," I said. "That's the way it is, then. But I got to tell you something too, Dave. You never been up against a carbine before." I let my finger curl over the trigger. "I don't have to draw, like you do. All I got to do is just tilt her up a little, and pull the trigger. That's all I got to do. I don't think you can beat me."

Agony was in his face, agony and a kind of uncertainty. I felt sorry for him, and for me, too, but it didn't do any good. The only way you could ever do any good with Dave was stick with him, and make him see you meant it.

"One," he said.

It was still and quiet in the sun for a minute. Then someone yelled. "Sic 'im, Dave!" I saw Dave's lips work, and I swallowed hard. The muscles of my forearm tightened. All I had to do was swing her up and—

"No," Dave said. He let his arms fall flat to his side, and his fingers curled empty. "No."

Chaffee's gang yelled at him again, jeering. Maybe it was Bluejaw. "Scared, Dave?" Someone else took up the cry. "Let that kid make you back down, Dave?" There were catcalls, and angry shouts. "Go git 'im Dave! For Christ's sake!"

"No," Dave said again. He smiled at me, the old crinkled smile that twisted his face. I hadn't seen it for a long time. "I can't do her," he said. "I believe you would have, Joey. But I can't do her."

Seeing how they had us all bottled up in the house, Chaffee's gang had pulled in close. They were scattered around the yard within a score of paces. They sprawled behind rocks and stone walls, crouched behind the wickiup, skulked in the cover of a haystack next to the pole corral. As I watched, Scudder popped up from behind a bale of hay. Nothing was there but his pale face, and the flat-crowned black hat, level on his head. There was a gun, too. It wasn't pointed at me. It pointed at Dave.

"Get on with it," Scudder said. "Draw on that loudmouth kid. Don't let him talk to you like that."

Dave half-turned, looking over his shoulder. He was still smiling. "You go to hell," he said to Scudder.

I never knew what Scudder had in mind. Maybe he didn't like Dave talking to him like that. Maybe he was just put out at Dave's backing down to me. Maybe, and more likely, he saw a quick way to get rid of Dave and slide into Chaffee's chair himself. Whatever his reasons were, he pulled the trigger and shot my brother Dave in the back. Dave's arms flew wide, and he stumbled and fell forward. I threw up my carbine and fired, but Scudder was quick. He dropped behind the bale of hay, and my shot went over his head.

It all happened so fast it caught everyone flatfooted. But someone in the Texas house was thinking. "Run, Joey!" a voice screeched behind me.

Scudder's gun poked out from behind the hay-bale, and I dropped flat on the ground as his shot whipped the air over my head. Behind me, almost trampling me as they came, ran George Mowry and Casey and Turner and the rest of them, in one last desperate rush, blasting and banging. No one had expected a break like that, and the pressure of it, all the days of waiting and hoping, drove the settlers across the yard like slugs from a shotgun, and they were hollering all at once. There was a kind of shock to it, because Chaffee's men, caught short by the surprise, fired wild and crazy and scrambled away to cover, slipping and falling and cussing. They emptied their guns, and there wasn't time to reload because the settlers were on them like a swarm of bees, buzzing and stinging. Bluejaw tripped and fell over one of his own men, cavalry great-coat flapping as he ran, and Casey clubbed him to death right there with the butt of his rifle. Bluejaw's thick hand came up to protect his face, and then the butt smashed down on it and crushed the felt hat into his head. A man I didn't know, with no shirt—just the top part of a set of red flannel underwear—dropped his gun and ran, and Turner gave him a charge of buckshot in the back. It hardly showed against the red of the flannel, but the man flung his head back, arms wide and fingers spread, and toppled backward. He took three desperate steps that way, and then the life oozed out of him and he sank down, legs doubled under. All around me the settlers beat and slashed and shot, driving Chaffee's men before them like quail in a grain field. They were furious, indignant men, and they wouldn't be denied.

I don't how long I lay there, half-stunned, watching the carnage. I might have been there yet, with that terrible sick feeling, but for seeing Scudder break loose and try to get away. One minute George Mowry had him by the coattails, trying to wrestle him to the ground, and the next Scudder had twisted away, striking George across the forehead with the barrel of his gun. He sprinted away, running low and fast toward the corral where Buster was tied. Scudder getting away was like a shower of cold water on me. It banged against every nerve in my body with a shock that made me gasp for breath, and it drove the fog out of my mind. Suddenly I was running after him, not realizing I'd dropped the carbine beside Dave. I ran like the wind, the air wet and cold in my face, my boots pounding into the dust, feeling my clothes whip and ripple over my body as I ran.

"Scudder!" I yelled.

He threw a leg over Buster, and slashed the reins with a knife. Over his shoulder he looked at me with his pale flat eyes, and then slapped Buster on the rump with the flat of his hand. I was almost up to them, and as Buster charged away I got a hand around Scudder's ankle and clamped down. Buster drove hard, the way he always did when he was scared, but I hung on, feeling my feet fly into the air. I banged and slammed and dragged that way for a dozen yards, stuck like a leech to Scudder's boot, and he cursed and raved and tried to cut me with the knife but I held on.

My eyes danced out of their sockets and the world spun around in a welter of smoke and dust. But I still held on; I don't think the Lord Jehovah could have loosed my grip that day. Rattling and banging and bouncing, I hung on, and the pull told. Scudder slipped sideways from the saddle, clutching at the horn with one hand and ripping at my arm with the knife in the other. I didn't feel it at all. I could see my sleeve flutter into red ribbons, and I knew my arm was being hacked into a dime's worth of cat meat, but I didn't care. With the last strength I had in me, I gave a hard jerk, and Scudder tumbled off Buster.

For a moment we lay there, stunned. He was a small man, but he'd fallen from atop Buster, and when he fell his shoulder drove into my stomach. I gasped, and tried to roll from under him, but he scrambled to his feet, looking wildly around. A hundred yards off, Buster pulled up and looked back at us, his flanks heaving.

"You haven't got any gun," I said.

He had the knife, though. He stepped toward me, holding the knife low, ready to rip my guts out. From somewhere behind us drifted yells, and from the corner of my eye I could see a movement that might be someone starting to my rescue. But it was no good. Scudder was on me, snarling like a hungry alley-cat.

I let the shock of his first rush carry me over backward, but I pushed up and out as I fell, getting a knee into his chest. He flew over my head, squealing with rage, the knife flashing in the sun as it snicked by. In an instant he was up again, facing me, and I wondered how he ever kept that flat-brimmed black hat on so neat. He ran at me again, and the air whistled with the sweep of the knife. I fell flat and it hissed over me, driving to the haft in the dirt next to my ear. Before he could wrench it free, I caught his thin wrist and staked it to the ground, getting my forearm across his throat. His eyes widened under the pressure, and I flattened my body against his, pinioning him flat, laying my bleeding forearm against his throat, pushing harder and harder. After a while his face purpled, and his eyes closed. His body went limp under me, and then I put both hands around his skinny throat and clamped them together till my fingers met. I held them there until somebody—I think it was Casey—pulled me off. They said later my fingers were laced so tight they had to pry them apart. But Scudder was dead. And that was one for old man Coogan. *Too many people,* Ike always said. This was one less.

I buried Dave myself. I wouldn't let anyone help me. I dug the hole on the bluff that overlooked the Wells. I found a kind of red flower growing up there, and I cut an armful with my knife and spread them over the grave.

When I came down, Tom Morgan and George Mowry were waiting for me. Tom had his arm in a sling. They didn't say anything. I didn't either. I brushed past them and went into the Texas house. I put the little stuff I had in a gunny sack and threw it over Buster's withers. I went past them again into the house and stood for a long time. Saul's trench he'd dug—the water trench—was gurgling again. The room was dark and cool. The oak rocker stood there, the shawl he'd worn over the back. I went over in the corner and took the old dulcimer Eda had played and stamped it into a mess of splintered wood and a tangle of wire with my heel. Then I walked out into the sunlight.

"Where you going?" Tom asked.

I took a deep breath. "I don't know. West, someplace. A man offered to give me a job in Sacramento if I ever got up that way."

I worked the action of my carbine and stuck it in the saddle boot. Sacramento was as good a place as any. The Oggs were there.

"I think you're making a mistake, Joe," Casey said.

What was I good for anymore? I'd loved the Wells, I'd wanted to die there, I'd never be happy anyplace else. It was home—all the home I'd known for five years. But I couldn't stay there. Not after what had happened.

"You belong here," Tom said.

I was a legal man now. I could ride, and shoot. I could wrangle cattle, and I knew a smattering of Apache. But the Territory was full of men who could do all that, and more, No, I didn't draw much water in the Territory. I'd better light out.

"Goddamit," Casey said. He wiped his red face with his sleeve. "You can't just pull out like this, Joe! Hell, we all been through a lot together." He waved his hand. "Look, we get the fields plowed up and planted again—build a couple of new houses—"

I shook hands with them. "I got to go."

"Joe," Tom Morgan said, "you're the man with the *cojones* around here. We need you."

I didn't know what *cojones* meant. I didn't care. "You don't need me," I said. "Not any more. The fighting's all done. It'll be easy from here on in."

"Don't you owe us something?" Mowry asked.

I'd heard that question before. I'd asked it of Saul once. Dave asked it of me, too.

"I owe you my life," I said.

Casey spit into the dirt. "Hell, that ain't what we mean!"

"I got to go," I said again. "I won't ever forget any of you. But I got to go."

As I rode away they stood in the shade of the Texas house, and Tom Morgan raised his good hand in farewell. That was all. That was the end of it. Not Boston Wells, anymore. No, Bloody Wells.

Tucson wasn't any different. It was as noisy and dirty as ever. The Legislature was in session, and everything was crowded and filled with people. Politicians, pimps, hangers-on, drunks, loafers—it wouldn't ever be a decent town, anyone could see that. I rode Buster through the crowded streets, and he walked high and dainty, careful not to step on anyone.

Down on Camp Street I saw her again—the little Spanish whore that took my eight hundred dollars. This time she couldn't get away from me. I swung down off Buster and grabbed her arm, spinning her around to face me. But all of a sudden she was a fat, dirty-faced girl, scared as hell, and blubbering. It was the same girl, all right; I'd know her in hell. But it was different.

"*Vamos*" I said.

I shoved her away, and watched her scuttle through the crowd like a scared rabbit, holding her black skirts high with her hand as she ran. Had she ever been beautiful and mysterious to me? It seemed impossible. She was fat, and her eyes were small and set too close together. I got back on Buster and rode away, wondering if she'd changed, or if I had. It didn't make any difference, though; the thing was, something had changed.

I looked up Eda before I left town. She was down on Soapsuds Row, the Landrys told me. I found her bent over a steaming wooden tub, dragging clothes out of the dirty water. She didn't see me at first, and she straightened up like her back hurt and stood for a minute looking down the row of officer's quarters toward the river. It glinted in the sun, like a jewel in tall grass.

"Eda," I said.

She turned to face me, one hand pushing the red hair back from her eyes. Her lips opened silently, and she stared at me. Then she ran and flung her arms around me, burying her face against my chest, laughing and crying at the same time.

"You're all right?" she asked me. "Oh, what's the matter with your arm!"

"I cut it a little," I said. "It isn't anything."

The heavy tresses were still rich and fine, like milkweed down. But it hurt me to see her doing other people's washing.

"Some soldiers came in from Fort Bowie this morning," she said. "Corporal Schrader told me there was some kind of a fight at the Wells. A big fight. Schrader said Saul was gone, too."

"That's right," I said. "He went back to Columbus."

"I guess we're not married anymore," Eda said. "I paid a lawyer ten dollars to file my case with the Legislature. If Saul isn't here to object to it, I'll get the divorce easy. That's what the lawyer said."

"Saul won't be here," I said.

I pulled her to me and put my cheek against her hair, hating to leave her, hating to go away and leave Eda in Tucson. But there wasn't anything else to do. I was riding west alone. I didn't want any woman tagging along, even if she'd go. And I'd never ask her. I couldn't.

"Dave's dead," I said. "He got killed in that fight."

Her body was tense against mine. "I heard."

A fat quartermaster sergeant, with yellow chevrons big as a circus poster, waddled down the line of washtubs and started to raise hell with the laundresses. When he came to us, I looked him in the eye.

"On your way, soldier," I said. "You didn't lose anything around here."

He puffed out his cheeks, and his mustache stood up like there was electricity in it.

"Mister, you're trespassing on a military post."

"I don't care where I trespass," I said. "I'm talking to this lady, and there'll be a strange face in hell in the morning if you don't go on about your business, and that damned quick."

His eyes popped but he stomped away huffing and puffing and raising sand as he went.

Eda giggled. "That was Sergeant Hoefer." She pushed away from me, holding her head back, but still hanging on to my arms. "No wonder you scared him! Joey, you're the roughest-looking article in Tucson! I declare! You look like a pirate, with that long hair and that dirty buckskin jacket and your toes coming out of your boots!"

"That's right," I said. "I guess I don't look very good."

She shook her head, and there were tears in her eyes. Where they came from so fast, I don't know. Women cry so damned easy.

"You look all right. I didn't mean that. You look fine to me."

I dug my toe into the dirt.

"I came to say goodbye."

"Goodbye?"

Not trusting myself to speak, I nodded.

"Where?"

"Oh," I said, "west. Sacramento. With Carl Ogg. He's got a farm out there. Might give me a job. I'm good with horses."

Her face was unbelieving.

"You don't mean that!"

"Of course I meant it," I said.

"But what about the Wells?"

"What about the Wells? I don't give a damn about the Wells. They're nothing to me anymore. They don't mean anything to me."

She pulled me down beside her on the wooden bench.

"Now, Joey, you know you're acting the fool. You can't run away from things like that. They'll just follow you. All it is, you've been hurt and you—you've found out what grief is." She looked down at her hands, cracked and yellowed with the Army's soap. "I guess everyone finds that out sooner or later. I was pretty young when I found out."

"Stop it!" I blurted. "You talk like you're an old woman!"

"Then you stop acting like a little boy."

The other laundresses stopped their rubbing and tubbing and were watching us. One of them—a fat Irish-looking lady—put her hands on her hips and winked at me.

"All right," I said. "But I'm of age. I know what I'm doing. I'm free, white, and twenty-one. I can make my own bed."

Eda shook her head. "It's more than that. It's—" She bit her lip. "What I'm trying to say, Joey—or maybe not say—anyway, what I mean, you can't leave the Wells. You just can't!"

"That's just what I'm going to do."

She didn't seem to hear me.

"Joey, the Wells are yours. They belong to you. You belong to them. Don't you think I remember the way your face used to light up when you talked about the Wells? It was everything to you. You told me all about the blueberry vines, the way the creek splashed, the deer up in the rocks someplace. You told me about the wind at night and the sun going down red and the smell of dust in the moonlight. Don't you remember all those things now?"

I swallowed hard. It was all true.

"I feel like I know the Wells myself, like I'd lived there. I was only there once, for a short unhappy time. But it's—it's almost like home to me too, in a way. Just because it's home to you."

"I don't owe anybody anything," I said. "I'm free and unfettered. That's why I'm moving on."

"Listen," Eda said. Her voice was low, almost rough. "You listen to me, now! Maybe I'm nothing to you but a kind of a sister, but if that's all I am, I've got a right to talk to you like a sister. What I say is this, Joe Boston. You've got a responsibility to the Wells!"

"How?" I growled.

The look on her face was eager. The way she had changed, she was tan and whiplike, the old soft loveliness gone, but something new and better in its place. She was a woman grown—a woman who'd known hard times, but hard times have a way of tempering the right kind of person.

"Joey, doesn't what's happened at the Wells mean anything to you? A long time ago, old Mr. Coogan could have had the Wells. He was the first white man there, maybe, and he loved the Wells as much as you. But he was always a restless kind of man. He said so himself. And the Wells weren't for him. Then—" Her voice softened. "Saul came. He loved the Wells too, but they weren't for him either. He was a lonely man. I'm beginning to see how lonely. But Saul didn't have the knack of knowing people, and working with them, and bringing out the best. Now he's gone, and the Wells are still there."

"Chaffee," I said.

Her eyes were hard and fierce.

"He couldn't take the Wells either. The Wells was never meant to be taken that way, by that kind of a man. And Dave—"

We both knew about Dave.

"Dave was nice to me sometimes," Eda said. "He bought me a red dress, once, when he had some money."

"He liked red."

She gripped my arm suddenly, and it hurt. "Don't you see, Joey? Not one of them was right for the Wells. They were all wrong for it. The Wells needed someone to grow with it, to love it and respect it and care for it. Doesn't it make sense?"

Something else was beginning to make sense to me. It was too vague to put a name on it, but it was in my mind, building.

"The Wells are like a woman," I said, "Those are the things a woman needs, too."

In spite of her brown cheeks, she blushed. The flush was lovely, staining through the brown. "Maybe."

The idea was growing in me. It was a beautiful idea, and all of a sudden it flashed up like lightning, completely formed and perfect. It made my scattered life fall into place and take a shape and a meaning that was there all the time, only I'd missed it. At first, though, I was scared to mention it. My throat got tight and hurt, and sweat broke out in the palms of my hands. But I finally took the plunge and blurted it out, gasping like a stranded trout.

"I'll go back," I said. "I'll do her. But not unless you go with me, Eda."

She caught her breath in an agonized little gasp. "No!"

"That's it," I said. "That's the bargain. I won't do it any other way. If you won't come with me, I'll go on to Sacramento, alone."

"You don't want me!" In one of those quick changes, she was defiant and reckless. "You're talking the fool, Joey!" Her fingers rubbed at the brown V in the neck of her shirtwaist. "I've—well, I've been around too much. I'm not for you."

"Then neither is the Wells."

She laughed, a touch of grimness in it. "Don't make it so hard for me, Joey."

"I wouldn't ever hurt you," I said. "Not for anything, and you know it. But the Wells don't mean a thing to me without you. And with you, they mean everything in the world to me. I'll never leave either one of you."

"You don't know what you're saying." A trace of panic was in her voice, and she looked around desperately, like an animal in a trap. The washerwomen were silent, busy with their tubbing, but watching us from the corner of the eye.

"For the first time in my life," I said, "I do know what I'm saying." I reached out and drew her to me, pressing her against me. She looked thin and hard, but she was soft against me, and a feeling went through me I never knew before. This was something different. Maybe I was inexperienced in a lot of ways, but I knew when I had the right woman in my arms. "Eda," I said, "I love you. I guess I always did."

She didn't say anything. She didn't have to. I picked her up in my arms, away from the washtubs and the fat Sergeant Hoefer and the dirty water, and set her on Buster before me. We rode away like that, and all the washerwomen on Soapsuds Row cheered us to the echo, and waved after us. We were going back to the Wells. Boston Wells. I knew I'd never be happy again till I saw it on the horizon like that first day—a low green haze, rising out of the sunbaked land, beckoning to us.

www.ingramcontent.com/pod-product-compliance
Lightning Source LLC
LaVergne TN
LVHW091144080826
845145LV00008B/2249